THE HALLOW

S.A. PERCHEZ

THE HALLOW

ABERRATION CYCLE

THE HALLOW
THIS BOOK IS PART OF THE ABERRATION CYCLE

First published 2026
Copyright © 2026 by S.A. PERCHEZ

This is a work of fiction. All characters, names, places, and incidents are the product of the author's imagination. Any resemblance to real persons, living or dead, events, or locales is purely coincidental.

All rights reserved.

No portion of this book may be reproduced in any form or by any electronic or mechanical means including information storage and retrieval systems without permission in writing from its publisher or author.

Cover design by David Gardias
Map illustration: Rob D
Editing: K.A. Tutin, Tutin Editing

www.aberrationcycle.com

S.A. PERCHEZ

For my wife—
who stood beside me through every chapter,
and made this journey possible.

Serrin Peaks
The Bastion
Lake Serrinth
Vitel
Rodin
Thalor
Aelvir River
Rodannis River
Avriel
Orvain
The Veiled Heights

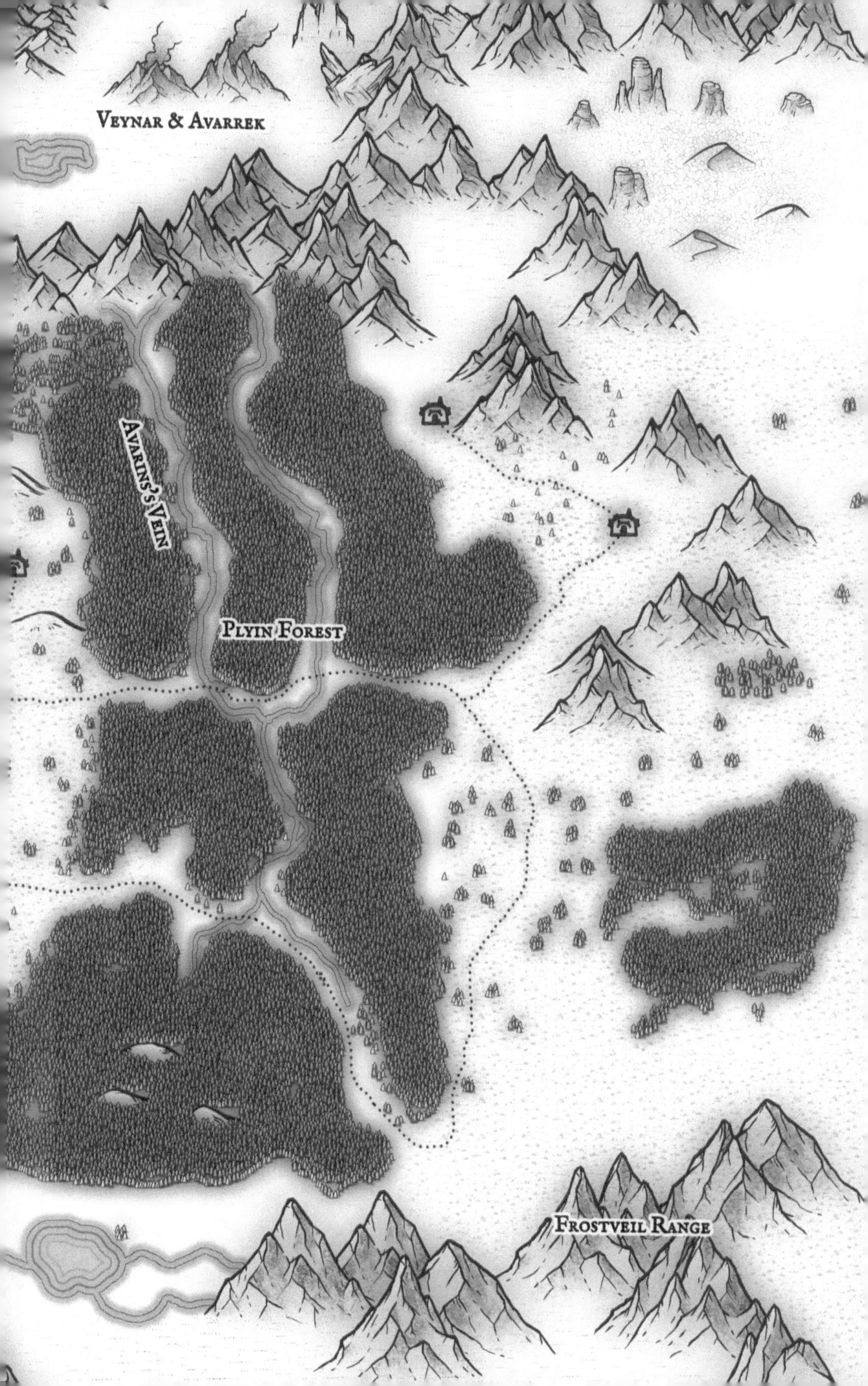

Veynar & Avarrek
Avarins's Vein
Plyin Forest
Frostveil Range

CONTENTS

PROLOGUE

The woods were quiet again.

Too quiet.

Morning light crept through the trees in thin, colorless strands, brushing over leaves still wet with dew. My legs ached from running. My lungs burned. I didn't remember when I stopped, only that I had. My hands were shaking. My feet were bare, cut open by roots and stones, caked with blood that wasn't all mine.

I'd run all night.

The cold hadn't mattered then. Neither had direction. Only distance.

Now the forest thinned behind me, giving way to open prairie that shimmered pale under the early sun.

I hated the sight of it. Too much sky. Nowhere to hide. The trees had been cruel, but at least they were cover.

The chill of the forest shade gave way to the sting of open air. Sunlight pressed against my skin, harsh and unfiltered. Even the wind felt like it was watching.

The hem of my dress hung in tatters, stiff with blood and dirt. The neckline was torn where he'd grabbed me. One of the sleeves was gone entirely. My throat still ached from where the second man had tried to hold me down, though the rain had washed most of his blood away.

I didn't remember screaming. Only the light.

It had come without thought. A rush, a pulse that burned through me and out of me, blinding and hot.

I'd stood there afterward, waiting for something—guilt, horror, relief.

None came.

Now, as the sun broke over the horizon, the forest behind me smelled of rot and iron.

I moved on.

There was nothing behind me worth turning for.

Every step burned, tearing at raw skin until pain blurred into rhythm. Blisters had split open across my heels, and the cold air stung the cuts. I found a narrow stream near the tree line and followed it east.

The water was clear and bitter. I knelt to drink until the taste of metal faded from my tongue. The reflection staring back didn't look like me.

My eyes were still green, too bright, almost feral against the grime, but they sat hollow in my face, stripped of anything soft. Blood had dried in the hollow of my throat, cracked and dark against my skin. Dirt streaked my jaw and collarbone.

My hair should have been a blaze of red. Instead, it hung knotted and dull, snarled with sweat, clinging to my cheeks like it belonged to someone else.

I looked like prey that had already been run down—standing only because it hadn't accepted the end yet.

The cawing of crows drew my gaze upward. A pair circled overhead, wings black against the morning light. I pulled what was left of my torn cloak tighter and started walking again.

The stream curved into the open plain. The air smelled of wet grass and smoke. Distant fires, maybe. I thought about following the scent, about finding people, but the idea of being seen made my stomach twist.

Better the open land than another pair of hands.

By midday, the trees were little more than a shadow on the horizon. I hadn't eaten since yesterday, but hunger felt far away, muted beneath exhaustion. The wind pushed against me as if trying to turn me back. Every time I closed my eyes, I saw flashes of light. My own power still echoing behind my lids.

I didn't know what I'd done. I only knew I couldn't let anyone see it.

When the sun reached its peak, I stopped long enough to tear the lower half of my dress into strips and wrap my feet. The strips soaked through with blood almost immediately, but they kept the pebbles from slicing deeper.

They'd have found the bodies by now.

The thought should have scared me more than it did. But fear had burned out long before, leaving only ashes behind.

I kept walking.

The prairie stretched ahead, pale and endless, rippling with wind. The kind of place that promised freedom and death in equal measure.

By late afternoon, the prairie bled into farmland. Fences sagged, half collapsed beneath years of neglect, and the fields lay bare except for a few grazing sheep in the distance. Smoke still rose from the chimneys farther east with thin trails against the pale sky.

I stayed low, keeping to the shallow rises and hollows of the field.

The first house I saw looked abandoned. Boards nailed across the windows, roof sagging.

The second wasn't.

A line of shirts and trousers hung behind it, stirring in the wind.

I waited until the yard was still. No dogs. No voices. Only the sound of a door closing somewhere inside.

My legs trembled as I crossed the field, stumbling until my knees hit the dirt, then crawling the rest of the way.

The laundry line creaked when I touched it. The short shirt fit close, the fabric light and unrestrictive. The trousers were worn but well-cut, meant for travel rather than trade. They allowed me to move freely, no excess cloth to snag or slow me down. Clean, and better than anything I'd worn in months.

The reflection in the kitchen window looked narrower, all edges where there had once been softness. I stared too long before I realized I didn't quite recognize her.

The air smelled of bread. My stomach cramped at the scent, but I didn't risk the door. I turned toward the pasture instead.

Two horses stood near the fence, one chestnut, one gray.

The chestnut still had a worn saddle strapped on, reins hanging loose as if someone had left in a hurry. I reached for it slowly, whispering nothing words to calm my own shaking hands.

The horse flicked an ear but didn't move.

When I swung onto the saddle, my thighs protested the stretch, weak from months of disuse, and I steadied myself against the pommel. The motion felt foreign, wrong, but my body remembered enough.

I glanced once toward the house.

The door hadn't opened. Smoke still rose from the chimney.

Then I kicked the horse into a slow trot, keeping to the rise of the hill until the farm disappeared behind me.

I didn't know where I was going. Only that the world behind me couldn't be home again.

1

Dinner twitched once, then went still.

The shard of Ice protruded from its skull. I knelt, tied the rabbit's legs, and slung the weight over my shoulder before turning back toward camp. It wouldn't make much of a stew, but it would feed one man for the night.

Pylin Forest wasn't easy to navigate. The woods here were dense, the ground a tangle of roots and hidden dips. Most travelers stayed to the main roads farther north, where the paths were wide and worn, with just enough clearance for horses and wagons.

Down here, the trail narrowed into something far less forgiving. That suited me fine. The forest demanded attention. It didn't allow drifting thoughts or sloppy movement, and I trusted places that demanded discipline.

Traveling on a horse would only slow the journey, at least compared to the way I moved.

A faint shudder ran through the ground.

I stopped.

At first, the sound was low, nearly lost beneath the rustle of dry leaves. Then the rhythm resolved—hooves striking earth, leather creaking, metal shifting.

Riders.

Unusual this deep in the forest. More so at that speed.

I crouched beside a cluster of mossy stones and waited as the noise grew clearer.

More than one rider. They moved in formation, forcing their way through the brush, horses high-stepping over thick, exposed roots. One of the riders cursed as they passed. They ran no more than twenty paces downhill.

Curiosity edged out caution as I drifted toward the slope's edge, slipping between twisted limbs of tree trunks until I had a clear view. From there, I studied their formation.

Flashes of movement cut between the trees. They rode fast—too fast for anyone who knew this forest. Loud, careless. Branches snapped and scraped against cloaks as they passed. They muscled through, reacting only after the branches struck.

I kept pace from the higher ground, running parallel to their line. My feet made no sound as I stayed out of sight. The rabbit dangling from the rope thudded lightly against my back with each step.

My shirt was going to be stained with blood by sundown. The thought irritated me briefly, then it passed.

I drew on Wind Casting. The air parted ahead of me, carrying my stride faster, weaving between the trees in near silence. When they broke into a clearing, I finally got a good look. Nine riders, one leading a few paces ahead.

The riders crossed the glade, cloaks shifting like shadows slipping free of the trees.

That was when I saw her.

While the others wore full cloaks, she stood out in her short black shirt, making no attempt to blend it. Her fiery hair caught the light like a beacon in a sea of green. Her face tensed each time she looked over her shoulder. She looked young, early twenties, maybe. A small dagger hung at her waist.

There was desperation in the way she rode. Then I realized she was trying to get away.

Now that the forest thinned, they began to close the distance.

I stayed on higher ground, remaining unseen. Their focus never left the chase.

I considered dropping the rabbit to free my hands but dismissed the thought. I hadn't tracked it this far just to waste it.

She was losing ground. No matter how hard she pushed, they were gaining.

The group's frontrunner, an older man, raised a hand.

Lightning ripped through the trees, crackling with violent energy.

The strike hit the horse low and hard—a crack of brilliant force. The animal screamed, bucked, and collapsed mid-stride, dragging her down with it.

She recovered quickly, but instead of reaching for her dagger, she raised both hands, palms open before her.

The others ushered their mounts forward, spreading out as they went. One by one, they dismounted, crossbows coming up in practiced unison. Every shot was lined up—yet no one fired.

They wanted her alive.

This wasn't an ordinary group. Something about them set my nerves on edge. Eight riders, and one of them a Lightning Variant—one of the unnatural affinities—was trouble, even for a skilled Caster. At this distance, I couldn't tell how many more there were.

Even outnumbered and unarmed, she still made them wary. By the way she held her hands out, it was obvious she was a Caster too.

She scanned the clearing, breath coming hard after the fall. Dirt streaked her face and clung to her clothes. Her eyes moved from one man to the next, watching for the next blow.

Everything about her said escape. And these were the ones sent to take her back.

I recognized that look on her face. I'd worn it myself, once.

I should've kept moving. That was the plan. No stopping, no getting involved. I huffed a breath, annoyed at myself as I felt the direction I was being pulled.

I looked back at the girl, her hands still raised.

She showed none of the tells of the four pillars of Casting—not Wind, Earth, Fire, or Water.

If she were a novice, they would've rushed her already.

They hadn't. Which meant she was the other kind—a wielder of one of the unnatural affinities.

Like the Lightning Variant who'd dropped her horse. Casters outside the natural order.

A rider pushed back her hood and stepped forward. A burly woman from the pursuing group. Broad-shouldered and solid, maybe in her forties, with gray streaks threading her dark braid. There was a steadiness in the way she held herself, the kind that came from giving orders more than taking them.

"Celeste," she called out, the single word cutting through the clearing. "Give it up already. I'm tired of chasing your skinny ass through these damned woods." She advanced with the confidence of someone who saw no threat, only another chore. "You're bleeding, limping, and outnumbered. Put up a fight, and I'll haul you out by your hair when it's all over."

She shook her head, almost impressed. "For fuck's sake, you killed Kaelen and Davos. Sure made a damned mess back there."

The girl didn't even flinch. "Fuck Kaelen. And *fuck* Davos." Then she turned, locking eyes with the Lightning Variant. "And fuck that pig too," she said, spitting in his direction.

The tension thickened, like the air charged before a storm. Celeste and the Lightning Variant held each other's gaze, and whatever passed between them had nothing to do with orders.

As they closed in around her, I wondered what they truly wanted.

Capturing her alive made sense, at least on the surface. But there was more to it than that. She wasn't just a fugitive. The way they circled her, cautious, yet careful not to kill her, suggested she was worth more than a simple runaway should be.

They stood quietly at an impasse. Neither side willing to make the first move. Celeste and her would-be captors simply studied each other, evaluating the next best approach.

From the way she squared her shoulders, the weight in her voice and the look in her eye, it was clear she had no intention of surrendering. She'd die here before she let them take her.

She edged backward, careful to keep them in front of her. But the circle only widened.

Lightning Variants burned through a tremendous amount of power. But given the old man's age and control, it was doubtful he struggled with the same limits most did. Even so, too many wasted shots would take their toll eventually.

While they held their stalemate, I moved closer. I slid the rabbit from my shoulder and tied it to the tree I'd been perched in, then dropped down, sprinting low toward a thicker trunk closer to the group.

A handful carried swords. They barely registered beside the Casters.

The true threats were obvious: the Lightning Variant and the burly woman. The way she carried herself marked her as a Variant also. It was a kind of control I knew too well.

Two Variants in a group of eight weren't odds I'd call favorable.

The woman leading this band of misfits held her sword low, her hand trained on Celeste—wrist angled just enough to betray her affinity as an Ice Variant.

In a duel between Casters, every second mattered.

The Lightning Variant spoke. "Look, you little bitch, you're coming with us. Mouth off again and I'll take a few teeth for Davos."

"Jacque, I won't have her toothless; those don't grow back," the large woman snapped.

"Teresa—" Jacque started, but the look she cut him was enough and he shut his mouth.

Celeste had escaped. And if she was a Variant, that explained their desperation. These traffickers likely already had a buyer lined up—someone willing to pay a fortune for her.

Without warning, Teresa thrust her hand forward. Three icicles tore through the air, streaking toward Celeste's leg.

Celeste sprang backward and answered with her own attack. A brilliant burst of light exploded from her palms, streaking toward the bowman flanking her and Jacque.

Jacque dodged.

The bowman didn't.

The beam struck him square in the groin with a wet, bone-deep crack. He let out a high, strangled cry, as his knees buckled beneath him. His hands clutched uselessly at the ruin between his legs, blood spilling through his fingers and darkening the dirt. He writhed once, then went slack, breath hitching in shallow, broken pulls.

Celeste was an Ardor Variant.

Ardor Casters were rare—rare enough that a person could go a lifetime without ever seeing one. Their Casting expelled energy so concentrated it shone to the naked eye. Condensed further, it struck with piercing, explosive force.

The second bowman loosed his arrow. The string snapped, and the shaft whistled through the air before burying itself in the back of her thigh with a dull, meaty thud.

Pain twisted her features as her leg gave out beneath her, and she dropped to one knee, breath hissing between clenched teeth. Blood ran down her calf, darkening the dirt, but she didn't scream.

Jacque hurled another bolt of Lightning. Celeste threw herself flat to the ground, the current crackling past where her head had been.

Without hesitation, she snapped the fletching off the shaft and pulled the arrow clean through her leg.

Blood streamed from the wound.

I was stunned at the speed and grit it took to do that without so much as a flinch. Then it struck me what she was—and her worth increased tenfold.

The rest of the group surged forward.

That was my cue. I'd seen and heard enough to know exactly what was happening.

And whose side I was on.

I slipped in near silence, closing the distance between a crossbowman with his back turned.

In one swift motion, I drove my bastard sword clean through his neck. His eyes went wide, but it was already over. With a faint shudder, he slid off my blade and crumpled to the ground.

Most Wind Casters relied on their hands to channel air. I was a bit different. I shaped it around myself, wrapped my body in its hush.

As the crossbowman fell, a sudden flash flared to my left. A blinding bolt of Light struck a charging swordsman, punching through his abdomen with such force it hollowed out his chest. He hit the ground face-first, dead before he could cry out.

The power behind that shot wasn't just raw—it was desperate. It took too much force to tear through a man like that.

Too much energy.

Celeste panted as the last pulse of Light faded from her palm. Sweat clung to her skin, matting strands of hair to her temples, but she didn't wipe it away. Her eyes swept the clearing, still fixed in the opposite direction.

By now, they knew they weren't alone. I had arrived—uninvited and unwelcome.

Good. Confusion was leverage.

They hesitated, caught between finishing her and turning on me.

I didn't wait for them to decide. My gaze locked on a swordsman just to the right of Teresa, and I moved.

"Now, who the fuck are you?" Teresa growled, her voice low and rough, like gravel grinding against stone. Her glare promised violence. She didn't wait long for an answer. A snap of her wrist sent three icicles screaming toward me, each a lethal spike of frozen air.

I twisted clear.

Ice was dangerous, but not fast as Lightning. He was the real threat.

And for now, his focus was on Celeste. I saw it in his stance that he had made his choice. He ignored me, raised his hand, and hurled a bolt of electricity straight at her.

Jacque thought I hadn't Cast at all. An easy mistake to make. He assumed I wasn't a threat. That assumption would cost him.

I drove my blade through the next man's neck, steel sliding clean as flesh parted with a wet gurgle. His body jolted once before crumpling like a sack of dried barley. His head struck the ground a breath later, eyes wide and empty. I stepped over him without pause, already hunting the next.

Jacque's strike landed true.

Lightning tore through Celeste, hurling her to the ground. Her body convulsed, muscles locking as the charge seized her. For a moment, I thought she might not survive it.

Then—against all odds—she began to rise. Shaking. Straining. Fighting the current ripping through her.

Jacque didn't relent. He stepped closer, holding the charge between them, feeding her a continuous stream of Lightning that crackled and screamed through the air.

With their prize twitching on the ground, I decided it was time to end this. My hand extended toward the Ice Variant. She was too busy barking orders to notice the change in my aim.

I released a jagged shard of Ice straight at her head. It screamed through the air.

She tried to lean away, but her reaction came too late.

The icicle struck her jaw with a stone-shattering crack. Bone splintered. Flesh split. Her head snapped sideways from the force, the lower half of her face collapsing, her jaw swinging loose by cords of tendon and muscle.

She stumbled back.

Shock flooded her eyes. She clawed at her ruined face, blood pouring through her fingers as she dropped to one knee, choking on a wet gurgle that might have been words.

Yet, nothing comprehensible came out.

With a rush forward and a swing of my sword, I finished the job and took off her head.

Jacque cut off his assault on Celeste and turned his focus back to me.

Two others were already on the move, closer than he was, and closing the gap fast. But when the Ice tore through their leader's jaw, they hesitated.

One skidded to a halt, eyes locked on the twitching body of the woman who moments ago had been shouting orders like nothing could touch her. The other slowed mid-step, sword wavering.

Neither advanced. The fight drained from their stances.

I didn't wait.

Wind wrapped tight around my limbs and I pushed forward, the ground blurring beneath my feet as I closed the distance.

The closer one lunged to intercept my attack.

I met his blade with mine, steel ringing against steel. Using the force of the clash, I twisted with it, spinning into a tight arc. Mid-spin, I shifted my grip, letting my right hand guide the blade as I pivoted toward the approaching second swordsman.

There was no pause. He was a beat too slow. He brought his longsword up in both hands, but my blade sliced through his fingers before he could react, severing them cleanly and sending his weapon clattering to the ground. His yell barely left his throat before I ended him—another hand-sized icicle driven straight into his face.

His body dropped.

I stood alone, Jacque at my back and the last swordsman in front of me. He hesitated, eyes locked on mine, weighing the risk. He didn't charge. Whether out of caution or fear, the pause stretched thin.

I didn't linger on him. I could feel Jacque at my back now, only a few paces away. He'd strike any second.

I braced—and then I heard it: the sharp, crackling whine of power building, ready to be unleashed.

A split second before the charge peaked, I threw myself aside.

I let go of my bastard sword, twisted, and thrust both hands forward. Wind detonated beneath me, hurling me backward through the air.

At that exact moment, Jacque's charge tore through the space I'd occupied and slammed into the last swordsman.

The bolt hit him square in the torso.

He'd been gripping his sword in both hands, ready to swing, but the force drove it back into him, the edge carving a deep gash across his own shoulder before his weapon was ripped free. A strangled sound caught in his throat.

The arid stench of scorched flesh hit the air, thick and immediate. His mouth fell open in a silent scream, lips peeling back from his teeth, eyes wide as confusion curdled into horror. He staggered, clutching at the ruin of his chest as if he could hold himself together.

Where the armor split at the collar, blistered skin curled inward like old parchment, exposing raw sinew and the pale gleam of bone. The blast tore through him as if his body were nothing more than brittle ash.

He swayed—then dropped sideways.

Dead.

I tumbled through the air in a backward somersault and hit the ground hard, landing square on my ass.

No time to clear the dizziness.

I forced myself up, heart pounding.

Jacques was closing in. I might have been thrown five paces back, but he didn't hesitate. If anything, it only seemed to make him more desperate.

Before I could decide whether to strike or dodge, a flash of Light tore through the air.

It punched clean through Jacque's abdomen. A hole the size of a fist gaped on the left side of his stomach, the edges charred and smoking. He didn't move. He just stared down at the mess of his gut as if it belonged to someone else.

His mouth parted, breath caught somewhere between a gasp and a groan. His sword slipped from his fingers and thudded to the dirt. Eyes wide and unfocused, he swayed on his feet.

As he staggered, turning blindly to face Celeste again, I moved.

Wind coiled around my legs like a drawn spring. I launched forward, fist aimed straight for his head.

The impact landed with the sound of an explosion.

The force hurled him forward, and when he hit the ground his hair ignited, flames racing across his scalp in a sudden blaze. Jacque's gurgled cries echoed through the forest as Fire consumed what remained of him. The stench of burning flesh hung thick in the cool autumn air.

He twitched once.

Twice.

Then stilled.

Silence fell over the clearing.

Jacque was dead.

And yet, as I stood there, I couldn't shake the feeling that killing him had opened a door I'd never be able to close.

2

My body ached. Every muscle screamed, as if I'd woken from the worst muscle spasm imaginable.

I tried to take a deep breath, but my body seized instead. With what little Healing I had left, I eased the spasms and sealed the hole in my leg.

A charred black mark, the size of my fist, stretched across my left breast and climbed the side of my neck, etched there by the Lightning Jacque forced through me.

The burn was healing slowly, along with the rest of my body. I didn't have the strength or luxury to keep Healing beyond what it took just to sit up. When my vision finally focused, I looked around.

Teresa was dead.

Half her face was gone, her head severed.

Teresa had been the kindest of them—but only because everyone else was worse. But she kept the men in line. No one dared touch the prisoners while she was present.

That didn't make her merciful. Only useful.

Earlier, while locked in the fight with Jacque, I'd heard shouting behind me. From the sound of Teresa's voice, I'd guessed someone else had joined the fray.

When I turned my focus back to the three men still standing, Jacque had his back to me, advancing on the new arrival.

That was when I caught a glimpse of the stranger who'd thrown himself into the fight. I didn't know where he stood in all this. But he'd helped kill a few of my captors.

That earned him a pass—for now.

I'd sort him out later. Assuming Jacque didn't kill him first.

At this distance, my attack wouldn't pierce Jacque's skin. Even if it could, the cost would leave me empty. I tried to stand anyway. My legs buckled, and I dropped to my knees.

My body was still recovering from the electrical hell I'd endured. Nerves fired beneath my skin, muscles twitching with leftover static. Even breathing hurt, the air itself seeming to bite back.

I fought to stay upright, eyes locked on the three men.

Jacque was closing in, hand raised, ready to unleash another charge.

But then—the strangest thing happened.

Just as Jacque released the attack, the stranger jerked, hurled backward by an unseen force. His cloak snapped as he tumbled through the air before slamming into the dirt and rolling to a stop.

I blinked, stunned.

One moment he'd been standing his ground. The next, he was debris in the wind.

A scream ripped through the haze—the other swordsman.

Jacque didn't stop. Didn't even glance my way. He was already moving, charging the intruder with brutal focus.

My mind scrambled. *What was that?*

I snapped out of it, lurching forward on shaking legs, every step a battle, momentum dragging me closer.

Close enough.

My fingers twitched as I gathered what little energy I had left. Another charge of Light kindled in my palm. Jacque was too fixed on his target to notice me behind him.

Ten paces away.

Near enough to strike.

I raised my hand—and faltered.

What if I waited?

If I let him fire first, the stranger would almost certainly die. But Jacque might fall with him.

The thought tempted me more than it should have.

Wait. Conserve what remained. Let Jacque kill the stranger—and take Jacque before he ever saw it coming.

Then make him look at me.

Let him know I lived. That I survived.

The ideas slid into me like poison dressed as relief. Killing him slowly. Watching fear take him before death did.

He deserved that.

Jacque left cruelty in his wake. Cruelty I still carried with me.

The crack of leather across my back when exhaustion won. How he allowed other men to linger while we were forced to wash, their gazes stripping what their hands could not.

The boy Jacque killed for dropping a slop bucket on his boots. His temper flashed as fast as his Lightning, cutting the boy down before the apology finished forming on his tongue.

A single strike for a single mistake.

Jacque deserved to suffer. To be erased.

They all did.

And yet, despite everything in me screaming for revenge, I didn't know if I could let someone who *might* have been trying to save me die.

But sparing him didn't mean I trusted him.

Once this fight ended, I'd have nothing left. No strength to fight again. And I still didn't know who he was or what he wanted. He'd cut down my captors, yes—but that didn't make him an ally. For all I knew, he was clearing the way to claim me for himself.

Rescuer. Abductor.

It made no difference.

Jacque raised his hand.

That was all the time I had.

I made my choice.

With my right hand, I poured every last ounce of energy into the Light. I aimed for Jacque's back and released.

The beam punched through him—clean and hot. For a moment, I saw daylight on the other side.

Blood bloomed across his back, soaking into his shirt in slow, spreading waves.

He turned around. Our eyes locked.

I smiled.

My legs gave out. I dropped to both knees, too drained to stand. But I was still upright, still conscious.

Still able to meet Jacque's eyes as he glared at me with the hatred of a man staring at his brother's killer.

If I had the chance to do it all over again, I would've made him scream first.

They had captured me because I could Heal. That was my gift, and the only thing that made me valuable in their eyes.

Most Casters hurled Fire or bent Water. Not me. I was rare. A "regenerating investment," one of them joked.

Traded from slavers to slavers, but they kept me breathing. Kept me alive. Someone out there was willing to pay a fortune for a girl who could Heal others—and who didn't die easily, no matter how badly they tried.

And so they didn't hold back.

I was nothing but a commodity with a heartbeat.

The explosion ripped me out of the past.

Jacque flew toward me. He hit the ground hard, his skull caved in, blood and smoke rising from what was left of him.

Sputtering. Dying slow.

I hoped he felt every moment of it.

His chest shuddered once, then he took his last breath.

Then I was left with the stranger.

Just in time to help.

Far too late to trust.

He walked toward me. I stayed on my knees, too weak to rise. We both knew I couldn't fight.

He knew I was at his mercy.

As he stood over me, I finally got a clearer look at him.

Pale gray eyes, so light they were almost white. Staring into them felt like looking into something not entirely human, like an ethereal force reaching in, ready to strip me bare. His dark hair was tied back, though loose strands had fallen across his face in the chaos of battle. A short, well-kept beard framed his jaw. A tattoo curled along his left arm; silver glinted at his ear.

In any other situation, I might have called him handsome.

Right now, I called him a threat.

Unfortunately for me, I had no way to defend myself.

He offered me his hand.

"I appreciate the assist," he said.

I took it, letting him haul me to my feet.

"Glad you finished him before he decided to shoot me again," I muttered dryly. "Shame, though. I was looking forward to ending him myself."

Standing, I realized he was a head taller, probably more. If this turned sour, I knew exactly how it would end.

He didn't look winded in the slightest. A few strands of hair clung to his cheek, his clothes rumpled from the fall. But there was no strain in his movements, no heavy breathing. Whatever energy he'd used, he had barely scratched the surface.

And that bothered me.

Now that I thought about it ... what kind of Caster *was* he?

I could've sworn I saw him use Wind Casting to hurl himself away from Jacque's strike. But that explosion earlier? As far as I knew, no Casting art could make a body erupt like that from a punch.

Unless he was more than he seemed ...

Unless he was like me.

An Aberration—a Caster with more than one affinity.

"So," he said, studying me like a solved puzzle, "you're an Aberration."

My stomach dropped.

Shit.

I didn't know how he'd figured it out, but it put me in a dangerous position. Aberrations weren't just rare—they were condemned. Tools to use. Pets to cage.

"I know you're an Ardor Variant." He glanced at the scorched bodies. "The holes kind of gave it away."

Was that what I was?

I already knew I was different. Healing alone had proven that. It wasn't one of the four natural affinities, so I'd always known I was a Variant.

And this new power—this light that burned through flesh and bone—wasn't one of them either. I just hadn't known it had a name.

I'd only ever called it Light.

Not that I'd ever tell him that.

He stepped closer. "But you're also a Healing Variant, aren't you? You bounced back a little too fast. Most people cooked half to death would be face-down by now. Either dead or begging for it." He tilted his head, a grin tugging at his face. "Yet here you are. Still standing and breathing. And after all that, you had enough left to fire off one more blast."

He gestured lazily toward my leg. "You took an arrow. Yet you're moving just fine."

He had named both my affinities.

Two affinities alone made someone an Aberration—and both of mine were Variants.

I couldn't bullshit my way out of this one. The truth was obvious.

So I shoved the spotlight back on him.

"You're an Aberration too, aren't you?"

His smile widened, amused. "Now what makes you say that?"

If we were pretending to be honest, I'd keep going.

"You used Wind Casting earlier to dodge Jacque's strike. Then you blew his head apart with something I've never seen. And Teresa ..." I swallowed hard. "You may have cut her head off, but her face told another story. Whatever ripped through her—that wasn't your blade. That was something else."

He stayed silent. But silence could say plenty.

"Whatever you did to Jacque, you did to her too. So why didn't she burn the same way?"

He let out a soft laugh. "Wind fed the Fire and forced it to erupt." He paused. "As for the woman—Teresa, was it? That was Ice."

He tipped his head, almost amused. "You're welcome by the way."

Fire. Wind. Ice.

If he used Ice, that meant he could cast Water too.

Four elements.

I leaned back on my heels, putting a sliver of space between us. "I've never heard of an Aberration Casting more than two affinities. Yet you used four."

"Stories exaggerate. And Ice is just Water behaving under pressure."

I stared at him.

Of all the things he could've said, he chose to argue semantics.

Yes, Ice was technically a branch of Water Casting—but very few ever reached it. And here he was, brushing it aside like it was nothing.

I wasn't about to feed his smug satisfaction with awe or admiration. He knew exactly what he'd done wasn't ordinary.

So I didn't correct him.

Instead, I asked the only question that mattered.

"So what's next?"

What was to happen to me now?

All I could think about was getting out of here before any stragglers showed up. I didn't know how many were after me. For all I knew, this had only been the first wave.

I'd killed two of them and slipped into the night like a rat.

So much for escaping.

I might be hard to kill, but if they caught me again, it wouldn't matter. I'd rather die than go through that again.

His smile faded. He studied me for a long moment before answering.

"Nothing," he said at last. "I did what I came to do. There's a rabbit waiting to be cooked. From here, we part ways."

That was it.

Anticlimactic, but probably the best outcome I could've hoped for.

He turned and walked back toward the woods.

Thanks to his flashy entrance, there were no horses nearby; they bolted the moment that explosion shook the ground.

And I could barely stay on my feet, let alone walk leagues through this cursed forest to the next town.

My exhaustion was bone-deep. I didn't have the strength to do anything but sit down and wait for my body to recover. Even if I could still Cast Healing, fatigue was beyond repair.

At most, I could've forced a little energy into my leg, enough to dull the ache. The wound was already closed. Maybe I could've cleared the burnt skin along my neck and chest from Jacque's last strike.

But that was it. The rest would take time.

And time meant waiting.

Only problem was, what little food I had was buried beneath my dead horse. With the other mounts scattered, there was nothing nearby to scavenge. No packs. No supplies.

I glanced up. He was still walking, his silhouette shrinking as he climbed toward the wooded hills.

I forced myself to shout, the effort scraping my throat raw. "That's it? You help me kill men you don't even know, and you won't even give me your name?"

He stopped. Then turned.

That grin slid back into place like it had never left.

"Name's Artemis," he said. "But you can just call me Art."

3

After telling her my name, I found myself walking back toward her.

It wasn't the first time she'd surprised me.

She was filthy and bruised, worn thin from days without rest, but none of it could fully hide the beauty beneath. Strands of red hair cut through the grime, vibrant despite everything. Her light green eyes caught the sun—bright and unflinching.

The burn that stretched from her neck down across her left breast was impossible to miss, charred black and cruel in its severity. Only her Healing kept her upright. With how small she was, it was a miracle she hadn't already collapsed.

If there was one word for her, it was *resilient*.

Being a Healer didn't mean stamina came back without rest. Casting at that level would drain anyone. And with her reserves spent, even mending a simple bruise was likely beyond her abilities now.

If I wanted her trust, the best thing I could do was walk away—prove I wasn't a threat.

I'd been ready to do exactly that.

I knew what it felt like to trust someone with the truth, only to have them sell you out for a handful of coin.

Still, she wasn't walking anywhere in her condition.

When I reached her, I kept my tone casual. "Would you like some rabbit stew?"

She gave me a look of open suspicion. I didn't blame her. A stranger who nearly left without offering his name, only to circle back with food, any sane person would hesitate.

She studied me for a second, then nodded. "Sure. I could really use a meal right now."

I wrapped her right arm around my waist, careful not to press against the burn seared across her left side. She leaned into me, and together we made our way toward the edge of the clearing, up the gentle incline that led back into the woods.

Once we reached the tree line, I eased her down.

"I'll be right back," I told her, turning to jog up to where I'd left the rabbit hanging.

"You're bleeding," she called after me, her voice edged with concern.

I froze and glanced over my shoulder, confused. I looked down. Arms, ribs, nothing.

"It's in the middle of your back. How badly are you injured? I might still have enough strength left to stop the bleeding."

I reached back, pressing my hand to the top of my spine. My fingers came back wet with blood.

I couldn't help but laugh. "Not mine," I said, grinning. "It's from the rabbit we're about to eat."

She blinked, clearly confused.

"I'd just finished hunting it when I slung it over my shoulder. Guess it bled more than I thought."

I nodded back toward the woods. "I need to grab my gear if I'm going to make stew out of it. Give me a few minutes."

I left her at the edge of the clearing and started back toward camp. The path was uneven, littered with fallen branches. The faint smell of smoke still clung to the air.

The rush from the fight had faded, leaving the usual quiet behind—the kind that came after bloodshed. The kind I'd grown used to.

I called the Wind, letting it coil around my legs and spine. The first step always felt like pressure dropping before a storm. Then the world blurred. The ground rolled beneath me in long, effortless strides. Branches whipped past, the forest streaking by in green and gold.

My camp lay half a league away, far enough to be safe from the fighting, close enough to return before she started to worry.

The fire had burned low by the time I arrived. My gear was still where I'd left it: the pack, the small pot, the waterskin, the herbs I'd traded for back in Orvain.

I moved quickly, gathering what I needed.

For a brief period, I let the silence settle. Just the wind whispering through the trees, the faint pop of cooling embers. Normally, that quiet was a comfort. Proof that I was still alone, that the world hadn't caught up yet.

Now it felt different.

What, exactly, was I doing?

I'd told myself not to get involved again. Not to show anyone what I could really do. Not to risk it.

But a part of me—small but reckless—wanted to. A flicker of something dangerously close to anticipation at the thought of not having to hide. Of sharing even a fraction of what I was with someone who might understand it.

Yet here I was, cooking for a stranger who'd seen more of me in one day than most ever would.

Fool. Age was supposed to bring wisdom.

I tugged the strap on the pack tight and exhaled slowly.

Her Casting was strong. I knew that kind of strength.

I knew what it cost.

The thought sat heavy as I stepped forward and called Wind again.

One more night, I told myself. Then I'd be gone.

When I returned to the clearing, rabbit and supplies in hand, I noticed her immediately.

Celeste was slumped over, and for a terrifying moment I thought she'd collapsed, until I saw the slow rise of her chest.

She was asleep.

Her knees had fallen to one side, her back leaning toward the ground, her head tilted sideways. The tension she carried had eased, softening the sharp lines in her face. Even in sleep she looked guarded, but the raw edge had dulled.

I set the supplies down and stood there a moment longer than I meant to, watching her breathe.

She looked young. Not in years, but in the way pain could finally let go when it ran out of strength.

I knelt beside her. The charred skin down her neck had faded, smaller than before.

She'd pushed herself again.

Too far this time.

Enervation, most likely. No wonder she was out cold.

I exhaled through my nose, half impressed, half concerned. She didn't know her limits yet. But she was getting closer to understanding them.

Healing alone wouldn't make her a fighter. Most Healers never saw a real battle. They kept to the rear, stitching the fallen back together while others broke apart at the front.

They weren't built for this. But she wasn't just a Healer. Aberrations were rare enough, and her affinities weren't standard.

Healing. Ardor. Variant powers.

A Variant Aberration.

She hadn't yet grasped what her abilities were truly capable of—but one day she would.

Without a word, I pulled the blanket from my pack and draped it over her, easing her into a more comfortable position. Autumn's chill had crept in with the lowering sun. No sense in letting her freeze.

I slid a hand behind her head and lifted it just enough to tuck my travel pillow beneath. It was worn and flat from years on the road, but better than cold ground.

She stirred, then drifted deeper into sleep.

"Rest easy," I murmured, not expecting a response.

I turned to the fire pit, laying stones in a small ring before clearing space for kindling. Then I started on the stew, the rabbit and supplies set neatly at my side. The clearing quieted again.

I stripped the rabbit with practiced hands, setting bones and sinew aside. I worked slowly, guided by routine rather than urgency. It gave my thoughts somewhere to rest.

Across the fire, she shifted in her sleep, curling in around herself as if even rest couldn't quite convince her she was safe.

I'd seen that posture before.

I'd worn it once.

A long time ago, I had been the one in the dirt—half dead, wondering when my own hell would end. Trust given too freely. A boy too young to know better.

All it took was a frightened friend and a price he couldn't refuse.

I was taken.

And the torture began.

I wasn't strong then. Not like now. I remembered the chains. The smell of rust and sweat. The long nights spent staring into the dark, waiting to find out what the next day would bring.

I made it out. Not clean. Not whole. But I got out.

And I learned. Not just how to fight or Cast or keep moving—but how to wear a mask. Act kind enough not to draw suspicion. Remain distant enough not to invite questions.

Even now, in towns I passed through often, no one really knew me. Not the barkeeps I shared drinks with. Not the traders I helped on the road. The fewer people who knew what I could do, the fewer chances there were to be betrayed again.

I glanced over at her, still asleep, blanket drawn to her chin and hair tangled from the fight.

I cut the onion next, the only other ingredient I had besides the rabbit. Adding what little seasoning and dried herbs remained in my kit, I stirred the pot. The scent rose, earthy and sharp.

It was moments like these that made me feel oddly melancholic.

People like us didn't get peace, only pauses.

Brief ones. Between battles. Between betrayals. And sometimes, if we were lucky, that was enough.

I let the fire burn and kept my eyes on the horizon, one ear always open.

When the stew had simmered and cooled, I ate my half, then went to move the bodies out of the clearing.

By the time I returned, she was stirring.

Celeste blinked against the low light, her movements sluggish from recovery. Then she jolted upright, eyes sweeping the clearing until recognition settled in. She frowned at the blanket draped over her, then the fire, before finally meeting my gaze.

I scooped out a generous portion of stew into the same bowl I'd used earlier and extended it toward her.

"Here," I said. "You should eat while it's still warm."

She hesitated, eyeing the bowl like it might bite. After a few seconds, she took it. The first bites were careful, until hunger won out and she ate in earnest.

I returned to my place by the fire and let her eat in peace. I picked up my charcoal, steadied the paper on my knee, and began to sketch.

The silence between us wasn't uncomfortable. Just quiet. The soft scrape of charcoal. The faint clink of her spoon against the bowl.

When she finished, she set the bowl aside without a word. The quiet stretched, neither of us in any rush to fill it.

Then I heard it.

A faint hum, gentle and low. The familiar sound of a Healer at work.

She was Casting again.

I watched from the corner of my eye. Her brow was furrowed in concentration, jaw tight. She was pushing herself.

I waited a moment. She didn't strike me as someone who welcomed orders, especially from a stranger. But the hum deepened, and I could feel the strain in it.

"She's going to burn herself out," I muttered to myself.

I set the charcoal aside.

"You don't need to force it," I said, keeping my voice calm but firm. "You've already done enough. Push too far and you'll pass out again."

She didn't answer at first. The hum lingered a moment longer, then faded as the light around her chest dimmed.

Good. At least she was listening—to her body, if not to me.

When the glow finally vanished from her hands, she straightened slowly and glanced over. "How long was I out?"

"Not long. A few hours at most."

She nodded, gaze drifting back to the fire. Her posture was looser now, but tension lived in her shoulders, like she braced for something that hadn't come yet.

I didn't let the silence root itself again.

"Didn't have much to work with," I said, nodding toward the pot. "Hope the stew came out halfway decent."

Her eyes flicked to my hands, then lifted to me again before she answered. "It was good. Best meal I've had in a while." She curled into herself, arms wrapping around her legs. "They would've fed me rabbit skin, not rabbit stew."

"Want to talk about it?" I asked.

She shrugged, studying the firelight dancing in the pot. "Not really." No edge in her voice, just fatigue. "Talking didn't do me much good before."

I nodded once and let it be.

"Fair enough. Then tell me this—where do you plan on heading next? You're welcome to stay here a few days and rest. I was camped nearby when I came to investigate the commotion. I'm headed toward Thalor."

"Not Thalor," she said flatly.

I raised an eyebrow.

"It's not because it's your destination," she added quickly. "It's just …" Something flickered behind her eyes. After a moment, she sighed. "I was held somewhere near Rodin. It's on the way."

"Meaning these weren't the only ones. There's a larger group and you were moving east to get clear before they caught up."

She nodded, expression grim. "That's why I can't stay here longer than a night. Come morning, I have to keep moving. I need to get out while I still can. I don't know how many more are after me, but it only took them a few days to catch up. And now I'm without a horse. It won't be long before they find me again."

I tested her reasoning. "You're not wrong," I admitted. "But cutting straight through Pylin Forest instead of sticking to the roads worked in your favor."

She frowned.

"This place is vast. No mapped trails. Just old hunter paths and growth thick enough to swallow a wagon. Most people won't risk it without a guide. But with the horse you rode, you left signs everywhere, even with the head start."

The fire's crackle filled the space between us.

"If we move camp in the morning, deeper and more remote, it'll be near impossible for them to track you. I know these woods. I've spent weeks here over the years."

My gaze drifted toward the tree line. "Trust me, if you want to disappear, there's no better place than this forest."

Her expression grew thoughtful. "If you're right ... then staying one more day might actually give me an edge."

The last of the sunlight spilled through the trees, gilding the camp in a soft, fading warmth.

"I think it'd be best for you to rest. If you plan on leaving the day after tomorrow, you'll need your strength. I'll put the fire out early and I'll stay awake a few more hours to keep watch."

She hesitated, then nodded. Turned and lowered herself back onto the bedroll.

"Thank you," she murmured. "You've shown me a kindness I may never be able to repay."

Her voice faded with the dying fire. A moment later, her breathing evened.

I stayed where I was, listening to the forest breathe around us—the wind through the leaves, the distant call of something wild—and told myself I'd only keep watch a little longer.

4

Morning light broke through the trees, chasing away the shadows, and with them the weight of yesterday's battle.

I pushed myself upright, forcing my sore body to obey. Each movement sparked pain, a reminder of what we'd endured. Still, I rose, even as my muscles protested with every step.

Blinking against the light, I scanned the camp.

Art was gone.

The campfire was cold and smothered. The pot and supplies he'd used to cook were stacked neatly at the base of a nearby tree. Even the bodies he'd dragged out of the clearing were gone. He'd been up before me, already erasing every trace of our presence.

I must've been more exhausted than I realized. For him to do all this without waking me ... he was either unnervingly quiet, or I'd truly been dead to the world.

Maybe both.

With no clue where he'd gone or what his intentions were, I decided to stay put and wait. There was little else I could do. I turned my thoughts instead to preparing for tomorrow. Escaping into the forest had been my only goal—a desperate, directionless bid for freedom. But now that the immediate threat had passed, I faced a harder question.

Where would I go?

I couldn't return to Avriel, even if I wanted to. There was nothing left for me there. No family. No friends. No one I could trust. I didn't even know what state my hometown was in now. Going back would be foolish.

In prison, there was the little blond-haired boy they sometimes let out of his cell, probably no older than nine. His eyes always looked swollen from crying.

And then there was Faylen.

The girl with the soft voice. The only person who'd kept me sane, whispering stories of her life and family through the cracks in the stone between our cells. She told me about her younger brothers, how one of them had recently awakened as a Water Caster. He'd been so excited he ran across town to the tavern where she worked, just to tell her the news.

I could hear the joy in her voice when she said he was the first Caster ever born in their family. Her tone always turned wistful when she spoke of home. Picking flowers in the hill villages or riding beside her father on trips to Orvain to sell wares.

She missed them terribly.

She had been a dreamer, always talking about escape and the things we'd do together once we got out, like it was a promise. How we'd find a place far from all this and start over. That I was welcome in her family's home.

Tears slipped free before I realized I was crying.

But I hadn't waited for her. When the moment came—when Kaelen and Davos dragged me from my cell that final time and into the dark beyond the compound, and I Cast my first Ardor and killed them ...

I ran.

I didn't look back.

And now I lived with that.

I didn't even know if she was still alive.

The guilt was there, raw and festering. It lingered like a wound I couldn't heal. I kept telling myself there was nothing I could've done. That if I'd stayed, they would've sold me off anyway, just for someone else to continue the torment.

But none of that mattered now. Because if she was still in that place, still whispering hope through the cracks in the stone ...

There was nothing I could do. I wasn't strong enough to go back.

Not a hero who could return and save everyone.

An Aberration—yet even that wasn't enough. I still needed someone else to save me.

If only I had been stronger ...

A twig snapped nearby. I wiped my tears and turned toward the sound.

Art stepped out from between the trees.

"Good morning," he said.

"Morning." The word caught faintly in my throat.

He moved to pack up the blanket and pillow, folding them before tucking them into his satchel. Then he turned back to me.

"We should get moving soon. I followed the trail the horses left but didn't see anyone. That doesn't mean they're not out there. There's a creek not far from here where we can wash up before we continue. Figured you might like that."

"I haven't had a proper bath in ages." I gave a brittle smile. "You sure the creek's deep enough?"

"Well, it's not exactly a hot spring, but it'll do. You'll come out cleaner than you went in—mostly."

I let out a soft but rough laugh. "So, no scented oils or rose petals? What kind of service is that?" The words came out lighter than I felt, but I forced them out anyway.

A faint smile tugged at his mouth. "Not unless you count wet leaves. Come on. Creek's this way."

We started up the slope, weaving between trees as the morning light filtered through the canopy. Our exchange had been small, but it lifted my mood more than I expected. For the first time in a long while, I was actually looking forward to something. A good wash would do me some good. Maybe I'd even clean his blanket and pillow as a quiet apology for getting my stench all over them.

As we made our way toward the creek, Art told me a bit about the forest. While scouting for any trackers earlier that morning, he had seen a family of gray foxes drinking from the stream.

He'd said it would take a quarter of the morning to reach the creek. Yet somehow he'd managed to get there, scout for trackers, and return all in the same stretch of daylight.

I knew he was a Wind Caster, but that wasn't any kind of Wind Casting I'd ever heard of.

Was that how he moved so fast?

I kept my questions to myself. I still had my own secrets; it wouldn't be fair to ask about his.

And I wasn't ready to give him that kind of ground.

He then explained that if I ever needed a drink of water and wasn't near a stream, I could cut into the vinewood and drink the clear liquid inside. As we passed a tree, he peeled back some bark and showed me fireleaf. It burned hot and fast, making it a perfect fire starter.

With how much he knew about the forest, he could've told me he'd lived here his whole life, and I would've believed him.

His voice was easygoing, almost fond. "If you see a squirrel throwing nuts at you, that's Nettles. We've had disagreements," he said with a straight face. I couldn't tell if he was joking or not.

He paused at a nearby bush and gestured toward the berries. "These are frostberries. Bitter, but safe to eat. Good for energy if you've got nothing else."

I eyed them suspiciously. "After you."

He chuckled. "I'm not hungry at the moment."

We reached the creek. The water was clear, and cold, whispering softly as it wound between smooth stones and moss-covered banks. The sound was serene, lifting a heaviness in me I hadn't known was still there.

Art set his bags down and unpacked supplies, including something wrapped in leather. He walked over and placed it in my hands. A solid white block that looked almost like cheese.

"Here," he said. "Use this to wash up. It's lye soap I picked up on my travels. Don't worry about using too much, I've got more. Works on clothes, too."

I glanced down at the worn, homemade soap. Even the idea of washing felt like a luxury. It had been so long since I'd felt clean—not just rinsed off in dirty rainwater or wiped down with torn fabric. A real bath. Even if it was only a cold stream.

He hesitated, then reached back into his bag and pulled out a slender wooden stick wrapped neatly in cloth, one end frayed into stiff fibers. He held it out awkwardly.

"For your teeth. It's unused."

I eyed it, then looked up at him. "I'd hope so."

The corner of his mouth twitched.

He rummaged through his bag again and pulled out a clean shirt and pair of pants, holding them out to me. "Wear these while your clothes dry."

I blinked, caught off guard by his preparedness and by the quiet way he kept offering kindness without asking for anything in return.

I wasn't sure which unnerved me more—the thought that it was real, or the fact that I wanted it to be.

Before I could find the words to thank him, he was already turning away.

"I'll stay within earshot. Just shout if you need anything," he called over his shoulder.

I stood there, soap in hand, clothes draped over one arm. For a moment, I didn't move. Overwhelmed by how simple it all was.

I wasn't used to this kind of consideration. Not since the stone cells.

I exhaled slowly and stepped toward the water.

I set the borrowed clothes on a dry patch of stone and peeled off my own. They were stiff with sweat, dirt, and blood. My fingers brushed the burn mark going up my neck. It hadn't fully healed yet, but if I kept at it over the next few days, I might be able to avoid scarring.

I waded deeper into the creek. The shock of the cold wrapped around me, and I plunged under all at once to adjust faster. When I surfaced, I sank waist-deep, letting the current swirl around me. For a long moment, I just stayed there, still, letting the cold seep into my bones and wash away some of the exhaustion.

I lathered the soap between my hands, catching a faint scent of pine and ash. It was comforting. I worked it over my skin and scrubbed hard, as if I could erase the last remnants of that place. I dragged the soap through my hair next, combing my fingers down to the scalp, until the water ran cloudy and then clear again.

When I finished with my body, I reached for the small bundle he'd given me. Inside was the wooden brush and a pinch of pale powder wrapped in cloth. I dipped the bristles, scrubbed at my teeth, and rinsed, repeating it once more for good measure.

Unused, he'd said.

I eyed the brush, then tucked it back into the cloth. I'd keep it. If he asked for it back later, I'd have my answer.

When I finished, I gathered my clothes and scrubbed those too.

Back on the bank, I wrung out the damp fabric as best I could and spread it across a sunlit rock to dry. The shirt Art had given me hung a little loose, the pants cinched at the waist with a simple drawstring.

I squeezed the water from my hair and followed the path he'd taken. He must've thought I needed half the forest to myself, because it took forever before I finally spotted him sitting on a rock.

He turned his head when he heard me approach.

"The clothes fit perfectly," he said with a teasing grin.

"Keep that up and I might not give them back," I shot back, a small smirk tugging at my lips.

He lifted another bar of soap and a fresh set of clothes from the top of his pack, slinging them over his shoulder.

"There's some waterfowl eggs I boiled earlier. Help yourself while I go get cleaned up," he said, nodding toward the pot before heading off the way I'd come.

I watched him disappear into the trees before turning back to the pot. Inside, a few boiled eggs waited.

I crouched beside the pot and cracked one open, the steam still clinging to the shell. The first bite was soft and warm. I closed my eyes briefly in appreciation.

"Looks like the man can cook," I muttered under my breath, popping the rest of the egg into my mouth. A sly smile tugged at my lips. "Maybe I really should keep the clothes."

By the time the eggs were gone, Art returned, his hair still damp and the edges of his beard freshly shaved along his cheeks, a clean shirt clinging to his frame. He glanced at me. "How was breakfast?"

"Better than rabbit skin, I'll give you that." The words came out caught somewhere between playful and wary.

"Good. I'm glad you've enjoyed your fill," he replied with a faint smile.

Lifting a hand to his head, he began using Wind Casting to dry his hair. I'd only ever known one Wind Caster—Garron, back in my village—but he was older, and the rare times he would Cast, it came in heavy gusts, as though he had to wrestle it for control.

Art simply held up his hand and the wind obeyed.

I couldn't help but smile at the sight. "Must be nice, having your own personal windstorm on command."

He glanced sideways at me, water still clinging to a few loose strands. "You could do the same, you know. With a little practice."

I raised an eyebrow. "I doubt that."

He chuckled. "It's true. Control is everything. For example, I can only move small amounts of air this way. If I wanted to expel more force, I'd have to draw more from my core first."

His tone changed, more serious. "Ardor's about precision, not just power. You've already shaped it—controlled the size and force behind your attack, directed it where you wanted. That's not something most beginners manage."

I tilted my head, considering his words. "How do you know I'm a beginner?"

He gave me a look—assessing, almost amused. "Because control and instinct aren't the same. You can direct it, even rein in its size, but I can feel the strain when you do. That means you don't own it yet. It still owns you."

"So you're saying I could use heat, too?"

He nodded. "With refinement. Light and warmth go hand in hand. Focus enough, and you can generate heat without burning. Just takes discipline."

I glanced in the direction of the creek. "Never thought of it like that."

"Few do," he replied, lowering his hand now that his hair was mostly dry. "Most people live their entire lives without ever seeing Ardor. It doesn't behave like Wind or Fire. It requires a different kind of control—but with the right technique, it's incredibly versatile."

I studied, puzzled. "If it's that rare, how do you know so much about it?"

He held my gaze, something unreadable flickering behind his expression. "I met someone once who could Cast Ardor, like you. But unlike you, he wasn't an Aberration."

I blinked at him, a small laugh slipping out. "So according to you, that's two Ardor Casters in one lifetime? You really do get around."

He gave a noncommittal shrug. "I've been to a lot of places. Seen more than most."

I watched him for a moment longer. He didn't look much older than me—mid-twenties maybe. His eyes were keen, but they didn't carry the weight I'd expect from someone claiming to have seen so much.

So how?

How did someone so young know Ardor like second nature? How had he met two Ardor Variants, moved through the forest like he'd lived in it his whole life, and Cast so many elements as if it was nothing?

I didn't understand him, any of it, but for once, that didn't matter. I didn't need to unravel his secrets; I just wanted to understand my own.

"Then maybe you could show me a few things. Just enough to keep from burning myself out next time."

I hated how much I needed him to say yes. Not because I trusted him—but because I needed what he knew.

His expression didn't change, but I thought I saw a flicker of surprise.

"I'm not asking for much," I added quickly. "Just ... guidance."

He didn't respond right away. His gaze drifted toward the fire, expression unreadable, the stillness stretching just long enough to make me wonder if I'd said too much.

The flames cracked softly between us. After a moment, he gave a faint nod—barely there, but enough.

I didn't push the subject. That was probably the closest I was going to get to a yes.

The late morning air carried the scent of pine and ash. Maybe, just maybe, things were beginning to turn.

5

He didn't say anything for a while after that. Just stirred the fire with a stick, sending a faint curl of smoke into the air.

When he finally spoke, his tone was even. "You understand I can't teach you everything in a day."

"I figured as much."

He nodded once, eyes still on the embers. "Good. Because learning control isn't about power, it's about patience and focus. You push too hard too soon, you burn out. Or worse."

I folded my arms loosely around my knees. "Then where do we start?"

"Nowhere yet," he said, standing to check his pack. "You're still recovering. When your body's drained, your focus is the first thing to go. And control without focus is chaos waiting to happen."

There was something grounding in the way he said it. Like he'd learned that lesson the hard way once and didn't want to see me repeat it.

He adjusted the strap on his shoulder and gave me a sidelong glance. "Rest for a bit. Once the sun's higher, I'll show you a few things. Enough to keep from tearing yourself apart next time."

That was all he said before he turned toward the trees with a waterskin in hand.

I watched him go, the faint echo of his words lingering in my mind. *Enough to keep from tearing yourself apart.*

It wasn't a promise. But it was a start.

I waited until he was gone before I let myself breathe again.

The clearing felt different now, quieter. Maybe it was because he hadn't said *no*. Maybe it was just the first time in weeks I'd felt like I wasn't completely alone.

I glanced down at my hands. They trembled, the faintest pulse of heat flickering beneath my skin. A remnant of power I hadn't yet learned to command. If I could just hold onto that feeling without burning out, maybe I could learn something before this all slipped away.

When Art returned, the waterskin slung over his shoulder, I straightened instinctively. He set it beside the fire, crouching to check the pot. The smell of broth and ash lingered in the air.

He pulled out his worn leather-bound notebook and flipped it open, muttering. His charcoal scratched softly against the page, the strokes neat and precise. I sat nearby, watching the slow rhythm of his scribbling.

The silence stretched. Not tense, just ... awkward.

I wasn't used to quiet like this, not without the shadow of fear behind it.

Finally, I cleared my throat. "You write a lot?"

He didn't look up. "When there's something worth remembering."

"What is it this time?"

"A recipe," he said flatly.

I frowned. "You're joking."

One corner of his mouth twitched. "Mostly."

The scratching resumed.

My curiosity gnawed at me, and before I could stop myself, the words slipped out. "So where were you coming from before all this?"

He looked up, considering the question before answering. "Orvain. Passed through there about a month ago."

"Orvain," I repeated, nodding. "And now?"

"Thalor."

"That's a long way from here."

He shrugged. "Good food. Better ale. There's a festival coming up next month. Thought I'd stay for a while."

It sounded casual enough, but something about how easily he said it felt rehearsed. Like he'd picked the answer out of a pile of half-truths.

"You're just … wandering?"

"More or less." He closed the notebook and rested his forearm across his knee. "I travel when I feel like it. Stay where I don't get chased off. That sort of life."

"No family? Wife or kids?" I asked before realizing how personal it sounded.

His brow lifted, amused. "Do I look like someone's husband?"

Heat rose in my face. "I didn't mean—"

"I know what you meant," he said, a faint smile pulling at his lips before fading. "No wife. No kids. Too much road, not enough reason."

His gaze held mine, like he was assessing me. "You?"

"Same answer," I said quietly.

"Good," he said simply. "Less to worry about."

The conversation faded after that, the silence returning, softer this time. The sound of the forest filled it in: wind threading through branches, the crackle of the fire, the faint rush of a nearby stream.

Art leaned back against a log, flipping open his notebook again, content to let the hush linger.

The sun had climbed a little higher, its light slanting through the canopy, dappled and warm. The fire had burned low, its smoke rising in thin, lazy ribbons.

Rest for a bit, he'd said. Easy for him.

I glanced at him once more. He was scribbling something in his notebook again, focused, completely oblivious to the rest of the world.

I took a slow breath and reached inward, finding that flicker of warmth that lived somewhere behind my ribs. The energy stirred, eager, pulsing in tandem with my heartbeat. I guided it to my palms, careful, focused.

Light began to bloom between my fingers. It shimmered weakly at first, then brightened as I fed more energy into it.

It was working.

Then—

"Should I be concerned about you setting yourself on fire," Art interrupted lazily, "or is this part of your meditation routine?"

The Light faltered, slipping though my control. I whipped around. "I was practicing. You said I needed focus."

He looked up from his notebook, utterly unfazed. "I said you needed rest. I also said patience. Good to know you listened to neither."

I narrowed my eyes. "I was trying to be productive."

He shut the notebook with a quiet snap. "And I'm trying to make sure you don't explode before lunch."

He stood, brushing the dirt from his hands. "Well, since resting clearly isn't your strong suit, let's put that stubbornness to better use."

Crossing his arms, he nodded toward me. "Go on, then. Show me what you were doing."

"I *was* trying to get a handle on it," I said defensively. "I almost had it too."

"I noticed. That's when most people lose it." He stepped closer, the faintest trace of a smirk tugging at his mouth. "You're trying to control something that doesn't answer to force."

I frowned. "You make it sound like it has a mind of its own."

"In a way, it does. You don't command Ardor, you cooperate with it. Push too hard and it pushes back."

He stopped in front of me and gestured to my hands. "Try again. Slowly this time."

I hesitated. "So you can make more jokes when it fails?"

"Hopefully fewer," he said, tone flat but eyes amused.

I inhaled and focused again, drawing the warmth from my chest into my hands. The Light sparked, faint and unsteady, flickering with every heartbeat.

"Don't reach for it," he murmured. "Just notice it."

I exhaled, letting the air leave me in one slow stream. The glow steadied for a moment, then wavered again.

"Better. Now keep breathing. Let it respond to you, not the other way around."

The air between us felt different now, charged with something invisible. I could sense him watching, studying every flicker.

"Good," he said at last. "You can stop."

The Light blinked out, leaving only the faint warmth on my skin. I looked down at my hands, surprised.

"That was ... easier than I expected."

"That's because you stopped fighting it. Control isn't about holding on. It's about knowing when to let go."

I flexed my fingers, watching the faint shimmer fade completely. "It's not the same as when I Cast Healing," I said. "That feels ... different. Calmer somehow. Like it moves on its own once I start."

"That's because it does," he replied, crouching to poke at the embers. "Healing wants balance. Ardor wants direction. They may both manifest as light, but they behave differently. Each element has its own way of being Cast."

He used his stick to trace idle lines in the dirt. "Every Cast begins in the body. Fire, Water, Wind, Lightning—those start in the Caster. You shape the energy first, then release it. Earth is different. You can't create it inside yourself the way you do the others. It already exists. All an Earth Caster does is move what's there."

I frowned. "So they can just raise a wall anywhere?"

"Not unless they're a strong Caster. Most have to be in contact with the ground, and distance weakens the connection."

He nudged the dirt with the stick. "And once something's Cast, it belongs to the one who made it. A Fire Caster can't steal another Fire Caster's flame. They can fight it, overwhelm it, counter it—but they can't take it."

His gaze flicked up to meet mine. "Wind answers movement. Fire, emotion. Water listens. Earth endures. Healing restores. But Ardor, it *reflects*."

"Reflects?" I echoed, brow furrowing.

He nodded. "It mirrors the Caster. Your intent, your focus, even your doubt. The more you push against it, the more it resists."

I let his words sink in. "It's stubborn."

He chuckled. "I'd call it discerning. It only listens when you mean it."

I looked down at my hands again, the faint warmth still lingering beneath my skin. "Sounds like me."

"That's why you were able to use it at all," he said, standing and brushing the dirt from his palms. "You didn't think. You just reacted. Instinct can wake a gift, but it won't keep it steady. That's where discipline comes in."

He paused, eyes following a shaft of sunlight cutting through the branches. "Ardor isn't something you force into shape. You learn to meet it halfway. The only other person I ever saw Cast it said the same thing."

I glanced up, remembering what he'd told me before. "The other Ardor Variant?"

He gave a curt nod, the corner of his mouth tightening. "He was good. Too good, maybe. He taught me enough to recognize when someone's about to burn themselves alive trying to control it."

That earned a quiet laugh from me. "So that's your way of saying you're worried."

Art exhaled once. "Call it cautious."

The silence that followed felt easier than before. Comfortable, almost. A breeze stirred through the clearing, cool and comforting.

Art glanced at the sky, gauging the sun. "We should move soon. We've stayed near the trail long enough."

"Where to?" I asked.

"South. The forest thickens that way. Less traveled, fewer eyes. If they're still looking for you, they'll expect you to head east, out of the forest and toward Moira."

I hesitated. "But that's the opposite direction from where you were going."

He gave a small shrug. "I can make my way west later. You can't exactly travel alone in your condition." His tone was casual, but his meaning wasn't lost on me.

I lifted a brow at him. "You do realize I'm a Healer, right? I can manage a few bruises."

He gave me a sidelong glance, unimpressed. "Healing doesn't fix exhaustion—or bad decisions."

"Then it's a good thing I'm getting better at both," I said, my voice just dry enough to make him grin.

"Sure you are," he said, adjusting the strap of his pack. "But south still makes more sense. You need rest, and I'd rather not have to kill again just because you decided to prove a point."

The corner of my mouth twitched despite myself. "Are you saying you'd protect me?"

"I'm admitting you attract trouble," he replied evenly. "Keeping you alive just happens to overlap with my plans for a quiet life."

I snorted. "You're doing a terrible job at that."

He smiled but it didn't quiet reach his eyes. "Story of my life."

Finally, I nodded. "All right. South it is."

He returned the nod, moving to gather the few things we'd unpacked. "Good. We'll travel until dusk, then find higher ground to make camp. Should keep us clear of the trails."

I watched him, the easy way he moved, the quiet confidence in every action. For the first time in days, I wasn't running blind. I had a direction.

6

Nearly two weeks had passed since we left the creek behind. I'd stopped counting somewhere along the road. Time blurred when every day looked the same—walking through trees, stopping when the light thinned, sleeping under the whisper of rain.

Each morning, I told myself I'd leave soon. That I'd had enough time. Enough lessons in control.

Yet, each evening I found another reason to stay.

Part of it was practical. I could tell the training made a difference. That I was stronger than I'd been when Teresa and her men had found me.

But that wasn't all of it.

I told myself it was. I tried to believe it.

We talked enough to fill the quiet, but nothing that mattered. Nothing real.

Aside from that story he'd told me when we first met, Art hadn't said much about himself. And I hadn't offered anything in return. Whatever we shared stayed safely on the surface. Never the past. Never the things that still hurt.

Still, there was something about walking beside him—about knowing he would wake at the smallest sound, that he could read the forest like a map—that made the night feel less lonely.

I didn't like what that meant.

Some quiet moments didn't feel empty; they just ... stayed, like a truce neither of us wanted to test.

If he wasn't writing in that small leather book, he was teaching, showing me how to call Ardor without burning myself out. He'd say the same thing over and over: *Control. Not strength. Control.*

And if he wasn't teaching, he was cooking. If he wasn't cooking, he would vanish for a while, soundless as mist, and come back with fish or herbs or nothing at all.

I never asked where he went.

It was easier to keep our questions tucked away. Easier to walk beside someone you didn't have to explain yourself to.

Still, I found myself wondering about that book sometimes. What he filled its pages with when he thought I wasn't watching. Names? Memories? Things he didn't want to forget? Whatever it was, it wasn't meant for me.

Maybe he preferred it that way. Wrapping isolation tight around him like another layer of armor. Maybe I wasn't much different. Leaving things unsaid was safer than the truth, and safer than whatever might come if I asked the wrong question.

It didn't matter. We were only passing through the same stretch of road. That was all.

At least that was what I kept telling myself.

The air cooled as we moved south, touched by the promise of rain. The ground softened beneath our boots, and the forest seemed to hush around us, the wind moving through pine and rocks. By the time we stopped for the night, even the birds had gone still.

We made camp near a rise of stone, hidden from the trail.

A creek wound close by, shallow and clear, surrounded by moss and roots. Art had already taken his turn, washing the dust from himself and his clothes while I ate. When he finished, he left me the space and went to gather wood.

The chill bit at my skin as I stepped in, but it felt good to scrub away the grit of travel, the weight of days that all blurred together.

I brushed my fingers across the raised edge of the scar that crossed from my collarbone up along my neck. I'd healed most of it, sealed the flesh and numbed the pain, but the mark refused to fade. Lightning left its memory behind, etched deep beneath the skin.

The scar was only on the surface, but the pain dug deeper.

The sound of the running water left too much room for thought. Of Faylen, her voice in the dark, the stories she used to whisper through the cracks in the walls. I could almost hear her laughter, soft and breathless, pretending she wasn't afraid. She used to tell me that someday the sky would open for us both. That we'd breathe air not choked by stone. I'd promised her we would.

And then I'd left her there.

The water shimmered around my hands as I submerged them. No matter how cold it was, it couldn't wash that memory away. The guilt had sunk too deep, a burden I'd carried longer than a wound.

Maybe running wasn't enough anymore. Maybe surviving wasn't the same as living.

Faylen was still there. Still waiting in the dark while I walked beneath open sky.

If I ever meant to go back for her, I would need more than just a few tricks to control my Casting.

Two weeks of telling myself I would leave soon had finally worn thin. If Art was willing to have me, I was staying.

A faint rustle sounded from the trees behind me.

I stilled, listening.

There, perched on a low branch, was a squat little squirrel with fur too full for the season and cheeks stuffed with nuts—or something he'd no doubt stolen. He stared at me without blinking.

I narrowed my eyes. "You again."

It had to be the same one. The same shameless creature who'd watched us make camp more than once, bold as if he owned the forest. Art had mentioned a squirrel he called Nettles—claimed it once threw nuts at him. I still wasn't sure if he'd been joking.

Every time I spotted the creature, I would turn to ask Art if it was the same one. But the squirrel always vanished before I could point him out. I swear he was mocking me.

The squirrel twitched his tail before disappearing into the trees.

I stood there for a long moment before climbing back onto the bank, sunlight warm and bright on the water behind me.

At camp, Art was crouched near the fire, stirring the coals. The midday light spilled through the trees, painting him in flashes of gold and shadow.

He didn't look up right away, but I could tell he knew I was there—the subtle roll of his shoulders, the brief pause in his stirring.

When he finally did look up, he studied me for a moment, something thoughtful in his expression, as if he'd been waiting for the right time to speak. "You've come a long way. Wasn't long ago that you couldn't keep Ardor steady for more than a breath."

"Still can't do much with it," I muttered.

"Control comes first. Everything else follows."

I nodded. He meant well. But control wasn't enough anymore. Not for what waited ahead of me. Not for the people I'd left behind.

I gazed into the fire, watching the light shift and curl.

"Art," I said. "When you're ready ... I want to learn how to fight."

He didn't look up right away, but his hand paused over the fire. "That's a bigger lesson. And a harder one to walk away from once it starts."

"I'm done walking away."

The words came out easier than I expected. At first, he said nothing. The space stretched between us, filled only by the stream's soft rush.

When he finally spoke again, his voice was quiet. Not dismissive. Not even surprised. Just calm. Like he was weighing something I couldn't see. "Why now?"

I hesitated. Not because I didn't know the answer, but because saying it out loud would make it real. And I wasn't sure I was ready for that.

Still, I managed. "Because I don't want to feel powerless anymore. Not the way I did back there."

His head tilted, as if that answer wasn't quite enough.

I swallowed. "Because there are others still trapped. I got out, but they didn't. And I can't go back unless I can fight."

He nodded, eyes dropping to his hands. His sigh was heavy. "I figured there were more," he said quietly, almost mournful. "Since you said others might be chasing you, I assumed you weren't the only one held there."

Just as I thought he was about to agree, his gaze lifted—and he shattered that hope.

"I can't, in good conscience, teach you how to use your power if it means you'll just throw your life away on a suicide mission."

The only sound was the wind moving through the branches, soft enough to make the silence cut deeper.

I stared at him, at a loss for words. He was right. Even if he did teach me, even if I learned quickly, I couldn't storm that place alone. The compound I escaped from was heavily guarded.

But I couldn't forget the only friend I had in there. I couldn't enjoy my freedom knowing she was still rotting away in that place.

I opened my mouth to argue, but he spoke first. "I'm not saying no," he said gently. "Not completely."

His gaze softened. "But if I'm going to teach you the way I learned, there can't be any half-truths between us. That kind of training requires trust. I'll need to know things about you that'll leave you feeling exposed. There are parts of Casting—especially your Casting—that can't be taught without that level of honesty."

He studied me for a moment, composed and unreadable.

"You've been through something most people wouldn't walk away from. I can see the strain it left on you. But what comes next will test you in new ways, both physically and mentally. If you want to learn what I know, you'll have to share parts of yourself that may be hard to face. And in return, you'll learn things about me that no one else knows."

The creek murmured in the distance.

"This isn't just about saving your friends. If we do this—if I train you—then this is only the beginning."

I didn't hesitate. "Yes."

There was nothing left to think about. I couldn't keep hesitating—not anymore. I had nowhere else to go, no one else to turn to.

Maybe it was selfish to ask more of him after everything he'd already done, but if he was willing to train me at all, it meant he wasn't leaving. He wasn't just helping me survive. He was helping me fight.

I wasn't naïve enough to believe I could do this alone.

I'd seen what he could do. I knew he was powerful.

"Good," he said. "Let's get started. How much do you know about Casting? Not just your own ability, but Casting in general?"

I took a moment to think before answering. "I'm from the peasantry. What I learned wasn't from a book. I can read, but we could never afford anything worth reading. Most of what I know came from my parents—things they heard and passed down—but neither of them were Casters, so a lot of it might be wrong. There was a boy in the village named Jorran who awakened as a Fire Caster not long before the raid. Aside from him the only others were two elderly Casters who lived there for years, but they were long past proving anything to anyone. I rarely saw them Cast."

A memory surfaced, and I almost smiled. "There was one other person I met who could Cast Fire. A boy who visited our village each spring. His family traveled for the festival on their way to Vitel—the capital, far north of us. Every year, when they stopped to rest and resupply, we'd play together."

A faint smile tugged at my lips. "One year, he told me he'd become a Fire Caster. Showing off, he made flames dance in his palm. It wasn't the first time I'd seen someone Cast Fire, but it was the first time it felt real. Knowing the person who could do it. Seeing it up close.

"He said it happened a few months after their last visit. He'd gotten angry one day, and it just ... happened." I let out a soft laugh. "He tried to shoot the flame at a stump, but it didn't go anywhere. It just flared up, grew too fast, and nearly swallowed his whole arm. I had to throw a bucket of water on him."

Art smiled. "It was his mixed emotions. Fire is a raw and volatile affinity. Powerful, but quick to turn if not kept in check. It's also one of the more emotion-driven elementals. He couldn't control it because he was too excited. Too nervous." He paused, the corner of his mouth lifting. "And if I had to guess, there was a bit of infatuation in the mix, likely directed at you. When feelings get tangled without focus, it turns wild. That's why it lashed out."

I smiled back. "I already knew he liked me. His little sister once told me he had secret plans to marry me when we grew up," I said, teasing. "But over time, he stopped showing off his Casting. The following year, he told me his family had hired a Warden to help him control it better." I paused, my smile fading. "Not long after, they stopped visiting the village altogether."

Art didn't speak right away. When he finally did, his voice was calm. "Wardens can be expensive. They're skilled Casters—masters of their element—who usually have their own school or will travel for the right coin. Did you know what a Warden was?"

"I did. I knew they were teachers who came to your home if you could afford them. But not everyone has that kind of privilege."

He nodded faintly. "Were you also aware you can't just hire any Warden? Each one only teaches their own element. A good Warden won't take on a student who Casts something different."

He studied me for a moment before continuing. "Do you know why that is?"

I considered it, then shook my head. "I always assumed any Warden could teach any kind of Caster."

He shook his head. "A Warden might master their own craft, but that doesn't make them suited to teach another. Sure, they can teach the basics. Breathing. Focus. But paying a Warden just for that would leave most people feeling cheated."

We started walking back toward camp, the sound of water moving softly through the trees.

"Every element has its own temperament," he said. "If a Warden doesn't understand the true nature of a Caster's affinity, they're no better than a non-Caster. Teaching with the wrong mindset can do more harm than good. It can stunt a Caster's growth, maybe even push them back."

I watched the ground pass beneath my steps. "So ... if someone has to share the same affinity to teach properly, does that mean you'll only be able to teach me the basics?"

He gave me a mischievous grin.

"I picked up a lot from that other Ardor Variant I told you about. He wasn't exactly a master, but he'd been Casting for a few years and managed to teach himself most of the fundamentals. You don't always need a teacher to learn how to Cast, but it makes things a lot easier. And it helps keep you from getting hurt by blowbacks. Just like your friend." He grinned. He then stopped mid-step. "Also ..."

I paused, uncertain. He didn't say anything more. Instead, he lifted his hand and reached toward me.

Instinctively, I flinched.

Every part of me wanted to pull back. But I stopped myself. I'd agreed to trust him. I told him I would.

So I stayed still.

His hand remained suspended, hovering—not waiting for the right moment, but for silent permission.

I gave a small nod.

Then, without a word, he closed the space between us.

The oversized shirt slipped off my shoulder, exposing the scar running from my collarbone to my neck. Art's hand found it without hesitation, his palm settling against my skin.

His touch was warm.

In that suspended moment, a soft glow rose between his fingers and began to sink into me. The light pulsed gently, folding into my skin with quiet purpose.

Neither of us moved.

The warmth spread, slow and constant, not only across the wound but somewhere deeper. A calming hum radiated from his touch, easing something tight inside me. I hadn't realized I'd been holding my breath until it left me in a soft exhale.

After a minute, the glow faded. He lifted his hand, gentle and slow.

Where the scar had once carved a leathery mark into my skin, there remained only a faint impression—a pale pink shadow of what was.

It was practically invisible now.

Healing? He can Cast Healing, too?

"So ... you're a Healer as well. Can you Cast every element there is?" I kept my tone light, though the question wasn't.

He chuckled. "No. That was the last one I had tucked away. I'm officially out of tricks."

His expression softened, thoughtful now. "But truthfully ... being a Healer is the only reason I ever grew at all."

I gave him a questioning look.

He offered a small shrug. "It's a little long to explain. We'll get to it eventually. For now, I've still got a few questions of my own."

⸻◦⸻

A few hours later, we made our way back to the creek.

My clothes were stretched across a flat stone warmed by the sun. His hung on the branch of a tree.

I touched my shirt. It was mostly dry now.

Art had already taken his clothes from the branch and was heading toward the trail. He didn't say anything, didn't look over his shoulder.

It had become his habit—turning his back, wandering just far enough into the trees whenever I needed privacy. A small thing, maybe. But after everything, it was the first time in a long while that changing didn't feel like something to endure.

I slipped out of the oversized clothes and back into my own. After folding the shirt and pants he'd lent me, I gathered my things and followed the trail.

He was standing a short distance ahead, arms loosely crossed, facing the trees like he had all the time in the world.

I watched him as I walked.

He never asked for thanks—not once. Never pushed for answers. He simply kept giving me space.

And yet ... I couldn't shake the feeling that a debt was quietly growing between us.

I pushed the thought aside.

"So," I said as I reached him, "what am I supposed to learn first?"

He studied me for a long moment, then stepped toward a clearing near the creek.

"Before you learn to Cast, or to fight with a blade, you need to learn how to fight with your body."

I blinked. "Hand-to-hand?"

He nodded once. "If you can't stay on your feet, no amount of Casting will save you. The body and mind move together. Until you learn that, the rest won't matter."

He gestured for me to follow him onto the open patch of ground. The soil was soft and cool underfoot, damp from the creek's edge.

"Out here, you'll learn balance first. How to move your weight. How to keep breathing even when you're scared."

I hesitated, then frowned. "I thought you'd be teaching me how to shoot people with Ardor. That's what I need, isn't it? I can hold it now, but I haven't fired it at anyone since the day they attacked me."

He studied with an unreadable expression. "That's because you were running on a rush. Instinct took over. It's what saved you."

I looked down. "So what? I can only defend if I'm terrified?"

He shook his head. "You can Cast whenever you want. But that day, your form was sloppy. I saw the blowbacks that hit, you were lucky they didn't burn straight through your arm."

The words stung, even though I knew he was right.

"You hit them because they were close. Practically on top of you. That's why we start here." He stepped back, folding his arms. "You'll be learning three things before we reach Rodin: hand-to-hand, sword fighting, and Casting."

I frowned. "All of that? While we're traveling?"

He nodded. "Every day. We'll train as we move west out of the forest, then north toward Rodin. I don't have time to teach you the slow way. You'll learn fast, or you won't learn at all."

He said it plainly.

And he meant it.

We trained until the light started to fade, the day folding around us in sweat and bruises. Art moved through each lesson like he'd done it a thousand times. First came the hand-to-hand. Stances, strikes, how to fall without breaking something. He corrected me with small gestures.

Then came the sword. Or close enough.

Art stepped toward a nearby sapling and lifted his hand. The sapling parted as if cut by an unseen blade. He caught the falling length before it struck the ground, then split it down the middle with another flick of Wind. "You'll use my sword when you're training on your own. But when we train together, we use these."

He stepped in close, positioning my hands along the length of the stick. "Grip here," he said, guiding my fingers into place. "Looser. You're not strangling it."

I tried to follow, but my stance slipped again.

When he moved behind me, his hand brushed my wrist—and I tensed before I could stop it.

He froze. "May I?"

My throat tightened, but I managed a nod.

Only then did his other hand rest lightly at my hip, steadying my balance. His breath stirred the hair near my temple.

"Weight on your back foot," he murmured. "Good. Now, let the strike come from your center, not your arms."

The first swing went wide. The second landed with a solid thud against his stick. The third jarred my shoulders so hard I nearly dropped it, but the quiet satisfaction in his nod made the ache worth it.

By the time my arms stopped trembling, I thought the lesson was over.

It wasn't.

Art set the sticks aside and motioned toward a stretch of open ground near the creek. "Now we work on Casting."

I stared at him. "Now?"

He gave a quiet nod. "You wanted to learn how to fight. That means learning when you're already tired."

I bit a groan and followed him.

He started simple. A single rock a few paces away. "Hit that."

I blinked. "That close? You're joking."

"If you can't land a clean shot here, you won't hit anything that's moving."

I raised my hand, drawing in light until it flickered at my fingertips. The pulse was steady for a breath, then jumped. The beam shot wide, scorching bark nowhere near the rock.

Art didn't flinch. "Again."

I tried.

Missed.

Again.

Missed worse.

Each blast left my arms tingling and my focus slipping. Sweat ran into my eyes, and my chest tightened from the strain.

"Breathe," he said. "Don't force it. Guide it."

I tried again, slower now. The Ardor didn't waver this time. I exhaled and let it go.

The beam struck the edge of the rock and sent a spray of dust.

Art lifted a hand. "Stop."

I lowered my arm, breathing hard. "What? I actually hit it that time."

He nodded. "I know."

I frowned. "Then why—"

"Because anyone can hit their mark when they're fresh," he said, stepping closer. "But control only means something when you're past your limit."

I didn't argue. My arms hung limp, muscles shaking. But under the soreness, something sparked.

I'd done it.

I thought that was the end of it—until Art lifted his hand again.

The glow that followed was soft and familiar. The ache in my shoulders ebbed, then the burns in my arms, until the weight of the entire day eased from my body.

When the light dimmed, I could breathe again. Too easily.

He nodded toward the clearing. "Good. Now we start again. From the top."

I stared at him. "You're serious."

He didn't even try to hide the grin. "You're Healed, aren't you?"

I exhaled, slow. The ache was gone. But the memory of it still lingered.

"I don't know if that's comforting," I said, voice quieter now. "Or cruel."

7

Days bled into weeks as we made our way west through the forest. Every morning began the same: training, travel, more training until the light faded. My body ached in places I didn't know existed, but Art kept his word. Hand-to-hand, sword drills, Casting—again and again until it all blurred. When the pain became too much, he'd lay a hand on my shoulder, mend the ache, and we would start over like it was nothing.

Some days I wondered if he ever felt tired. He trained me with a quiet, relentless precision—never raising his voice, never slipping, never softening. It wasn't cruelty, but it could feel like it. Especially when he stepped close, when his breath brushed my shoulder or he corrected my stance without warning. My whole body would lock up before I could stop it.

I hated that.

I hated how easily my mind could mistake discipline for danger.

But beneath all that, I still understood. He wasn't just teaching me how to fight. He was teaching me how to survive myself.

The forest felt endless. The density of the trees never seemed to break. Sometimes, when the wind changed, I thought I heard water or the soft, rhythmic thud of footsteps far off between the trunks. But it was only the woods breathing around us. When we first started this journey, we'd gone south to lose anyone who might have been trailing me. Now we were turning west, working our way back toward open roads and civilization.

Art said we'd take the route through Orvain, then north toward Rodin. Two weeks, if we found a horse. On foot, the days dragged like they meant to prove him wrong.

By then, I'd grown used to the rhythm between us. The stretches of quiet, the daily lessons, the rare questions that cut closer than I expected. They always came from nowhere, calm and disarming.

That morning was no different.

The sun hung low through the branches, scattering light across the path. Art walked ahead, his attention fixed somewhere far off. Then, without warning, he broke the silence. "So, when did you first learn to Cast Healing?"

It was an easy question. One I could never forget. "I was sixteen. That year, raiders came through our village. My father had already been gone three years by then. Sickness took him early. It was just me, my mother, and my brother. He was three years older."

I kept my eyes on the path ahead as I spoke, the rhythm of my steps carrying the words.

"Normally, we didn't have trouble with raiders. Our village was small, tucked far away enough from the main roads to escape most of the fighting. But that autumn ... things changed.

"Most of the men had left on a long hunting trip to prepare for winter. My brother among them. Our two Casters we had went with them, tasked with protecting the group and preserving what they gathered.

"The ones who came for us weren't part of the Triarchy. Not anymore. They were deserters. Former soldiers turned mercenaries, drifting between frontlines with no allegiance, surviving off whatever they could take. The war had only begun the year before, but already it was leaving men like them broken. Dangerous.

"They timed it well," I said quietly. "They must've been watching. Waiting until our strongest were gone before they attacked."

The forest around us hummed softly, indifferent to the memory I was unraveling.

"My mother told me to hide," I murmured. "She pulled up the floorboards in the pantry and stuffed me beneath them, told me not to make a sound, no matter what I heard. I did as she said."

The next words came slower. "I heard them break down the door. Heard their boots on our floor. They wanted her. I didn't understand at first—not fully. But then I heard her fight back. Screaming. Kicking. She bit one of them, and yelled something vile before he—"

My throat tightened. "That's when he stabbed her. When she fell."

A slow, shaking breath left me. "They didn't leave right away. I could still hear them outside, arguing, searching the house next door. When they finally moved farther down the road, I crawled out."

I swallowed. "She was lying on the kitchen floor. There was so much blood. I didn't even know I was Casting. I just kept pressing my hands to the wound, begging her to stay. I couldn't call for help. They were still out there."

My voice faltered. The copper scent filled my lungs again. I could see it—spreading between the cracks of the wood, dark and endless. My hands trembled at the memory, fingers curling into my palms.

That was the moment hope started to slip.

"The only thing I could do was beg," I said more quietly. "My hands wouldn't stop shaking. And then ... it happened. Light poured from my hands—out of me and into her. I didn't know how. I just knew I couldn't let it stop. Not until I was sure she'd be okay." I drew a breath, steadying myself. "The first time it happened, I felt completely drained. Like something inside me had been wrung out. But I couldn't stop. I wouldn't stop."

I glanced toward Art. "She survived. Just barely."

He was quiet for a long moment.

"What about the others?" he asked finally. "Did you have enough strength to Heal anyone else?"

I shook my head. "By the time I finished Healing her, I collapsed. When I came to, my mother was in tears. She was so relieved I was alive ... but she was terrified. She didn't want anyone in the village to know I'd awakened."

I hesitated before continuing.

"Under normal circumstances, it might not have mattered. But everything was so chaotic. People were scared. Suspicious. She worried someone might think the raiders had come for me ... or that if they ever came back, the villagers might try to trade me to save themselves."

My eyes drifted to a familiar, overly round squirrel perched high in a tree, tail flicking once before going still.

"When we finally stepped outside, the worst of the wounded had already been tended to. No one was in danger anymore. So ... I kept my ability quiet. Just like she asked."

Art nodded, his gaze distant. "It was a mixture of your emotions that allowed you to ignite. Fear and desperation, most likely. Those two are powerful catalysts for Healers. They were for me, and I've heard similar stories from others who awakened the same way."

He looked at me a moment, thoughtful. "They're not the only emotions that can trigger it, but in your case, I'd wager those were the ones."

He paused before speaking again. "My Healing ignited when I was eighteen. It wasn't noble. I wasn't trying to save anyone. I was just trying to survive. Someone stabbed me—cut through my neck and left me for dead."

His tone stayed calm, but quieter now, like the memory didn't get spoken aloud often. "My fear wasn't for someone else. It was for me. I was desperate to stay alive. Desperate not to be forgotten. Desperate to get revenge."

He exhaled, almost a laugh, but not quite.

"Healing like that ... It wasn't fast. I passed out more than once. It took the whole day before I could move again."

He said nothing more, and I didn't push. We fell into the easy silence of two people who had already given too much to words. That talk was the most I'd ever learned about his past.

After a long beat I asked, "Did you get your revenge?"

He smiled, though sadness touched the edges. "Yes. It took me several years to find the ones I wanted dead. When I did, I killed them myself. I nearly got myself killed doing it. Even after all that time, I still wasn't strong enough. But I went anyway."

He let the words hang between us, then met my eyes. "I won't let you make that same mistake. Not while you're with me."

Something in that sentence sank deep under my skin. I didn't answer. The truth sat plain and ugly in my chest: I didn't care if it killed me. If it meant they suffered first ... then it would be worth it.

The forest came alive around us; a pair of squirrels bolted through the underbrush, their quick scrabbling breaking the steady hush of the trees.

A third trailed behind them—rounder, slower. He barreled after them with far less grace, paused when they vanished into the brush, then sat back on his haunches as if reconsidering his life choices. Then he turned and loped in the opposite direction.

We kept moving, weaving between root and bramble, the conversation behind us folding into a companionable hush. I kept stealing glances at

Art, drawing quiet reassurance from the line of his shoulders, from the way his words replayed in my head.

We'd made camp the night before, deep in the southern stretch of the forest. Art had managed to bring down a boar, something he admitted was rare this time of year. Most of the larger game had already migrated deeper north, following instinct as the air grew colder in the south. With winter creeping in, only stragglers remained.

After we ate, he kept mostly to himself, sharpening his blade while I practiced a few of the movements he'd shown me. He didn't push me to train longer or to talk, just watched, corrected my stance once or twice, and then let the quiet sit between us again.

This morning, the chill came early. I hadn't said anything, but Art noticed. Without a word, he pulled a heavier coat from his pack and handed it to me. It smelled faintly of pine and smoke, like everything else he carried. I slipped it on and kept walking.

"How much farther until we're out of these woods?" I asked at last.

Art's gaze lifted to the sky, briefly tracking the sun's position. "We'll be walking another full day before we clear the forest."

My stomach sank a little, but I kept pace. It was ironic. After all the desperation I'd felt to escape that place ... now I couldn't stop thinking about going back. My only fear was whether I'd be too late when I finally did.

We walked a while longer, the soft crunch of leaves underfoot filling the forest hush. My thoughts drifted ahead, to the days waiting for us, the fight that would come, and everything I still didn't know how to face. Yet, despite it all, I wasn't as afraid as I should be.

Art glanced at me. "When you Cast Healing for the first time, how often did you use it after that?"

I thought for a moment. "After my mother recovered enough to walk, her stomach still had deep bruising and an open wound that would weep occasionally. The next night, I Cast Healing again. Only a faint scar remained."

I'd been so worn out after Healing her for the first time, but I couldn't stop. I couldn't risk the wound festering, not when we had no other Healers in the village.

I didn't know if I could Heal an illness before it took shape, before any sign of it reached the surface. I only knew I wasn't willing to risk it. Not when it came to her.

"Do you understand what you are?" Art asked.

I hesitated, unsure what he meant, then gave a small nod. "I'm a Healer and Ardor Variant. Together that makes me an Aberration."

"Aberrations are rare. Most Casters are born with only one elemental affinity, and that's all they'll ever have. Healing alone is already uncommon. But Healing and Ardor?" He shook his head. "That combination is exceedingly rare."

"You're an Aberration too. So what does that make you, some kind of legendary version?"

He gave me a crooked smile. "You could say that. A high-tier Aberration, maybe."

His voice dropped a note, the edge of humor fading. "I've only ever met one other person who could Cast three. Most can't handle the strain. Plenty of Casters live their whole lives without ever unlocking a second affinity."

"Why is that?" I asked.

He paused, as if weighing how much to tell me. "When someone is born, they can only hold so much energy. Think of it like a core. Some are larger than others, but everyone has a limit. As you get older, that limit can strengthen a little. With enough training and repetition, most Casters can push their abilities to the edge of what their body allows."

His gaze drifted. "But that's the thing. No matter how much you train, you can't force your core to hold more than it was made to. You can make your Casting cleaner, faster, more controlled—but the size of your core stays the same."

"Except there is a way," he said slowly, as if choosing each word with care, "to grow the core—to expand it. Most people don't even know it's possible. And those who do ..." His gaze met mine. "I've only ever known one person who could."

He didn't say it outright, but I knew he meant himself.

I held his gaze before he asked, almost as an afterthought, "Have you ever heard of Enervation?"

I shook my head.

Art exhaled slowly. "Enervation happens when you burn through everything in your core—when your body starts pulling from reserves it was never meant to touch. It's the point where your strength collapses. Your pulse slows. Your breathing falters. For most, it ends there."

We stepped over a fallen branch. The sun was slipping lower across the thinning trees, light catching on his hair before scattering into the undergrowth. Dry leaves crackled underfoot, sharp against the quiet.

"Most Casters spend their whole lives avoiding that edge. And they should. Anyone who crosses it is gambling with their life."

I didn't respond. The memory came back without invitation.

That first night after the fight, when he'd gone to grab his supplies and I was still bleeding into the dirt. The arrow wound in my leg had already closed halfway, but the burn on my chest kept sparking with pain. I hadn't trusted him yet. Not enough to let my life hang on his goodwill.

So I tried to Heal myself. Just enough to stand if I had to. To run, if I needed to.

At first, it worked. The burn dulled, the ache softened. But the light started to slip from my hands, dimming no matter how hard I focused. Everything around me blurred. The dark pushing in.

I thought it was just exhaustion. Something a little rest would fix.

Art's voice cut through my thoughts. "You've already done it."

I looked at him.

It wasn't a question.

"You were slumped over when I came back," he said. "Your breathing was shallow. But your wounds were mostly closed. You didn't just push too far, Celeste. You crossed the line. Enervation doesn't always stop at unconsciousness. Some Casters never wake up."

I slowed, the ground soft under my boots. "I didn't realize ..."

He nodded once. "Most don't. It feels like you're blacking out. But if your body keeps pulling energy once the cores empty, it starts feeding on itself. Heart. Mind. Everything."

A chill ran through my body. "Then why am I still here?"

"You were lucky," he said simply.

I looked away, the memory still raw. "I just didn't want to depend on you. I thought if I could Heal myself, I'd be safe."

Art's expression softened.

"I didn't trust you," I said quietly. "I don't trust easily ... Not anymore. Not after what happened."

He paused, gaze dropping to the path. "It took me years to stop seeing every outstretched hand as a threat."

"I didn't mean to ..." I murmured. "My body just doesn't listen. Even when I want to trust someone, it—" I swallowed.

He gave a small nod, a quiet knowing gesture, like he understood more than I meant to say.

"You did something few ever attempt," he said softly. "But when you pushed that far, you didn't just survive—you changed. You pulled yourself back from the brink and reshaped your core. Just a little."

He glanced toward the trees, his voice carrying a weight that felt lived-in. "Think of your core like steel under heat. You have to bring it to the right temperature before it will yield. Too much strain, too quickly, and it fractures instead of forms. That's what kills most Casters."

I frowned. "But not you."

He met my eyes. "Because I was born with a core that can stretch. Most people aren't. Their limits are set. No matter how hard they train, no matter how strong their will, they'll never push past the boundary they were given." He paused. "But you could. That's why you survived."

I stared at him, unsure what to say.

"There are only a few people in the world like that. Casters whose cores aren't just deep, but elastic. And if they survive Enervation more than once, they don't just recover. They evolve."

And then the truth clicked into place. "Healing. That's what lets me survive it. What lets me keep growing without dying in the process."

He nodded. "Exactly. Your ability to Heal—even when unconscious—keeps you from tipping over the edge. Most Casters, once they collapse, are gambling with their lives. But you ..." He paused. "Even when you pass out, your body keeps working to repair itself. It buys you time others wouldn't have."

I let that sit. The wind stirred the branches above us, soft and cool, carrying the faint scent of pine in the air.

Before I could stop myself, the question slipped out. "Have you done it ... a lot of times?"

A faint breath escaped him, almost like a laugh. "Yes. Hundreds of times."

I blinked, unsure I'd heard him right.

He didn't elaborate at first, just kept walking, eyes tracing the fading light between the trees. The hush between us deepened until he spoke again, quieter now. "It's not something I do lightly. Every time I push that far, I lose consciousness. Same as you did. For minutes, sometimes hours. And during that time, I'm completely vulnerable."

He slowed a little. "That's part of why I'm out here. This is the kind of training I can't do anywhere else."

His shoulders eased, something guarded slipping out. "That's why I only do it when I'm alone. Far from towns, far from people. Places like this." He gestured faintly at the woods around us. "Pylin Forest is quiet. Untouched. I know its paths and I trust it to keep my secrets."

He fell silent again, and I didn't push. There was something reverent in the way he spoke—like he was recalling not just pain, but a kind of devotion. Like the forest wasn't just his refuge, but the altar where he bled himself clean.

"It's the closest I ever come to dying. And somehow, it's what keeps me alive."

A tightness stirred in my chest as his words sank in.

Hundreds of times.

I tried to imagine it, choosing to fall like that, not because he was desperate in a fight, but deliberately. Again and again. Alone, knowing how vulnerable he'd be.

Faith that he would come back each time.

That kind of trust—in himself, in his Healing—was terrifying. And awe-inspiring.

We walked without speaking.

But eventually, the question rose through everything he'd said. I glanced at him, my voice softer than I intended. "If that's true, why hasn't anyone figured it out? Surely some Casters have had Healers nearby. Couldn't they have worked through Enervation safely? Learned to grow their core that way?"

Art didn't answer immediately.

Instead, he looked at me. "How did it feel? After you pushed yourself that far?"

I frowned, taken off guard. "Tired," I admitted. "Bone-tired."

He nodded once. "Do you feel any stronger now?"

I thought about it—really thought.

I reached inward, the way he'd taught me. Searched for any change, any new depth or ripple of strength.

But there was nothing. "I don't feel different at all."

His gaze didn't waver. "Exactly."

He slowed his pace, the word hanging between us.

"It takes time," he went on, his pace slowing as he spoke. "I didn't notice a change the first time either. Or the second. It wasn't until I'd survived it a dozen times that I felt anything alter. And even then, it was subtle, just a little more reach, a little more endurance."

He looked ahead, toward the thinning trees where light fractured through the leaves. "Cold metal doesn't change, no matter how hard you strike it. Add heat and it becomes workable—but even then, one blow won't show you anything. Two won't either. It takes heat and hundreds of strikes before the shape finally starts to change.

"Most Casters never get both. They strike without heat and break themselves ... or they have heat without striking, so nothing ever changes. And even if they tried it two or three times together, the metal would look the same. They'd stop long before anything truly took shape."

The moment between us stretched, heavy and honest. He met my eyes again. "And that's assuming they survive the striking at all."

We continued walking. No more words, just the soft crunch of leaves beneath our boots and the distant rustle of wind through the canopy. A gray bird flitted across our path, wings flashing once before vanishing into the trees.

I kept my gaze ahead, but my thoughts drifted—circling the things he'd said.

Hundreds of times—at least.

How many times had he willingly let his body collapse into the dark, trusting it would pull itself back? How many times had he lain alone in the woods, breath shallow, pulse fading, with no one beside him if something went wrong?

I'd barely survived once, and only because he was there. Or because I was a Healer, I wasn't even sure anymore.

And yet he'd done it over and over, just to grow. To change what he was. Bit by bit. Quietly and alone.

Was that strength? Or madness?

Could they be the same thing?

I reached inward again, brushing against my Casting, searching for any difference. Any sign that my core had changed. But there was nothing. No deeper pull. Only fatigue. The kind that sank into your bones and made everything heavier.

Still, the thought lingered.

If what he said was true, if my core could stretch, then how far could I go?

How much more was hidden beneath what I already knew?

And what would it cost to find out?

The trees had begun to thin.

The path I'd taken into the forest was long behind us now, buried under weeks of walking and distance.

The canopy above grew patchy, letting in streaks of late-afternoon sun. Somewhere ahead, past the brush and the slope of the land, the forest would give way to open fields.

I didn't want to leave just yet.

Not because I feared what lay ahead, but because for the first time in a long while, the quiet between us felt like something I could breathe in.

I glanced at Art.

He hadn't spoken in a while. His eyes were alert, tracking the trees, listening in a way that made me instinctively do the same.

And then I saw it.

Half buried in the mud just ahead. Hoofprints.

Deep.

Fresh.

Art appeared beside me, his jaw tightening as he crouched low. He pressed two fingers to the edge of the track, then looked back up. "Multiple riders. They're moving fast."

My pulse quickened. "Are they tracking us?"

He stood, scanning the trees. "No. If they were, they wouldn't be coming from that direction."

I looked behind us, then ahead. "Then why are they here?"

He didn't answer right away. Instead, he studied the tracks again, the tension in his jaw giving away what he didn't say aloud.

"Could be coincidence," he said at last. But his tone didn't match the words.

I waited, but he didn't continue. So I asked, "You don't think it is, do you?"

He looked up, brow furrowed. "I think someone's looking for you." His gaze flicked toward the fading trail behind us. "And not just the ones you escaped from."

The wind slid through the trees. Somewhere deeper in the forest, a crow called once, then fell silent again.

8

They weren't bandits. That much I knew. The prints were too clean and too deep. Well-bred horses. Heavier than the wiry beasts raiders favored. These were trained for endurance.

One rider had dismounted briefly, leaving a firm impression in the mud. Square heel with a narrow toe. Boots like that usually meant military. But this wasn't a patrol route. And the spacing was too precise.

I rose, scanning the thinning trees ahead.

They hadn't come from our direction. They weren't tracking. They were sweeping, circling. This wasn't a coincidence.

I kept my expression still, but my thoughts had already begun mapping the terrain, tracking the distance between where we stood and where steel might break through the trees. If we kept walking, we might cross their path. If they circled back, we'd find another waiting.

I glanced over my shoulder. Celeste stood a few paces back, watching me with still concentration. She was catching on. Quicker than I'd expected.

But she didn't yet understand that escape was only the first step to staying free.

"We're not going through the field," I said, already turning back toward the trees. "Too exposed. If they spot us out there, we're pinned."

She followed without protest, though I could hear the tension in her breath.

"What do we do?" she asked.

"We vanish," I said simply. "If they think we crossed into open terrain, they'll follow. I'll make sure they see something worth chasing."

I didn't explain further. Just moved, weaving through the underbrush with the quiet precision of someone who'd done this before.

We circled back just far enough to put a ridge between us and the meadow.

"This is where we split," I said, voice low. "You head south. Not along the edge—cut through the trees. Keep a steady pace. No running. Quick and quiet."

She hesitated. "What about you?"

"I'm going back to the creek. I'll build a fire, fake a trail heading north. Make it look like we camped and moved that way. With any luck, they'll take the bait."

I didn't wait for protest.

"If you hear anything, don't turn around. Keep moving." I caught her gaze. "You get clear. That's all that matters."

Then I turned northeast, slipping between trees with the aid of Wind, just enough to stay fast, quiet, and light-footed. The forest bent around me like it recognized me.

The creek wasn't far. I didn't go all the way down this time, just close enough to feel the air cool and hear the murmur of water running over stone.

Still armed. Still moving.

The weight of my sword sat steady at my side, the blade wrapped in cloth to keep it silent when I ran.

I crouched beneath a leaning pine, brushing away loose needles and clearing a space. Then, with careful hands, I stacked a small ring of half-rotted wood. Pressing my palm to the base, I let the heat build until a tongue of flame unfurled from my hand into the kindling. The fire caught fast.

I fed it just enough to burn hot and bright, letting the blackened ends crackle, ash curling upward. It had to look used. Left in haste.

After a moment, I smothered it.

The smoke thinned. I left footprints leading east, then crossed the stream at a shallow bend, boots finding slick purchase on the stone.

Once on the other side, I angled north. Each step deep enough to leave a trail, but never careless.

Let them chase ghosts.

Nearly an hour had passed since I'd left her.

The sun had moved behind a thicker stretch of cloud, and the light filtering through the canopy had dulled to a faint gray-green hue. I moved slower now, backtracking with care.

Angled south, each step placed with care, my Wind Casting held tight and shallow. Used only to steady my movement rather than speed it.

Then I heard it.

A deep, echoing crack rolled through the forest—like a tree splitting.

I froze, eyes scanning the canopy.

A flare burst upward in the distance, climbing fast in a bloom of thick smoke. The sound of it, loud and thunderous, rippled through the stillness.

No mistaking it.

They'd found something ... or someone.

And it was coming from the same direction I was heading, the path she would've taken.

I didn't hesitate. Stealth meant nothing now.

Wind surged around me as I sprinted, brush whipping past in a blur. Branches clawed at my arms and shoulders, but I didn't slow. The forest became a smear of thorns and color.

⸻◆⸻

Celeste

I kept moving south.

Not rushed, just like he told me. Quick only when the ground allowed it. Keep south. Keep hidden. Keep away from the forest's edge.

The trees felt heavier now. Every branch I brushed past felt too loud. Every twig I snapped underfoot made me flinch.

He'd made it sound simple: move, stay low, keep going.

But the silence was starting to eat at me.

No birds calling. No wind. No sound except my own breathing and the soft crunch of leaves.

I paused once. Just long enough to press my hand to the side of a vinewood tree and listen.

Nothing.

I let out a slow breath and kept going.

A low branch caught my arm as I ducked beneath it, scratching a thin line down my forearm. I barely felt it. Just wiped the blood away with my sleeve and pressed on.

I hadn't looked back once since we'd split up. Not even when I wanted to.

His voice kept replaying in my head. *You get clear. That's the only thing that matters.*

I hated leaving him behind. But I hated the thought of making his risk mean nothing even more.

A sudden rustle filtered through the brush behind me. I spun—heart hammering—only to see a squat little squirrel dart past my boots and claw its way up the nearest trunk with frantic urgency.

My breath rushed out in a shaky exhale.

I almost laughed.

I took one more step—

And the world cracked open.

An echoing boom rolled through the trees like distant thunder. The ground didn't shake, but the air did.

I jerked my head up just as the flare burst through the canopy.

Close.

Too close.

Smoke twisted through the branches, curling fast into the sky and I froze.

Eyes locked on the flare.

That wasn't Art.

A sharp hiss cut the air beside me.

Thunk.

Pain flared in my thigh—not from impact, but from how close it had come. An arrow quivered in the dirt, a handspan from my leg. Another handspan and it would've taken me down.

A shallow burn bloomed across my thigh, followed by the slow, unmistakable warmth of blood trailing down my leg.

I didn't wait.

I turned and ran.

Branches tore at my arms. Roots clawed at my boots. The ground rose sharply, but I didn't care. I just kept moving, dodging trees, leaping over fallen limbs.

Shouts rang out behind me. Two voices. Both male.

Another arrow hissed past, flying wide. I didn't look back. I couldn't. My heartbeat thundered loud enough to drown out thought.

The sound of hooves followed, growing louder. They were closing fast. The trees here weren't as dense as the inner forest. Too much open ground.

I pushed harder. Lungs burning. Legs screaming.

Then the air grew heavy.

A low, rising rush of heat pressed against my side.

I threw myself sideways—just as Fire exploded against the trunk where I'd been. Bark split with a crack. Embers spat across the underbrush.

A Fire Caster.

That had to be the one who'd launched the flare.

I rolled hard and kept moving, the scorched scent clinging to my throat.

Keep going. Just keep going.

I thought about Casting Ardor—just enough to blind them, maybe slow them down. But with a Fire Caster this close, I couldn't afford to turn. Not without exposing myself and risking another arrow ... or worse.

The trees blurred past in streaks of green and brown. My boots skidded across slick moss stone, nearly sending me crashing. I caught myself on a low branch, breath ragged, then pushed forward again.

Another surge of heat rushed past—closer this time. I felt the sting near my arm.

They were closing in. I needed to do something.

A flicker of light flared against a fallen trunk behind me. Fire licked across the dry branches.

They were herding me like prey.

A sharp incline rose ahead, rocks jutting up like broken teeth, roots twisting through the slope. Climbing it would leave me exposed. Skirting around meant slowing down.

Neither option was good.

I chose the one that might get me away faster.

I started up the incline, half running, half climbing, my fingers clawing for purchase.

Something slammed into my back. Not Fire—no heat, just force. A solid wall of air that hit like a charging animal.

The impact stole the breath from my lungs. My feet left the ground.

I hit hard, shoulder first, tumbling back down the slope. Rocks scraped my skin and the roots tore at my clothes. The world flipped. My head cracked against something unyielding before I landed flat on my chest, the air wrenched from me.

For a moment, I couldn't move. Couldn't think.

Pain bloomed fast and brutal along my ribs. I gasped, hand flying to my chest, and Cast—broad and unfocused.

It wasn't efficient, but it worked. Raw, sweeping Healing flooding through me. Enough to dull the worst of it. The pain eased. Not gone, but bearable. Breathing came easier. My arms stopped shaking.

I pushed to my knees.

A shadow stepped into view—a cloaked figure, tall and broad. His bow was raised, arrow already trained on me.

⚫◇⚫

Artemis

The flare had long since faded, but smoke still clung to the trees, thin wisps trailing through the canopy.

I caught the scent first. Burnt bark, sap hissing from a tree trunk split clean by heat. I slowed, scanning the trail. Scorched leaves. Vines curled black and brittle. Hoof ruts in the dirt. They were fresh.

Close.

A rush of compressed air cracked through the forest. Wind Casting. Strong enough to feel the vibrations in my chest.

I broke through the last of the brush just in time to see Celeste tumble down a rocky slope, arms curling in as she hit the ground hard.

A Caster, tall and broad-shouldered with sun-browned skin, swung off his horse and grabbed a bow from the saddle. He strode toward her as she fought to rise.

Behind him, still mounted, sat a wiry man.

From this distance, I couldn't tell which one was the Wind Caster.

There were only a few paces between me and the mounted rider. He hadn't seen me. Not yet.

I drew my sword and moved fast.

One clean strike—low and swift across the neck, separating head from spine. The horse reared.

With a panicked snort, it bolted.

The bowman turned, eyes wide, shock flashing before hardening.

"Fuckin' whoreson," he spat.

He hadn't expected backup. Good.

Celeste moved.

While his attention shifted to me, she raised her hand and Cast. A burst of Ardor flared from her palm, strong enough for me to feel the white-hot ripple.

He reacted faster still. Swinging his arm wide, he used the motion to whip himself sideways. The light shot past his coat like a heated blade.

He didn't waste time.

He landed, boots digging in, and loosed an arrow at me in the same breath—quick, with a practiced hand. I deflected it with a twist of my blade. He threw his bow aside before the arrow even hit the ground.

He swept his hand outward, and the air answered violently.

A crescent of force rippled through the air—dust lifting in its wake as it sliced low toward Celeste.

The force wasn't just air. It was a blade.

The arc cut clean across her upper arm, deep enough to tear through skin and muscle.

Celeste screamed, a raw, guttural sound.

Blood soaked through her sleeve in an instant, darkening the fabric. She stumbled back, hand clamped over the wound, teeth bared.

I didn't hesitate.

I surged forward and Cast mid-stride, Ice forming sharp and jagged, shaping into a spear that I threw at the Wind Caster. He was ten paces out and opening the distance with every step back.

He moved fast, thrusting both hands forward. A burst of Wind hammered sideways across the clearing. My Ice veered with the gust and shattered against the tree trunk in a spray of glittering shards.

He was already retreating, putting distance between us, smart enough to stay far from my reach.

The ground trembled beneath me with the pound of hooves.

More are coming.

I didn't look back. It didn't matter how many if I couldn't reach Celeste first.

I hurled a second shard, low and angled to clip the Wind Caster's knee. Another gust bent my Ice just enough that it lost its mark, veering wide.

I used that moment to move.

Wind surged around my legs as I Cast.

Celeste had pushed herself up to one knee, faint Healing light shimmering around her wounded arm. She was still bleeding, but she held on.

Her face was pale from the blood loss, but her eyes locked on mine the moment I dropped beside her.

"I've got you," I muttered.

Three riders burst through the trees, dismounting before their horses had fully slowed. Dirt spat under their boots as they advanced, fast and direct. The horses barely flinched, snorting once before settling, like they were used to chaos.

The Wind Caster regrouped with them, falling into formation without a word. A glance toward the headless body slumped near the slope was his only acknowledgement.

They traded clipped phrases of information. Shock flickered across their expressions, but fear never came. Fury replaced it.

"You son of a whore," one of them growled, hand drifting to his weapon.

Another two riders broke through the trees moments later, slowing only long enough to drop from their saddles before joining the line.

Six in total now. Each armed. Likely all Casters. They didn't shout demands or threats. Didn't posture for courage or dominance. They aligned with practiced ease, spacing themselves out, ready to move at a moment's notice.

These weren't raiders looking for coin or deserters trying to survive. These men moved like they'd done this together a hundred times. Their tight formation marking them as trained, disciplined, professional bounty hunters.

Six against two.

One of us wounded.

Let them make the first move.

I'd make the last.

9

I glanced toward Celeste. She'd Healed most of her injury. The bleeding had slowed, and the deepest part of the gash was sealed, though the edges still wept.

Her breathing was shallow, shoulders trembling, worn from both the chase and the Casting.

The bounty hunters kept their distance, watching us in silence. They hadn't moved. Not yet.

I weighed my options.

Celeste was stable enough to move, but her arm would still slow her down.

The Wind Caster had seen her Cast both Healing and Ardor. He'd seen me use Ice, but the Wind I'd used had been nothing more than a surge of speed—I doubt he'd marked it as Casting.

One of them stepped forward, boots crunching the leaves. His hand rested casually on his weapon's hilt.

"We're here for the girl." His voice was rough. "She's got a bounty on her head. Alive." He let the words hang, eyes flicking between us. "You, we might've let walk. But that's done now." He jerked his chin toward the corpse. "You kill one of ours, we return the favor."

I let my blade drop slightly, casual, but ready.

"Leave," I told them. "Or stay and bleed like he did."

A few of them moved, fingers tightening around their weapons.

I tilted my head. "Go on then—prove you're worth the trouble."

Birdsong cut through the forest, each call unnaturally loud. The Wind Caster's jaw flexed, but he didn't bite. They held their composure better than I'd hoped. If I'd had any doubts about what we were up against, their calm erased them.

The break came fast.

The Wind Caster surged forward first, a compressed blade of air tearing toward us, displacing leaves in its wake.

Almost in the same instant, Fire blazed to life from the left flank, a burning arc launched to catch whichever of us dodged the Wind. A coordinated opening, clean and efficient. Something they must have done before.

Stepping in front of Celeste, I let my sword drop. Steel was useless against the speed of Casting; it would only slow me down. I raised both hands. With my left, Wind snapped outward, distorting the incoming blade, bending its edges just wide enough to shear past us and carve a furrow through the dirt.

With my right hand, Ice burst forward, a concentrated strike that met the fireball mid-flight. Flame hit frost with a violent hiss, smoke and steam twisting upward as the fire sputtered out in fragments of dying ember.

I didn't wait for the smoke to clear.

Wind coiled at my back and I launched forward. The ground blurred beneath my feet, twenty paces gone in the span of a single breath. I caught the flicker of surprise in the Wind Caster's eyes as I closed the distance.

He threw up his hand for another Cast.

Too late.

Ice snapped into being, not a single shard but a tight cluster, driven by a burst of Wind from behind my strike. At this range, there was no bending their path.

They struck him square in the torso. His breath left him in a shocked grunt as his legs folded beneath him, body hitting the dirt before the steam behind me had even thinned.

He hit the ground, dead before the others fully understood what they'd seen.

There was a moment of stillness, wide eyes, a ripple of disbelief. Wind-borne movement always came with visible Casting for them. I'd left that limitation behind years ago.

The cluster of five moved as one as everything snapped back into motion.

To my right, the Fire Caster thrust his palm toward her. Flame roared to life, a direct, punishing strike meant to erase her before she could raise a hand.

At the same moment, crackling blue light flared from the center line. Lightning, a streak of blinding force rippling toward me with a sharp, metallic snap that raised the hairs on my arms.

Using Wind, I pivoted hard, letting the bolts tear past close enough to sting. Static bit the air where my body had been.

Wind gathered at my back again and I surged toward Celeste, closing half the distance.

The Fire was almost on her when I lifted my right hand.

Ice slammed forward in a wide, sweeping Cast. It struck the incoming Fire from the side, overpowering the blaze with a violent collision of steam and scattered embers. Celeste shielded her face against the lingering vapor.

Steam curled between us, still rising when the ground lurched beneath my boots. A pull of softened soil, darkening underfoot and swallowing my ankles.

Advanced Earth Casting. He was trying to root me where I stood.

I didn't fight the drag. I Cast down instead, Wind funneling into a tight spiral, blasting the softened earth apart while Water thinned the muck clinging to my boots. The ground spat me free in a rush of mud and torn grass.

The reprieve lasted less than a moment.

Ice whistled through the air from both flanks, not a volley, but two simultaneous Casts, tightly grouped and meant to cut my retreat in one clean sweep.

I didn't dodge.

I sheathed myself in a skin of Water just before Flame roared from my palms in twin torrents, wide and hungry. Fire met Ice mid-flight, exploding into white-hot steam before they ever reached me. The air snapped, hissing and violent, the clearing swallowed in boiling mist that curled around us like smoke from a forge.

Wind surged around my legs and torso as I leapt back from the haze. Turning, I ran to Celeste's side. Shapes shifted in the mist. Shadows broke, regrouping.

I landed beside her just as the fog began to thin. Celeste's breath was ragged, her fingers glowing faint with leftover Light.

"I hit the one on the right," she murmured, eyes tracking movement ahead.

My gaze caught the Fire Caster she meant, his stance lower now, his coat singed and a hand pressed tight to his ribs. Blood seeped between his fingers, dark and steady. Hurt, but still standing.

The mist thinned further, unveiling the rest.

"A Fire Caster, Earth Caster, Two Ice Variants, and a Lightning Variant," I warned Celeste. "These aren't strays—they're trained. The Earth Caster can mire your feet if you stand still, but he can't raise walls anywhere beyond his immediate reach. And you already know how dangerous the others are."

They were a trained unit with practiced formations. Whoever sent them hadn't hired cheap blades. And they'd seen enough of me too. They knew what I was. Only one piece of my hand remained hidden.

They moved as one, closing ranks around the Earth Caster. Fire stepped to the front, the Ice Variants flanked on either side, and Lightning lingered behind them all.

The Fire Caster pushed first, hands already burning. A surge of flame roared over the ground toward us, wide enough to swallow both of us whole. I once again blasted the flame away with an outstretched hand of Ice, a hard jet of frost cutting through the heat. The impact cracked the air, a white glare of vapor flooding the clearing and erasing everything beyond a few paces.

The moment my Cast met his, the real attack came.

Two shrill whistles cut through the haze, one from each flank, Ice shards slicing from opposite sides. And from the center, darker shapes punched through the vapor with a hurl of jagged stones.

Three converging lines and no clean escape.

I slammed my heel back and drew the Wind up hard. A torrential gale erupted outward, ripping through the steam in a violent rush. Ice veered wide, spinning off course; stone tumbled and shattered past us, jagged pieces cracking against trees and dirt. One rock clipped my shoulder, close enough to sting but not break.

Celeste didn't wait.

Ardor flared bright from her fingers, a concentrated beam that lanced toward their center, straight at the Fire Caster. It would have struck true—

—but stone surged upward, a wall erupting just in time to swallow the blast in a shower of earth and shattered light, the impact booming through the clearing.

The wall held, then sank back into the ground, crumbling away in chunks of dirt and dust. The moment the path cleared, they advanced again, a coordinated effort, closing the distance with careful, practiced steps. They weren't rushing. Their formation let them advance without fear of what we threw back.

They were preparing the same strike—now from closer range.

I exhaled through my nose.

If they fire together this time, I thought, *those attacks will land.*

My Wind had barely turned them aside before, and as they continued to close the distance, the Ice would hit harder, and the stones even faster. Burning the Ice wouldn't stop the rocks.

Lightning stayed at the back. He'd been willing to strike earlier, but now he was being kept in reserve. He should have been front and center if their goal was a clean kill—Lightning was too fast, too lethal. If they meant to end this, he would be leading the charge.

The spacing, the restraint, with Lightning being kept in the back, waiting. It wasn't lethal intent anymore. They'd changed the protocol once they realized what I was.

Celeste wasn't the only asset on the field now. And I was worth more to them alive than dead.

Fine. I could use that. If they were intent on taking us alive, then they'd already given me the opening I needed.

As the multielemental attack flew toward us, I swept my arms in front of me, drawing the moisture from the air. Thin threads of vapor coiled and stretched, pulled tight into a lattice only I could see. The shield formed with Water in an instant, strands crossing and binding, held firm by will and core, though I felt the first tug of fatigue deep in my center.

Before the first shard or stone reached us, I thrust both palms forward. Ice erupted from my hands, racing across the web, locking it solid with a loud crack as the frozen wall took shape, thick and unyielding.

Stone wasn't the only way to build a wall. If stone was his shield, Ice would be mine.

The impact hit like a battering ram. Fire blasted across the surface in a hiss of steam, jagged stones slammed and fractured against its face, and frozen shards shattered in bursts of white powder.

The wall trembled, chipped, and shrank under the force—but still held. It didn't need to stand for much longer.

I raised one hand and Cast Water, not outward, but inward, threading a thin line of moisture through the wall's core. The frozen lattice softened where I willed it, a faultline forming beneath the surface. Before it could spread, I drove Wind into that weakened center in a tight, focused burst.

The Ice collapsed exactly where I intended, breaking into a spray of jagged shards. With a second sweep of my arm, I caught the fragments in a rolling gust and sent them hurtling forward. Dozens of fist-sized chunks screamed straight toward the advancing hunters.

I didn't wait to see how well they handled it.

The moment the Ice left my control, I was already moving. Wind drove me through the mist as their formation staggered, arms thrown up to shield against the storm of frozen shrapnel.

I used the chaos they couldn't see through.

The Earth Caster reacted fast. Stone burst up in five narrow slabs, shielding their line from the barrage. While shards hammered against the rock, I cut to the flank, toward the blind side of the slab I knew the left Ice Variant sheltered behind.

If they wanted to capture us, they'd have to stop me first.

And I wasn't giving them the chance.

The moment my boots hit solid ground, the left-flank Ice Variant was already recovering, his silhouette wavering around the haze. His focus snapped to me, arms thrust forward, unleashing a piercing blast of Ice straight toward my chest.

I answered with Fire.

Flame erupted from both palms, twin torrents meeting the Ice head-on. I pulled Water tight around my skin as vapor exploded between us, the already clouded battlefield swelling with another burst of boiling fog. I advanced through the blur of white, drawing both streams together into a single, driving column of fire.

He reacted in kind, forcing more power into his Cast, frost thickening in the air around him, the temperature plummeting.

A lesser Caster would already be ash. He wasn't merely surviving the collision—he was contesting it.

His core was deep.

The impact lit the clearing in violent white and orange steam.

But my Fire finally drove through.

The heat intensified, devouring his Ice, turning it to mist before it ever reached me. His stance broke under the pressure, knees buckling as he tried to hold the torrent back. The flame punched past his outstretched arm and engulfed him.

His scream tore through the steam as he staggered, coat and flesh searing under the blast. He collapsed a moment later, flame still clinging to him as he hit the dirt.

The steam swallowed everything.

Shapes flickered within the whiteout. A split second later, the air erupted in a chaotic barrage of blind fire: A crack of Lightning lanced through the fog, a burning arc of Fire roared past, Ice shards hissed through the mist, and fist-sized stones hammered forward with brutal force.

A chunk of rock clipped the side of my head, exploding stars across my vision. Another piece—a shard of Ice—drove into the muscle just above my hip, biting deep. The Lightning strike missed by less than a breath, the heat and static burning a line across my cheek as it split the steam behind me.

I staggered back, pain flaring sharp in my gut. They couldn't see me, but I couldn't see them either.

I retreated, fast and low, slipping back behind the thinning veil of steam before the next wave found its mark.

The steam began to lift, curling upward in slow drifts, revealing fragments of the battlefield. I pressed my hand to my side, fingers brushing the jagged shard still lodged above my hip. The pain ripped up my side as I gripped it and tore it free. Blood spilled hot down my side.

I drew a tight breath and pressed my palm over the wound. Healing flared warm beneath my hand, light seeping into torn flesh and sealing muscle enough to keep me moving. The pull on my core came harder now, an ache blooming low and deep, reminding me of the price every Cast was stacking.

As the haze thinned further, shapes emerged from the white. The Earth walls were gone, crumbled back into the ground. All of the men remained standing—

All except the second Ice Variant, now sprawled on the ground.

It took me a moment to find the reason.

Celeste stood beyond the crumbled stone, having circled the outskirts during my attack. Her arm was still raised, fingers smoking with the last trace of Ardor.

A hole burned through the Ice Variant's abdomen told the rest. Smoke curled up from his open mouth, and a dim ember of light flickered faintly inside the charred wound in his torso.

The victory died the moment the battlefield fully came back into view.

Celeste stood a few paces from the remaining three, Fire, Earth, and Lightning.

She was too close.

Their focus was no longer on me.

My stomach tightened. From where I stood, I wouldn't reach her in time, not before three Casts tore through the space she occupied.

If they struck now, she wouldn't dodge all three. Neither could I.

The ache in my core pulsed again, deeper this time, a throb at the base of my ribs. But the pain meant little compared to what would happen if I hesitated.

I drew Wind, not clean, not controlled, but raw and heavy. It scraped along my nerves like gravel dragged through my blood, but I didn't stop. The gale built fast, pressure clawing up my spine, the tether to my core surging harder than I should have pushed it.

Look at me.

I let the Wind break loose and launched myself with it, the shockwave tearing across the clearing as I moved. Steam shredded into wild ribbons of white; leaves and dirt spiraled into the air in a sudden roar. Fire staggered sideways, bracing. Lightning flinched back a step.

But Earth recovered fastest.

His palms hit the ground. Three slabs of stone surged upward, forming a half-ring barricade around their line, cutting off my advance and shielding the three of them together. But every head had snapped back toward me before it went up.

My gambit worked, if only for a moment.

And Celeste used that moment.

A white-gold flash exploded from the flank, Ardor ripping through the thinning haze. The beam tore straight toward the Fire Caster, catching him before he fully turned.

She fired again, relentless, lurching to the side. I closed the distance toward the wall, and the angle vanished behind stone. I couldn't see if her attack landed or not.

Wind gathered, and I threw myself over the wall. I hit the ground hard on the other side, just in time to see the aftermath.

The Fire Caster was the first thing I saw—burned through and motionless.

The second was Celeste.

Welts carved into her side and arm, angry and raised. She stared at the Earth Caster with murder in her eyes.

Then she saw me.

The shift in her expression came a heartbeat before I felt it. The air crackled, charged, every hair along my arms lifting in warning.

Lightning.

I didn't think. Wind snapped from me in a violent burst, colliding with the oncoming strike. The bolt veered, just enough, its path skewing off-center—but not completely.

Pain detonated through my side as the edge of the strike clipped me, heat and static tearing through muscle. The rest of the bolt slammed into the stone behind, exploding against the wall in a blast of shattered rock and dirt.

The concussion hit like a hammer.

Debris slammed into my back and shoulders, driving me forward. I hit the ground hard, vision flaring, the taste of iron already in my mouth. My limbs spasmed from the jolt, fingers locked open, muscles twitching with the leftover charge.

I forced breath back into my lungs and lifted my head just enough to see through the settling dust.

The Lightning Variant was already resetting his stance. Earth mirrored him, palm pressed to the ground, the soil beneath his fingers darkening as it prepared to strike.

Celeste's eyes met mine across the clearing.

"Down!" she shouted.

I flattened instinctively, pressing my face into the dirt.

Light erupted. Even with my eyes shut, the flash tore through me.

The Casters cried out.

I lifted my head.

Both Casters clutched at their eyes, staggering, blinded and panicked.

I looked for Celeste. She was on the ground, one hand braced in the dirt, breath ragged. She driven herself to the brink of Enervation—spent and shaking.

I'd taught her how to use Ardor not as a beam, but as a burst: blinding and violent, trading precision for force. At range, it overwhelmed the senses, burning sight into chaos. Up close, it could steal a man's vision for good.

The cost was steep. A gamble taken only when there was nothing left to lose.

She'd chosen her moment well.

The ringing in my skull wouldn't fade. My muscles still twitched from the Lightning's bite, and every breath came with a tremor. The two Casters staggered, blind, cursing, groping for bearings they no longer had.

We were all hurting.

I put a hand to the ground, forcing myself upright through the haze in my eyes.

Lightning recovered first. His hand snapped up erratically, Casting blind, arcs of crackling blue tearing across the clearing. One shattered the stone slab behind me, peppering my shoulder with grit as I ducked instinctively. Another sizzled past close enough for heat to kiss my cheek.

I moved, forcing my legs to answer, pushing into a low sprint through the broken haze. Earth was closest.

He blinked hard, vision struggling back just as I closed the distance. His hand slapped toward the ground, stone answering. The wall only climbed halfway before I struck.

Ice left my palm in a tight, brutal cluster.

The first shard took him in the eye. The second buried itself deep in his throat.

He hit the dirt before he could finish forming the wall.

That left one.

I turned, breath shaking loose from my lungs in uneven pulls.

The Lightning Caster wiped at his eyes, blinking hard, the last of the blindness fading. He saw me first. Then the body of the Earth Caster. The clearing that had been a formation moments ago was now just him, alone and surrounded by the dead.

Lighting was the worst match for me. The strain in my core had become something deeper, like a hand closing around me and squeezing. Every Cast had been too much, too fast, stacked without space to recover.

I dragged in another breath, forcing my legs to lock beneath me.

The last Caster's gaze hardened. His hand snapped up with a clarity he hadn't had moments ago. Blue light ignited.

I moved.

Wind surged beneath each step, not smooth or elegant this time, just enough to hurl me forward in brutal, uneven bursts. Lightning lashed out, arcs ripping through the air, striking where I'd been seconds earlier. One of the branching arcs clipped my shoulder, searing flesh and numbing my arm to the fingertips. The taste of metal flooded my mouth.

Another crack split the air, the charge building faster now that his sight had returned. I felt the next strike coming, the pull of electricity reaching for the easiest path. I was closer now.

Instinct beat pain.

I dropped low, slamming my palm to the dirt. We were only a few paces apart now—close enough to see fear flicker sharp in his eyes. At this range there was no dodging; a clean hit meant death.

His arms snapped upward, panic twisting his features.

Ice erupted from my grounded hand, frost spidering across mud and shattered stone in a flash-frozen sheet. I ignited my other hand, Fire surging out in a tight, concentrated blast.

The world detonated.

Steam exploded upward in a deafening roar as Ice and Fire collided with raw earth, boiling water and shattered frost bursting between us—two clashing Casts meeting at arm's length. The pressure hit like a physical blow, flinging us apart as if the ground itself had rejected the fight.

I crashed onto my back, breath punched from my lungs, ears ringing so violently the world went silent beneath it. Steam billowed across the clearing in thick rolling waves.

For a long moment, nothing moved.

The steam thinned in slow, unraveling veils, the world returning in fragments. Scorched earth, fractured stone, the faint crackle of dying sparks.

Pain flared through my sides as I forced myself upright, pushing to my feet on unsteady legs. The ground swayed once, then settled beneath me.

Then I saw him.

The Lightning Caster lay twisted on his side, half propped against the splintered remains of a tree. His skin was slick and blistered where the steam had hit hardest, clothing seared and melted. He was still breathing, but shallow, ragged, steam rising from burnt cloth and blackened flesh.

His eyes found mine through the haze, wide and glassy. The last breath left him as a shudder. The light in his gaze went out.

And just like that, the clearing fell still.

The fight was over.

10

The smell of scorched stone and burnt flesh clung thick in the air. Heat still shimmered off the ground where Ice and flame had collided moments ago. My breath came ragged in the sudden quiet.

There was no one left standing.

We had killed them all.

The fading burn of Ardor ebbed from my palms, leaving my fingers shaking uncontrollably. The strength bled out of my legs, and I dropped to the forest floor before I realized I was falling. Every heartbeat echoed against the inside of my skull now that the roar of Casting had gone still.

The world felt too loud in its silence.

My arms were leaden, my chest tight. Welts burned along my side, climbing across my arm and neck, each one pulsing with its own beat of pain. A branded reminder of how close the strikes came to ending me.

I looked toward Art. The blast had thrown him back across the clearing, landing only a few paces away from me. He was breathing hard, shoulders rising and falling with each deep drag of air. His hands trembled too.

With a quiet exhale that sounded like it scraped its way out of him, he dropped to his knees. For a moment, he didn't move at all, head bowed, as if the weight of the fight had finally caught him and forced him still.

A pulse of panic cut through the fog in my head.

Had he pushed too far? Had he reached Enervation? If he collapsed out here, I didn't know if I could get him back on his feet.

"Art?" My voice cracked more than I wanted it to. "Are you—"

He lifted his head just enough for me to catch his eyes.

"Not there yet," he said, voice low and strained.

He shifted, lowering himself to sit with his back against the nearest tree, one knee bent. I crawled toward him and eased down opposite, the ground cold beneath me, grounding in a way that didn't quite reach my lungs.

I pressed a hand to my arm, light gathering faintly in my palm. The skin warmed under my touch, the ache ebbing, until the familiar pull tightened in my chest. My vision wavered at the edges, the world softening and darkening in a way I recognized too well.

If I kept going, I'd tip myself into collapse.

I pulled my hand back with a stifled grunt. The gash would have to wait.

For a while, neither of us moved. Our breathing was the only rhythm in the clearing, uneven pulls of air fighting to steady. Above us, the forest seemed to remember itself, leaves whispering faintly, as though sound was returning one small piece at a time now that the killing was done.

Art moved first.

He braced a hand against the ground and pushed himself upright, slow, testing, like he wasn't entirely sure his legs would listen. He stood a moment, catching himself against a tree, before moving toward the nearest body.

I watched him work through the aftermath. He moved from one corpse to the next, checking pockets, belts, and pouches. A few coins clinked faintly as he slipped them into his pocket. There was no reverence in the way he handled them, but no cruelty either, only necessity, as though survival had burned etiquette out of him long ago.

When he finished with the bodies, his attention turned to the horses. During that first quiet stretch, only three of the horses found their way back, filtering through the trees with flicking ears and cautious snorts. The rest had either panicked into the woods or gone down in the fight. Art stepped to the nearest, unfastening the leather satchel at its flank. A soft thud marked the supplies hitting the ground: dried rations, a waterskin, more coins, and a whetstone.

Then he stilled.

He pulled a piece of folded parchment free from the pouch, its wax seal broken but still clinging to the edges. Even from where I sat, I could see the elegant, formal script. The parchment was thick, the letter carved in ink dark and with purpose.

Art read it once, jaw tightening. Then his eyes flicked to me. "This wasn't some open bounty. They were contracted. Directly."

I didn't have to ask by who.

He began to read the paper aloud this time.

The bearer of this order is tasked with locating and securing the property known as Celeste Halloway, alive and physically whole. Lesser injuries are immaterial, as the subject's abilities ensure full recovery. The subject is considered extremely dangerous. She is an Aberration and a Variant, confirmed to wield Healing. It is believed—based on recent events—that she may also command Ardor. Delivery is to be made directly to the undersigned. Payment in full upon confirmation of delivery. Failure to comply will forfeit all compensation.

Authorized by: —

The bottom line ended in a jagged tear, the name cleanly removed.

"They cut the name out," Art said, his voice low. "Slavery's illegal. Harder to enforce with the war, but still illegal. Bounty hunters strip the names to protect whoever hired them."

Property. Extremely dangerous.

The words tangled together in my mind, cold and suffocating. They hadn't just priced me like cargo. They'd weighed me like a weapon.

Art's gaze lingered on the torn edge for a moment longer before he folded the paper and slipped it into his coat.

"Whoever paid for this isn't going to stop just because we killed these ones."

His eyes fixed on mine. "They call you property," he said, voice hard around the edges. "I think it's time we prove them wrong."

He turned back toward the nearest corpse and crouched, prying loose the sword still sheathed at the man's hip—Art's own blade lay somewhere back in the clearing where the fight began. He checked its weight, then tested the balance with a short, practiced swing. The blade sang faintly through the air before he steadied it again.

When he approached, I expected him to keep it. Instead, he held it out, hilt first. "Take it."

I hesitated, then managed a faint smile. "You planning on finding me sticks next?"

"Figured it's time we moved past the sticks." He nodded toward the blade. "It's lighter than mine. Shorter reach. You'll adjust quick."

I took the sword. The balance felt different from his bastard sword. Quicker, less weight behind the swing but easier to control. The real weight settled into my palm in a way that felt both foreign and right. The leather grip was worn smooth but solid, the steel faintly nicked from use.

The air between me and him was still, heavy with the smoke of what we'd done and what waited ahead. My arm ached, a reminder of how close I'd come to not being here at all.

Art turned away first, the moment passing as quietly as it had come. He crossed the scarred clearing to where his sword lay, dusted the hilt, and sheathed it before moving on to the remaining horses.

"We're taking these," he said over his shoulder. "Faster than walking. And I don't know about you but I'm too tired to even try."

I slid the sword through the empty loop at my belt and followed, matching his pace. As he approached, the nearest horse shifted uneasily, ears flicking. The black palfrey watched him without bolting, surprisingly calm despite the smoke and blood. Art took the reins, murmuring low, then checked the saddles and cinches.

He reached into a side pouch and pulled out a small, hardened stone the color of dark amber.

"Flare resin," he said, holding it up for me to see. "Highly flammable sap from a Seyler tree. You toss it in the air, light it mid-flight, and it burns bright enough to be seen for leagues around. That's how they signal when they've found something worth chasing." He slipped it into his pack. "We'll keep it. Could be useful."

I recalled the streak of red-orange light arcing above the treetops earlier, the way the air shuddered when it went off.

Art moved to the second horse—a dun mare—tossing me the reins without looking back.

"Ride light and don't get ahead of me," he said, eyes still scanning the tree line. "If anyone else is on our trail, I want them to see me first."

I climbed onto the saddle, wincing as the leather rubbed against my leg. Art mounted his horse, turning it by the reins.

"South. We'll make distance first. Then we'll worry about where we're going," he said.

The battlefield stretched behind us, scattered with bodies and broken gear. I didn't look for long. My fingers tightened on the reins, and I nudged my horse forward.

We kept to the deeper trees, steering clear of any open ground. My horse picked its way over roots and moss. Even as the clearing was swallowed by the forest, it didn't feel far enough.

The horses hooves thudded dully against the forest floor.

This was the second group to find me. The first time, Art had stepped in and killed them without effort. This time ... this time we'd barely made it through. He was strong. But these bounty hunters were faster, stronger, and harder to put down compared to Teresa's crew.

If they were sending people like this now, what would the next wave be like?

The thought lingered heavy in my chest. I'd put Art in danger again—worse than before—and he hadn't hesitated to throw himself into it. Again. I wanted to believe I was ready to fight beside him, but every labored breath reminded me I still leaned on him to survive.

I let my gaze flick toward him for just a second. He was slouched, one hand loose on the reins while the other stayed pressed against his thigh.

The wind felt colder now. The forest quieter. Too quiet.

We kept moving as the air continued to cool and the light dimmed, the scent of pine and damp earth thick around us.

Only then did Art stop.

We'd barely stopped long enough for the horses to steady their breathing when it came—a faint, rolling thump that didn't belong to the forest.

At first, I thought it might've been my imagination, my ears still ringing from the fight. But then another sound followed, clearer this time.

Hoofbeats. They were distant, but moving.

Art's head turned toward the sound, his whole body rigid. I didn't understand why until a streak of crimson tore up through the trees, staining the sky.

Another flare.

The red bloom hung in the air, searing itself into my vision.

A knot formed in my stomach.

If this group was like the last, we were already dangerously close. And if they were worse …

Art's voice cut through my thoughts, low and urgent. "Move. Now."

The flare still burned in my mind, even as its light faded into the night.

He didn't speak again. He just urged his horse off the faint path we'd been following, angling us deeper into the dark.

We moved where the trees grew tight enough to scrape my knees if I wasn't careful. The canopy swallowed the moonlight, leaving only thin ribbons of silver that Art seemed to navigate by instinct. When we reached open bands of moonlight, he timed our crossing with the drifting clouds, moving only when shadow covered us.

Our tracks vanished behind us as he worked. Wind swept loose needles and dirt across the trail while Water softened the deeper impressions, turning them to mud that sagged and filled.

When the sound of running water reached us, he steered us straight into it without a word. The shock of cold splashed up my legs, but I bit back a gasp. We followed the stream for what felt like forever, horses wading beneath the dark surface.

Only when the creek bent hard to the east did Art lead us out again. The horses came up dripping and shivering, the forest closing in. Damp, black, hiding us from the remnants of the flare's light.

Art slowed his horse, letting it drift to a halt beneath a thicket of low-leaning pine. The needles formed a curtain overhead, thick enough to muffle the wind.

"This is far enough for now," he said at last, keeping his voice low.

He dismounted, one hand on the reins, scanning the dark between the trees.

I could still hear the faint trickle of the creek behind us. No pursuit yet. No shouts. But still, my muscles stayed tense, waiting for the next flash of light to prove we hadn't outrun anything at all.

Art finally exhaled and loosened his grip on the reins. "We'll keep the horses close. No fire. No noise above a whisper."

I nodded, but my hands wouldn't stop trembling. Whether it was the cold or the residual tension, I couldn't tell. My heartbeat hadn't found its normal rhythm yet.

Art crouched, sweeping the leaf litter away from the scuffed patches of earth left by our boots. "We leave tracks, we invite company," he muttered without looking up.

I slid down from my saddle, my legs stiff from the ride. The horses shifted restlessly, ears flicking at the distant calls of night birds. Every sound in the dark felt louder. Closer.

Art straightened, scanning the forest, then moved to check the horses' tack in silence. His silhouette was a solid shape against the shifting shadows, the only thing keeping the knot in my chest from tightening further.

He looped the reins loosely around a low branch, close enough for a quick grab. He gave the horses a quiet pat.

Finally, he turned to a narrow patch of ground between two leaning oaks. "This'll do," he said, barely above the wind. "We keep to the shadows. If we need to move, we move fast."

I knelt beside him, easing my satchel down. The ground was uneven and cold, but we didn't bother clearing it. There was no time for comfort.

Art pulled a folded blanket from his pack and spread it thin over the damp earth, just enough to keep the chill from seeping into our bones.

The forest pressed in on all sides. Leaves whispered overhead, stirring in slow, restless patterns. My hands worked automatically, checking the edge of my boots, making sure nothing was tangled or loose enough to slow me if I had to run.

Art sat with his back to one of the oaks, sword resting across his lap. His eyes stayed open.

I sat beside him, leaving just enough space between us to reach for our weapons without bumping into the other. The cold bit through my clothes, but I forced myself still, matching his quiet.

"I'll take first watch," Art said, bracing his back against the tree. "You need the rest more than I do."

I frowned. "You've been through the same fight I have—"

"I'll be fine."

"You should at least—"

"Celeste." His voice held the force of an order. "Go to sleep."

I hesitated. "It just doesn't feel right."

His jaw tightened. "I said I'll be okay."

I waited a moment, before I tried again, softer this time. "Then we split the shifts. Half and half. That way—"

"Dammit, Celeste," he said, patience thinning. "My core runs deeper than you think. I've emptied it and crawled back enough times to know I'll survive. That's enough."

He looked away, eyes scanning the dark like nothing had happened. As if the outburst had never left his mouth.

But it had.

And the sting of it lingered.

I turned over, pulling the blanket tighter around me, and let the forest's hush close in gently. Sleep came slow, laced with the sound of his breathing and the faint rustle of leaves overhead.

11

Artemis

The forest was still.

I'd been awake for hours, long before first light began to creep through the branches. Sleep hadn't been an option.

Not after yesterday.

The horses stamped lightly now and then, ears flicking toward sounds too quiet for me to make out. Celeste slept beneath the blanket, her breathing light. If she was dreaming, the forest kept them.

I swept my gaze across the shadows between the trees, listening for anything out of place. The air felt heavy. Not with threat, but with the knowledge it could return at any moment.

No birds yet. No wind stirring the leaves. Just the faint trickle of the creek, somewhere behind us, the slow warmth of the sun filtering through the branches.

It had been one of the harder fights I'd had in years. Not the worst, but close. Protecting Celeste had made it harder.

I'd gotten used to fighting for myself alone, with no one else to guard but me. Yesterday, I'd had to cover someone else from every direction. Earth shrapnel, Ice shards, Lightning attacks.

Always tracking where Celeste was.

Always one misstep away from being too late.

It had slowed me. Pulled at my focus.

I told myself I could keep her safe. Hold the line long enough to end it. But even now, the thought crept in like a splinter I couldn't shake.

What if I can't?

She was quick. Determined. Smarter than she let on. But she'd never fought anything like that before.

And they'd been strong. Stronger than the last lot.

If there was one thing I'd learned, it was that the stronger the men, the more frequent the charge. Someone out there wasn't going to stop until she was back in chains.

And maybe that was the real danger.

Not the bounty hunters.

Not the Casters.

Her.

She was too much like me for it to be coincidence. The way she Healed. The way the Ardor bent to her hand like it had been waiting for her.

If I was right ... Walking away wasn't going to happen.

Not for me. Not for her.

But I wasn't ready to tell her that. Not yet.

It had been decades since I'd fought this hard for anyone but myself.

The last time, I'd been young enough to believe that will alone could keep someone alive. Young enough to think loyalty meant something in the end.

It hadn't.

I'd paid for that mistake with chains of my own, and when I finally broke free, I swore I'd never tie my fate to another's again.

A loud crack splintered the stillness. Then something pushed through the undergrowth.

I stayed seated for a moment, listening. The forest held its breath except for the faint whisper of branches shifting overhead.

Then it came again, heavier this time. A quick rustle.

I eased up onto one elbow, then to my feet, scanning the black between the trees.

When the shape finally broke cover, my grip didn't loosen.

A fat little squirrel darted up the nearest trunk and clung there, tail flicking once. He didn't flee when he saw me.

Nettles.

His dark eyes fixed on me, unblinking.

I exhaled slowly. "Go on."

The squirrel didn't run away. Instead he scrambled higher into the branches above me.

An acorn struck my shoulder and dropped harmlessly to the ground.

I looked up at him.

His tail lashed once before he climbed higher into the branches and vanished into the dark.

I glanced down at Celeste. She hadn't stirred. She breathed evenly, her face faintly silvered in the low light—sleeping too deeply to notice me standing over her.

I looked back toward the branches where Nettles had disappeared.

"You're right," I muttered.

Standing here watching her wasn't protection. It was just waiting to be caught. If there were more hunters, I needed to find them before they found us.

Leaving her, even for a short while, went against every instinct I had. But dragging her along when she was half spent and recovering was worse.

I dropped beside my pack and pulled free my charcoal and small leather-bound notebook. Flipping to a blank page, I wrote in tight, quick letters:

Stay put. I'll be back. –A

I set the book where her hand would find it if she stirred, weighing it down with my gloves so it wouldn't blow away.

Then I was moving through the trees, feet barely breaking the frost. The cold air burned in my lungs, but I didn't slow, not until I covered enough ground to circle back the way we'd come yesterday.

If anyone was out there, I'd find them before they found her.

I found tracks. The prints had softened at the edges, but not enough for time to have erased them. Three pairs of heavy boots. A branch snapped under weight and left behind. A young sapling bowed low across the path, still held in tension from being forced aside. The kind of trail left by people moving fast and not concerned about stealth.

I crouched, fingers brushing the fresh splinter of wood. Pale at the break, not yet darkened by frost or air. Hours old at most. They'd passed through heading south—same direction we'd taken.

No shouting. Not metal on metal.

I didn't like it.

If they were bounty hunters, the trail would have wandered, men spreading out, chasing shadows and guesses. This path was straight, confident, every step matching the last. Either they weren't after us ... or they hadn't found us yet.

Neither made me feel better.

I remained low and fast, letting Wind hug close around my calves to quiet the brush. The ground dipped and rose unevenly, old roots knuckling through the frost. I crossed a narrow game path, then another, widening the circle until I was past the line we'd cut yesterday.

A scuff on a tree pulled me up short.

I palmed the trunk. A fresh scrape, sap still sticky. Someone had shouldered through here in a hurry. A pace farther on, a thread of dark cloth clung to a thorn. I rolled it between my fingers. Tight weave, not homespun.

Boot prints reappeared in a shallow dip where the soil kept overnight moisture. They'd broken south or southwest.

I followed another fifty paces and stopped at a narrow run of stones half buried in moss. Someone had lingered long enough to leave a deeper print. I cut across the slope toward a stand of dark fir.

The air tasted faintly of oil. Metal. I crouched and ran my palm over the ground until my knuckles brushed something cold. A short brass tube lay in the dirt, crimped on one end, black soot staining the rim.

Flare casing.

The kind you load and fire fast. I'd seen them before, on walls, in fields, lighting the sky over men who wouldn't see morning. This one had a tiny stamp near the seam. Not a maker's flourish. An issue mark.

Regulation.

I slid it into my coat and waited as the forest stilled around me. No voices. No movement. Only the slow bleed of cold into my fingers and the distant creek murmuring somewhere far off.

I pushed another hundred paces.

A shallow divot where a knee had hit. The trail narrowed, not fading but committing, drawing a straight line south.

Whatever brought them into these woods, they weren't drifting after ghosts in the dark. They had somewhere to be, and it wasn't here.

I let a long breath fog the cold and forced the urge to keep pushing to bleed out. The rule was simple: Protect Celeste.

Anyone moving away from us could stay that way.

I angled west, then north, crooked and uneven, creating not a path but a problem for anyone trying to follow.

By the time I reached our hollow, light had begun to lift above the edges of the trees. The world wasn't brighter so much as less black.

The blanket lay half folded.

I stopped.

The horses stood as before. Ears forward. No sign of struggle.

But she wasn't there.

"Celeste?" I called softly.

I crossed the hollow in three strides, scanning for drag marks. Blood. Disturbed soil.

Nothing.

"Celeste," I hissed, louder now.

A rustle answered from the trees. I moved before I thought, sword half drawn, boots silent over root and moss.

I skidded to a stop.

She stood behind a low cedar, one hand braced against the trunk.

There was a long, suspended moment where neither of us spoke.

Her brows drew together. "Do you mind?" she asked, irritation plain.

I turned around immediately.

"Yes. Of course. I was—I thought—" I cleared my throat. "You weren't there."

"Congratulations. You found me. Can I get some privacy for a moment?"

"Yes," I answered immediately. "Take your time."

I walked back to the hollow and faced the opposite direction like a sentry who had just survived his own stupidity.

Behind me, the forest resumed its normal sounds.

My pulse took longer.

A few moments later, I heard her steps returning through the brush.

I kept my eyes fixed forward.

"You can turn around," she said at last.

I did.

She crossed the hollow without looking directly at me, brushing dirt from her palms. There was the faintest color in her cheeks—whether from the cold or the interruption, I couldn't tell.

"That was unnecessary," she muttered.

"You weren't where I left you."

"I went ten paces."

I exhaled slowly. "Next time, say something."

She hesitated, then shrugged. "I've had men watch me piss before. This is hardly the worst of it."

My jaw tightened. "That's not the same."

"No," she agreed. "It's not."

She glanced toward my book with the note I left her. "You left."

"Didn't go far. I checked our back trail."

She lowered herself onto the bedroll, the blanket gathering at her waist. "Anything?"

"Tracks. Boots. Three at least. Hours old. They kept moving south."

"After us?"

"Maybe. Maybe not." I met her eyes. "Either way, we don't linger."

She turned slightly, and that was when I saw it—the wound in her arm was still open, still oozing.

"Let me see it," I said.

"I'm fine." She didn't meet my eyes.

I crouched beside her. "You're not. That arm's going to slow you, and we can't afford slow."

Her gaze flicked to mine. "You barely slept. I heard you moving. Twice."

"I've got enough in me." My tone came out rougher than intended. "Better you're whole in case steel finds us again."

She hesitated, fingers curling in the blanket.

"Celeste." I didn't look away. "I've fought half dead and survived. I'm not letting you try the same."

Reluctantly, she extended her arm.

The skin was hot around the wound. I pressed my palm to it and let the familiar pull start. Her breath caught, but she didn't pull away. The light spilled between my fingers, warm and steady.

When it faded, the wound was gone, the skin whole again without a trace.

She flexed her arm slowly, then looked up at me. "That always feels … different. Not like when I do it." Her brow furrowed. "It's strange, having someone else Heal me. I'm so used to doing it myself."

I didn't answer right away.

It would feel different. I'd been doing this longer than she had. Pushed my gift to its edges and dragged it back again, reshaping it with every scar. My core was deeper. My control cleaner. But saying that meant pulling loose threads I wasn't ready for her to see.

"There," I said instead, straightening. "Now if you have to fight, you won't bleed to death doing it."

She studied me for a long moment, as if she knew what I wasn't saying. Then she nodded once and drew the blanket back over her legs.

"You should rest," she murmured.

"Later." I stepped away, letting the trees swallow the last of the dark.

She pulled the blanket tighter and settled back, eyes closing, the lightest edge of sleep tugging but never winning.

I stayed where I was, scanning the spaces between the trees. The cold sank in. Somewhere far off, a crow called once.

The forest felt like it was holding its breath.

For now, we could steal a little sleep, being safer than we'd been before. But soon, we'd have to move, before whatever lingered out there decided to close the distance.

12

I woke to warmth at my side.

The sun was high, light filtering through the branches in pale gold. Art lay beside me, one arm folded under his head, his breathing slow and even. The hard tension I'd grown used to in his features had eased in his sleep.

I wondered if anyone else had ever seen him like this.

A lock of hair had fallen forward over his brow, the faint shadow of stubble tracing his cheeks. His chest rose and fell in an easy rhythm, nearly in time with the creek's soft murmur. It struck me how deeply I'd slept—deeper than I had in months.

Of all the ways to be found in the forest, that hadn't been my finest moment.

A small breath left me.

My gaze lingered longer than it should have. He looked different without danger shadowing him—still dangerous, but in a way that made me think less of blades and more of how his hand rested over mine when he Healed me.

I stretched my legs, just enough to ease the stiffness in my calves.

His eyes opened instantly.

Something in that look made my fingers tighten in the blanket. Not fear. Not exactly. But close enough that I kept still.

"You were staring," he said, voice low, rough from sleep.

"Didn't want to wake you," I murmured. "Didn't know you were capable of sleeping that deep."

"I'm not." A ghost of a smile touched his mouth. "I heard you moving. I was just deciding if you were worth opening my eyes for."

My lips quirked despite myself.

"And?"

"Still undecided."

"Good to know I fall somewhere below sleep," I said dryly.

He stretched, slowly, as if to prove he'd taken his time for a reason. "Curiosity keeps me alive. Sleep keeps you tolerable before breakfast."

"Sounds like you're speaking from experience."

"Maybe." His smile widened just enough for sunlight to touch the edge of it. "But I don't hear you denying it."

My stomach answered for me, the low growl filling the space between us.

He arched a brow. "Subtle."

"Maybe I'll forgive you if there's bread involved."

"Don't have any bread, but I do have some meat." He pushed himself up, stretching once before reaching for his pack. "Dried what was left of the boar yesterday morning before everything went to hell. Figured it'd keep better that way."

I blinked. "You made jerky in an hour?"

"Not proper jerky." He pulled out a wrapped bundle. "Just sliced it thin and burned the moisture out. It'll be tough, but it's food."

I took the strip he offered, turning it over in my hand. "Smells like smoke."

"Better than smelling like rot." His mouth twitched. "Besides, it's my specialty."

I bit into it, chewing hard. "If this is your specialty, I'm starting to worry about the rest of your skills."

That earned me the first real laugh I'd heard from him in a while. It had a warmth to it that I needed right now.

His brow arched. "That sounds like someone volunteering to cook next time."

"I'll have you know, I'm better with a skillet than you are with that jerky." I took another bite, mostly to keep from smiling.

He leaned back on his elbows, a glint in his eye. "I'll believe it when I taste it."

I snorted, more out of habit than offense, and tore off another bite. "Fair. But I promise you, what I make doesn't fight back."

"That's debatable. You're awfully sure of yourself for someone without a skillet." His tone was softer now, the edge from last night gone, replaced with something easier.

We ate in a stretch of quiet that wasn't uncomfortable. The sun had risen clear over our heads, laying strips of light between the dense trees. Some-where beyond, the creek still murmured, a reminder that water wasn't far.

By the time I worked through the last strip of jerky, Art was already on his feet, eyes skimming the tree line like he always did. Even when he was still, there was a restlessness to him, as if he were already leaning toward the next move.

"You're thinking about leaving again," I said.

"Not far," he replied. "Just want to make sure the trail stayed cold."

The words were easy, but I saw the tension creep back into his shoulders.

I pushed myself up, brushing crumbs from my hands. "Then I'm coming with you."

He shook his head. "Not this time. If someone's still out there, I don't want you walking straight into them."

"That's not your decision," I said.

"Maybe not. But I'll make it anyway."

He glanced over his shoulder, that faint smirk pulling at his mouth. "You can yell at me for it when I get back."

Something in me wanted to. But instead, I just huffed and reached for my waterskin. "Fine. But don't take too long. I don't like being left behind."

His eyes softened a fraction. "Noted."

I watched him go until the trees swallowed him, the air becoming heavy again. The sunlight didn't quite reach the forest floor, but it caught in the frost, making the ground glitter faintly. I pulled the blanket tighter around my shoulders and sat back, trying not to think about how far away he'd be soon.

Somewhere behind me, the creek kept up its steady whisper. I focused on that instead of the memory of boot tracks or the flare resin he'd slid into his coat yesterday. If anyone was still in these woods, I'd have to trust him to find them before they found us.

And hope he came back just as quietly as he'd left.

The minutes bled into each other, the forest holding its own kind of stillness. A jay screeched once in the distance, then went silent again. My eyes kept drifting to the spaces between the trees, tracing shadows that might've been movement if I looked hard enough.

I tried to tell myself he wouldn't be gone long. That he'd know the quickest way to sweep the area and circle back.

I took a slow drink from the waterskin. My fingers had just started to thaw when I caught it. It was the faintest change in the air, like the woods had taken a breath it hadn't meant to.

I stilled, every muscle tightening.

The whisper of the creek suddenly felt farther away.

A shadow moved between the trees.

I gripped the blanket tighter—until Art stepped through, quiet as he'd left.

"Everything's clear," he said, but his eyes were already sweeping past me, tracing the forest like he was counting something.

I exhaled, trying to sound casual. "That quick?"

"Quicker than it needed to be."

His tone was even, but there was a faint edge to it.

He adjusted the strap of his pack, a small, quick motion that drew my attention to the faint smear of reddish clay along the back of his coat. The dirt hadn't come from around us.

I opened my mouth to ask, but he was already turning away. "We should get moving."

He didn't speak again, and I didn't push. Whatever he'd seen, he wasn't going to tell me. Not yet.

"We'll cut deeper into the forest first. There's an older game trail that bends south before it loops back west. Harder to follow."

There was no reason to argue with that. I crossed to my horse, gathering the reins, and guided her after him.

For the first two days, we moved with purpose and little else. No training. No unnecessary stops. We ate cold food and kept our fires low—if we lit them at all. Art doubled back more than once, breaking trail before rejoining it. At night, we rotated watch.

Still, every so often his head would turn, eyes flicking toward the deeper woods. And each time, the space between my shoulder blades tightened a little more.

By the second day, the forest began to change.

The pines thinned, giving way to bare-branched maples and low, knotted scrub. The air carried a cold bite that promised snow before long, each breath turning to pale mist between us.

We camped again that night beneath skeletal branches that rattled softly in the wind. Neither of us slept deeply.

On the third morning, the forest began to break.

Art slowed as the wood opened just enough for a strip of pale sky and the darker outline of distant hills to cut through the endless green. He stopped there, scanning the edge like he was looking at something I couldn't see.

A soft rustle sounded overhead.

I glanced up just in time to see Nettles perched on a low branch, tail flicking. He watched us with dark, unblinking eyes.

Then he turned and bounded deeper into the trees.

"That's as far as the trees will hide us," Art said, gaze lingering on the forest's edge. "Three leagues west puts us in a town."

I shifted the strap of my satchel. "We'll make it before nightfall?"

"If we keep pace," he said, already moving.

The air felt different out here, less muffled, clearer somehow. Every step away from the edge of the woods made the ground firmer underfoot, and the forest's scent gave way to something stronger.

The sky ahead was washed in a pale amber that deepened toward the horizon, promising no more than an hour of true light. Somewhere far to the west, the sun was sinking, drawing the shadows longer across the open ground.

We rode in silence for the first league, the forest receding behind us until it was only a dark wall in the distance.

For the first time in weeks, there was nothing overhead but open sky. Without the cover of trees, the wind reached us in low, constant gusts, pulling at my cloak and tossing strands of hair into my face. It carried the faintest trace of woodsmoke. Thin, far-off, but enough to stir something I couldn't quite place.

Gradually, the land began to change. The ground sloped down into the shallow valley where pale winter grasses swayed in the wind. A narrow road cut through it, the dirt worn into the twin grooves by years of wagon wheels.

The first village came into view just before dusk. Small homes, thin smoke, nothing remarkable.

We didn't ride straight through. We circled wide, watching the road from a rise before we approached. I stayed mounted while Art handled supplies.

We were gone before full dark.

Art remained vigilant for days after. But no riders appeared on the road behind us.

By the fifth day, I stopped checking the horizon as frequently. By the eighth day, I think Art did too.

We rose with the light and rode until the wind bit too hard to ignore. Art made me practice in every clearing we passed—hand-to-hand first, then Casting, then our blades. He corrected my stance more times than I cared to count.

We camped along the roadside most nights, far enough from travelers to avoid questions but close enough to hear wagons pass after dark.

Routine returned.

Not from safety, but from the absence of pursuit.

The road carried us steadily northwest and back on track toward Rodin.

By the time the smell of smoke reached us, it didn't raise alarm. It drifted thin through the cold air, faint and ordinary—clinging to every settlement this time of year.

Still, my hands tightened on the reins without meaning to. My eyes followed the lay of the land as the road curved around a low hill.

I knew that smell, the way it mingled with frost and damp earth.

And I knew this road.

It dipped the same way I remembered, with a watch post leaning at its far end. I'd passed through here years ago, heading west.

Art glanced over his shoulder at me. "Something wrong?"

I shook my head, burrowing deeper into my cloak. "Just … smells familiar."

"Most towns will, if you've spent enough time in them," he said, and turned his gaze forward again.

We crested the hill and the rest of the town unfolded: a patchwork fence lining the left side of the road, rails repaired with mismatched boards, a row of bushes rustling softly in the wind. The same crooked tree standing alone in the ditch-side grass.

I kept my eyes on the tree as we passed under the watch post, telling myself it was nothing.

Nothing but another town on the road.

13

Artemis

Dawn arrived on a cold, colorless light, carried on the rattle of loose shutters and the distant clatter of a cart on frozen stone. I'd been awake since before the dawn, listening to the slow stir of the town outside the inn. No trouble in the night. No riders. Just the soft bark of a dog somewhere down the street.

I'd chosen Dunwade for a reason. It was a small and quiet town.

I'd passed through before and knew it well enough to trust its habits. A place to get feed for the horses, dry bread for the road, and maybe a word or two about what was happening along the border.

I'd already checked the horses by the time Celeste came down from our room. Her hair was still damp from the washbasin, her cheeks flushed.

"We'll eat first," I said as we stepped out into the thin winter light.

The streets were still waking. Frost clung to the thatch roofs, catching what little light had made it over the hills. Smoke drifted in thin ribbons from chimneys, the smell of wood and rendered fat curling through the air.

A boy hurried past with a slop bucket, a woman strung laundry between two posts, and a shopkeeper glanced at us over his broom handle.

We made our way toward the market square, where a squat building with a wide porch sat near a well. The sign above the door read *The Broken Lantern*, its painted letters weathered to pale ghosts of themselves.

The door shut behind us with a muffled thud, holding the morning's chill at bay. Inside, the air was warmer, thick with the scent of baking bread and onions sizzling on a griddle. Rafters ran low overhead, darkened by years of smoke, with spiderwebs clinging to the corners.

A half dozen tables sat uneven on a warped plank floor, most already taken. Two older men played cards at the far end, their voices rising and falling with each hand. Coins clinked against the table with every bet. Near the hearth, a pair of merchants hunched over their bowls, their chat drowned out by the crackle of fire. A scarred mastiff dozed at their feet, its ears twitching now and then at the sound of boots on the floorboards.

We took a table along the wall where I could keep the door in sight. Somewhere in the kitchen, a pan hissed as something was dropped into hot oil.

A serving girl with dark hair in a kerchief came over, slate in hand. "Mornin'. Porridge or eggs? Both come with bread."

"Eggs," I said.

Celeste echoed me, and the girl scribbled it down before disappearing into the back. The warmth and low murmur of conversation drifted through the room. A farmer came in, stomping his boots, and called a greeting to one of the card players.

"Quiet here," Celeste murmured, her eyes drifting over the room.

"Most small towns are this early." My gaze slid to the merchants by the fire. They'd been watching us since we walked in, not openly, but enough to notice. Could just be curiosity. Could be something else.

The serving girl returned with our plates, the smell of fresh bread and fried eggs rising with the steam, still warm from the oven, the eggs gleaming in the firelight.

I waited until she was gone before speaking. "Eat," I said, sliding a plate toward her. "We'll get supplies after this."

I let her focus on the food. My attention stayed on the room, the card players, the merchants, and even the mastiff before I let myself relax again.

We left the tavern with the last of the frost still clinging to the eaves. The market square was busier now. Stall keepers calling out prices, the smell of pine from a woodcutter's cart mixing with the tang of tanned hides from the leather shop.

I stopped at a stall that was selling cured meat and hard cheese, trading a few coins while Celeste browsed the table beside it, her fingers brushing against old tin cups and worn blankets. She didn't linger long, moving instead toward the small general store at the far side of the square.

The narrow storefront was wedged between a cooper and a candle maker. Seemed fairly ordinary. Just a faded plank sign and jars in the window. Yet there was a faint spark in Celeste's expression I hadn't seen since we'd reached town.

I stopped beside her. "What is it?"

"Only proof civilization has its merits," she said with a grin.

Inside, the air smelled of starch and dried lavender. Bolts of linen lined one wall. Shelves of oil, twine, needles, and folded underthings filled the rest. An older man stood behind the counter.

Celeste stepped forward. "Do you carry blood rags?"

The man glanced at me once before returning his attention to her. "We do, miss," he said mildly. "Flow?"

"Moderate," she said without hesitation.

He nodded once and disappeared through a curtain at the back.

I watched her while we waited. There was something almost pleased about her posture, like a soldier finding proper boots after marching barefoot.

She glanced at me. "You have no idea how convenient these are for a lady during their month's blood."

"I imagine I'm about to be enlightened."

She snorted softly. "You'd say the same if you had to ride half a day through the forest with stomach cramps and nothing for supplies but scraps and hope."

"That does sound … inefficient."

"Oh, trust me, it is."

I folded my arms loosely. "Then I'm glad civilization has provided a solution."

She tilted her head. "Is that humor?"

"I wouldn't dare," I said. "I value comfort in my traveling companion."

"Good," she said with a mischievous grin. "Because I don't plan to suffer quietly."

The shopkeeper returned carrying a small wrapped bundle tied neatly with twine and then set it on the counter.

"Two coppers."

Celeste paid and tucked the bundle into her satchel with obvious relief.

When we stepped back into the square, the noise of the market rose around us again.

She adjusted the strap of her bag. "You don't have to ride slower."

"I know," I said. "I'm sparing myself the complaints."

She smiled sideways at me. "Look at you, learning."

We moved on through the square, drifting from stall to stall. Celeste paused at a rack of blankets, rubbing the edge of one between her fingers before letting it fall back into place. She didn't ask the price.

She then paused at a table of folded garments beneath a canvas awning. She lifted one, holding it up against herself.

"You need them," I said before she could.

Her mouth twitched. "I wasn't asking."

"I know."

She selected two shirts and a darker overskirt. The woman tending the stall measured her with a practiced eye and named a fair price. Celeste paid without haggling.

The crowd thickened as the morning went on. Traders argued over food. A child chased a small dog through the crowd, earning a string of curses from a merchant. The scent of pine pitch drifted from a cart of split timber, mixing with hot iron from the smithy across the way.

Celeste walked beside me, bundle tucked under her arm.

Near the western edge of the square, where the rooftops thinned and the hills rolled low beyond, her steps slowed.

When she spoke, her voice had lost its earlier playfulness. "My hometown isn't far from here."

I glanced at her. "How far?"

"A few leagues, half a day's ride. Smaller than this place." Her voice softened. "I haven't been there since the raid. Not since they ..." She trailed off, the rest caught somewhere in her throat.

I didn't push.

She drew a breath. "I told myself I wouldn't go back. But I need to see it. To know if there's anything left. Maybe someone came back after ... after the raiders left. And if not—" She shook her head. "At least I'll know."

The square felt smaller suddenly, the walls closer. I studied her a moment before speaking. "It's west of here," I said finally. "That's a bit of a detour."

"I know. But it's close. And if we cut through there, we can still reach Rodin without taking the main road."

That last part was the practical truth, but it wasn't the reason in her eyes.

I nodded once and kept walking, but I didn't like the idea of doubling back. We made a slow loop through the rest of the square, picking up a few last-minute items.

When we arrived back at the inn, I told her I'd settle the bill, and she nodded, saying she'd fetch the horses and pay the stablehand. We gathered our things before splitting up, Celeste toward the stables, and I toward the keeper's desk to cover our room and board.

The innkeeper had his sleeves rolled to his elbows, counting a neat stack of coins. He looked up and slid the tally board toward me, the figures scrawled in chalk. Room, supper, breakfast, and a pitcher of small beer.

"Fair rate," he said. "Feed for the horses is separate, but the boy'll have told your girl that."

I counted out the coins slow, enough to make him glance once or twice at the weight of my purse. Outside, boots clomped on the porch as someone passed, the sound fading into the murmur of voices that were inside.

I asked him how the roads were looking toward Celeste's village.

"Road to Avriel's been clear, so they say, but if you're headed that way, watch for ice on the north bridge. Last week a wagon nearly went over."

I made a noncommittal sound, let him keep talking. The longer I stood there, the less it looked like I was hurrying anywhere.

He gave the counter a wipe with a damp cloth, told me about a merchant who'd lost half his goods to a flood, then drifted into a story about some trouble near Elmswyke. I thanked him and tucked the receipt into my coat.

When I finally stepped back into the cold, the sun had edged higher, cutting long shadows between the buildings. The stables sat down the lane, the wide doors open to the smell of hay and horse.

Halfway there, I saw them, the same two from the tavern along with a third I didn't recognize, fanned out in the stable doorway, talking to Celeste. She had one hand on the mare's reins, her posture saying she was listening, but not inviting conversation.

I hurried over, keeping my steps quiet out of habit.

The younger one smirked. "Travel's dangerous these days. You make the trip alone?"

She hesitated but didn't answer. And in that pause, something flickered in the young man's eyes, interest that had nothing to do with idle talk.

"That depends on who's asking," I said.

The men turned, surprise flashing quick before they masked it. I let my gaze rest on each of the merchants in turn.

The older one, gray-bearded and weathered, gave a small shrug. "Just conversatin' friend."

"Then I assume you had a pleasant talk." I took the reins from Celeste and placed my belongings on the horse, the weight of her gaze on me now as much as theirs. "We'll be on our way."

None of the men moved to stop us, but I could feel their eyes on our backs as we led the horses out.

We didn't speak. Boots and wagon wheels still tracked damp prints through the packed dirt of the street.

Celeste walked ahead toward the edge of town, the mare following with a lazy flick of her tail. I stayed close, one hand on the reins, the other near my coat where my sword rested.

I could still feel the weight of those men's eyes, even with the stables behind us. A glance over my shoulder caught them just stepping out into the street, half in shadow. They weren't rushing after us, but they weren't heading anywhere else either.

We cut through the square, past the woodcutter's cart and a cluster of women trading loaves for a sack of grain. The noise and movement masked us for a while, but every so often I caught a shape in the crowd that looked too still.

The last of the buildings thinned into open road. Celeste glanced back, her eyes meeting mine briefly, just enough for me to know she'd noticed too.

"They followed us to the edge of town," she said.

"I know." I tightened my grip on the reins. "Let's get out of here."

I waited until the town was behind us before speaking. "What did they want?"

Celeste kept her eyes on the road ahead. "They were feeling me out. They acted like they were just making conversation."

"About what?"

"They said they'd seen me before, on the road yesterday. Asked where I was headed, and if I was traveling alone. They started talking about safe roads and dangerous ones. Noticed my horse, said the saddle was of a good make."

I glanced at her. "Anything else?"

She shook her head. "They kept coming back to whether I'd come far. The whole time they smiled like they were just talking. Glad you came when you did."

My jaw tightened. "Men who talk that much without saying anything usually already know the answers."

We left with an easy gait, only picking up speed once the town was safely out of view. The road wound between low hills and the occasional blackthorn hedge, the air crisp enough to sting the lungs. By midmorning, the roofs and smoke of the village were long gone behind us, leaving only the open country and the faint line of the western hills.

Celeste rode ahead by a few paces, her red hair bright in the pale sun. It caught the light with every small movement, impossible to miss against the muted browns and grays of winter. It made sense that eyes followed her, though not always for reasons she deserved.

For a time, we rode in silence save for the sound of the horses' hooves on the packed earth.

It was Celeste who finally broke it.

"The war between AurenVale and Morvain ... It's been going on for as long as I can remember." Her voice was steady, but there was pain in it that didn't come from the cold.

I didn't say anything. I'd learned that with some people, silence was permission to keep going.

"My brother was drafted two years ago. He wasn't a Caster—couldn't even light a lamp without flint. But they're taking everyone now. Even farmers. Even boys who've never held a blade." She glanced down at her hands. The mare's ears flicked.

"I don't even know if he's alive." She drew in a sharp breath, exhaling shakily. "Five months ago, I was out picking up grain from a farm less than half a day's ride. Trading that far wasn't unusual. Grinding was local, growing wasn't. I'd made the trip to the Branlow farm many times. The bag was still warm from the mill when I headed back. How stupid it was to feel proud about something so small. I made it back right as the sun set."

Her knuckles whitened as she tightened the grip on the reins. "I smelled it before I saw it. At first, I thought someone was burning brush. It wasn't like the first raid. This time, they weren't just after food. That's when I heard—" She took a second to swallow. "Yelling. Screaming. I came over the ridge and saw my village. Not gone, just ... torn apart. Fires everywhere. Men I'd never seen before hauling sacks of food out of homes. People in the street. People I knew. Some moving. Some ... not. Then I saw—"

Her voice thinned. "I found my mother by the well. Her dress was torn. Blood, just, everywhere ... She was still barely breathing. I dropped the grain, and I ran. I put my hands on top of her. Her whole body was ... I didn't even know *where* to put my hands ... I couldn't stop shaking. My

Healing light kept flickering. There was just so much blood. I just ... I couldn't. I didn't know what to do."

Her shoulders shook. I kept quiet.

"Men came over and stood nearby—laughing. Talking to each other. 'Let her patch her up,' one said. 'We'll break 'em both in after.'"

Her voice cracked, then the words spilled out. "I kept working—I swear I was—she was fading, I could see it, but they said I was taking too long and one of them just—he grabbed me—pulled me back—" Her breath hitched, chest rising fast. "They *pulled* me. I was screaming. I told them—told them I could save her, I could still save her—" She pressed a hand over her mouth, fighting for breath. "They wouldn't listen, they never listened, they just—" Her hand tightened against her lips as tears streaked her face.

For a long time she didn't speak, simply stared past the road.

When she finally went on, her voice was softer. "The last thing I saw as they dragged me away was her looking at me." She took a long breath. "And then—" She blinked hard, but the tears slipped free anyway. "Then she was gone. And I didn't see her again."

Her hands stayed in her lap, the reins loose now, but she didn't wipe her face.

We rode on without a word. The grasses whispered in the wind, bending in waves across the hills, but even that sound seemed distant.

When she spoke again, it was different. Hollow and worn down. Like she'd ground the edges off the words. "They kept me with them. Moved from place to place. They had seen I was a Healer, and that made me valuable in their eyes."

Her gaze stayed fixed somewhere far ahead. "They hit another village, doing the same thing there."

The mare's hooves clopped dully against the dirt. A crow called once from the trees and went quiet again.

"A few weeks later, they sold me. Sold me off to Teresa's group. I was there until I escaped."

And just like that, she was quiet again. But the weight of her story still lingered heavy between us, visible in the tight set of her jaw and the way her hands curled tight around the reins like she needed something solid to hold on to.

I didn't say anything. There was nothing to say that wouldn't sound small against what she'd just given me.

We'd been riding for a while, the cold seeping into my gloves. The road wound between knolls, each bend making me check the ridgeline before we passed it.

She rode ahead, shoulders drawn in slightly, hair pulled loose by the wind.

I'd seen wounds close. I'd made them close. But some things didn't knit back together, no matter how hard you Cast.

If any of the bastards from her story were still breathing, I hoped fate would bring us face-to-face.

Because if it did, I'd be sure to tear them apart until they begged for death. But I wouldn't give it to them.

We kept riding.

The hills swallowed the quiet rhythm of our passing.

14

C*eleste*

We crested the last hill at a slow pace. The trees thinned first, then gave way to a clearing. And then there it was—Avriel.

I thought I would never see it again.

Smoke drifted from the few chimneys, lazy and unhurried. The fields laid pale and sullen, the harvest long gone. All that remained were brittle vines and overturned earth. Some of the houses were shoddily repaired. They had the same crooked rooflines, new cracked plaster hastily patched with uneven boards. Familiar in all the worst ways.

I didn't know what I expected.

Relief. Anger. Grief.

But all I felt was hollow.

A few figures moved between the houses, too far to recognize. But something in their gait, their stillness; it struck me harder than I expected.

They looked older. Worn thinner. It was as though the last five months hadn't passed *over* them, but *through* them.

I spotted a silhouette near the well. He was bent slightly, limping. It was Rowan. An older man who used to be kind to me and my mother. I remembered his unusual laugh, like a cork popping loose under pressure. Now, even at this distance, he didn't look like someone who laughed anymore.

They moved like ghosts. Half there, half lost to something none of us had words for. Small as ants from a hill.

I just watched them, wondering how many faces I'd recognize.

And how many I wouldn't.

Someone looked up. A figure by the drying racks. They turned their head too fast. Or maybe they hadn't been looking at me at all. I didn't know why my stomach dropped either way.

I counted four people out in the open.

Four, in a village that used to buzz with voices by this time of day.

No children's laughter. No barking dogs. Just the wind and the faint clatter of firewood being stacked behind the houses.

The clop of hooves felt wrong here, like the village wasn't meant for noise anymore.

I pulled gently on the reins, slowing the mare, and Art followed without a word. We swung down from the saddles and walked the last stretch, leading the horses by their bridles. Our footsteps crunched softly over the frost-hardened earth, quieter, but no less noticeable.

I didn't know why I was afraid. I'd lived among them all my life. Walked these roads and pulled water from the same well.

But now, I felt like a stranger wearing my own skin.

And I didn't know if they'd look at me and see Celeste ... or the resentment meant for someone who lived when others didn't.

We kept moving, the road curling down toward the village, ushering me closer to the question I wasn't ready to answer.

I didn't look at Art. I didn't need to. I could sense his awareness heighten beside me, like he was watching everything and everyone without letting it show.

Every step closer felt heavier than the last. As we approached, I thought of my mother. I let out a slow breath, hoping it would keep the tears back.

She'd always had a calmness to her, even when everything else felt like it was falling apart. The kind of tired that never showed on her face, just in the way she moved slower at the end of the day, like every step cost her just a little bit more. She didn't leave behind wealth or legacy but instead left behind warmth where there should have been ruin. The world had taken plenty from her, but it never once took her kindness.

I didn't know what they'd done with her body after I was taken.

When the chaos finally ended, I hoped they'd been able to give her a proper burial. There would've been many to bury after that night.

And Caleb ...

I blinked hard and kept my eyes ahead.

He'd already been taken when it happened. He was pulled away like so many others when the war ramped up.

We never got letters. But that wasn't strange, not out here. Silence could mean anything. He could still be alive, but I told myself he was probably dead. He wasn't a Caster. And that made him easy to kill in a war built for power.

I didn't want to believe it. But it was easier than wondering whether he'd come home to find this—or never come home at all.

If he was gone, at least he'd never have to know. Never have to see the place where she died, or the spot where she fell. And never have to wonder why I hadn't stopped it.

I needed him to be alive. But I knew if he was, if he had come back and found the house empty, our mother dead, and me gone ...

Would he think he failed us? Or would he know the truth?

That I'm the one who failed.

I could still remember the last thing he said before he left.

Keep an eye on Mom. Don't let her overwork herself while I'm gone.

He ruffled my hair like I was ten and just smiled that lopsided smile of his. He always did that when he was worried, but didn't want to show it.

He trusted me. And I left her.

I reached forward and brushed my fingers through my mare's mane, like the motion alone might calm the restless edge in me. Her warmth was steady beneath my palm. Steadier than I was.

But it didn't stop the ache. If Caleb was still out there, still breathing, still fighting, then one day I'd have to face him. I'd have to explain, and I didn't know how. But when I did, would he look at me with grief ... or blame?

The road leveled as we reached the bottom of the hill.

A boy darted out from behind one of the sheds and froze when he saw us, eyes wide, his feet planted like they'd grown roots.

Edris.

The carpenter's son. He used to live near the edge of the village, always tagging behind his father and holding his tool bag for him.

"Celeste?"

My throat tightened, heat building behind my eyes. I couldn't break here. Not now. Not when I'd only just arrived.

"Edris. You've grown taller," was all I could manage.

He blinked at me like he wasn't sure I was real.

Beside me, Art said nothing. But I could feel him watching. Not just Edris, but everything. He didn't speak, just allowed me to have this moment.

Edris took a step closer, hesitant, like I might vanish if he moved too fast. "We thought you were ..." He didn't finish, his voice cracking.

"I'm not." The words felt too small.

A second shadow moved from behind the shed. An older woman this time, Calla. She paused when she saw me, a hand rising slowly to her mouth. Her eyes darted to Art, then back to me, before the tears started flowing.

The moment stretched thin, like the whole village was holding its breath, waiting on her reaction.

She rushed forward and wrapped her arms around me. I didn't fight it. Instead, I embraced her while my own tears slipped free, hot against my cheeks.

When we finally pulled apart, both of us hastily wiped at our faces, laughing under our breath like we'd been caught doing something foolish. "You're home," she whispered, voice thick. "We thought—" She stopped and shook her head. "Never mind what we thought."

I nodded, not trusting myself to speak again.

Calla turned to Art then, seeming to notice him fully for the first time. As she regarded him, her expression changed into the calm wariness of a woman who had long stood at the center of the village.

"I'm sorry," she said, straightening. "I should've introduced myself. I'm Calla. Thank you ... for bringing her home."

Art dipped his head in a quiet gesture of acknowledgement. "Don't thank me. She did the hard part. I just happened to be there."

Calla blinked, her gaze returning to me, and something warm flickered there.

She reached out, brushing a thumb along my cheek like she used to when I was little, when scrapes and bruises were the worst of my worries.

"She'd be proud, you know. Of the way you're standing here."

That almost broke me.

A door creaked open somewhere behind us, and then another, followed by footsteps. It wasn't long before more villagers emerged from their homes. It was slow at first, cautious. Faces I recognized. And faces that had aged in such a short span of time. People I'd known since I could walk, now staring at me like they'd seen a ghost.

I stood a little straighter, feeling like I couldn't show any signs of weakness.

Someone whispered my name from somewhere in the growing crowd. A few murmurs followed.

"Celeste?"

"I thought she—"

"She's alive."

The hush that followed wrapped around me like a blanket. Thick with disbelief, relief, and something in between.

Art didn't move. He remained at my side like a shadow with eyes, quiet and still, letting the moment belong to me. But I sensed the tension in him, like a blade not yet sheathed.

Calla squeezed my hand. "Come on. You should eat. You look like you've walked halfway across the Triarchy's Kingdom."

The laughter that escaped me was thin and tired. "Feels like I did."

"You'll tell us everything when you're ready," she said. "But not now. Right now, you just need to eat and rest."

We walked in silence through the heart of the village, the path winding back toward Calla's home. The horses moved quietly beside us, their hooves soft against the packed dirt, reins held loose in our hands.

I glanced around as we moved, trying to map the familiar onto what remained, but the place I remembered was gone. Houses that once stood proud were now collapsed or patched with mismatched wood. The square was emptier than it should have been. The last few intact buildings looked worn thin.

The village was unrecognizable, not just in shape, but in spirit. Like it had been hollowed out and was a shell of its former self.

When we reached Calla's house, Art moved ahead to post the horses to the porch. The animals nickered, tails flicking as the wind began to pick up.

Once we stepped into her home, Calla studied me again, like she wasn't sure I was real.

"We don't have much," she said, voice apologetic. "But we'll get you both something warm. What we do have … we share."

Calla disappeared into the kitchen. I heard the soft clang of cookware and the whisper of fire catching in the hearth. The smell of herbs rose soon after, curling through the air and drawing a tired kind of hunger out of me.

I stood near the doorway, not yet sitting. My eyes drifted across the small room. It hadn't changed as much as the village outside. The same worn table, the same clay pots lined up on the shelves. There was a new crack on the far wall which looked as though someone had tried to patch it with cloth and mud. Somehow that made it worse.

Art remained at my side, hands loose at his, posture deceptively relaxed. His attention never left the window.

"You can sit," I murmured.

He glanced at me, then the room, and nodded once before settling into a corner near the door. Not quite in, but not quite out either.

Calla returned with two bowls balanced in her arms. She set one in front of me and offered the other to Art. He took it with a murmured thanks but didn't eat right away. I didn't either.

The stew was thin, mostly broth and roots, but it was warm. I cupped the bowl in both hands, letting the heat soak into my skin.

"I didn't know what I expected," I said after a long silence.

Calla looked up from her own bowl. "From the village?"

I nodded.

Calla stared into her bowl as if searching for something. "No use pretending it was anything but awful. I'm not built for pretty lies."

I held her gaze. In it, there was quiet, bone-deep sorrow.

"It's been hard. Worse than hard. The night you were taken ... It broke something in all of us." Calla's gaze drifted past me, to a place only memory could see.

"I don't know how much you had seen before they took you," she said, voice thinning. "That day, they came all at once, setting fire to some of the houses as they swept through. They burned one of the grain stores during the initial raid. Broke down doors, raided our supplies, and even took some of our livestock."

She didn't look at me while she spoke, eyes distant, like she was seeing it unfold all over again.

"Mira was the first. She threw herself at them, screaming—trying to stop them from dragging her sister away, and they cut her down in front of the well.

"Jorran tried to Cast Fire, saints help him. But he was just a boy. Newly awakened. He still couldn't control his Casting. They didn't care. Swarmed him and drove their blades straight through.

"Never stood a chance without his brother. His mother stopped getting out of bed after that. Wouldn't eat. Wouldn't speak. She died last month, wasting away in silence. And his brother—the one they took for the war—he doesn't even know they're all gone. He's out there fighting for a realm that already took everything from him."

Calla exhaled slowly, like remembering had taken something from her.

Then her eyes shifted to mine. "I saw you, you know. That night."

My breath caught.

She didn't say it with accusation, just a quiet knowing, like the truth had always been sitting between us.

"You were kneeling beside her. Your hands were glowing, faint like moonlight through water. I'd never seen anything like it. Not in this village. Not from you."

She paused. Gave me a moment to respond. But I didn't.

Because I couldn't.

"You were trying to Heal her," she said gently. "I didn't tell anyone. I never planned to."

My fingers curled in my lap.

"I know why you hid it. Why you kept it to yourself all those years. Healing like that ... It's special. If word had gotten out, they would've taken you same as your brother. And your mother would've been left here alone."

I looked down. The old guilt twisted like a knife in my chest.

"You made the only choice you could." Her voice softened. "And still ... you didn't run when it mattered."

She swallowed, her gaze drifting to a memory only she could see. "I watched you fighting so hard when they pulled you off her before you could finish. Watched as you kicked and clawed, but they took you anyway ... I'm so sorry, dear. I truly am."

My throat closed.

Nothing moved. Not even the air. Then, slowly, she reached out and rested her hand close enough to feel the warmth between us. "You didn't fail her, Celeste. You were just one girl. And you gave everything you had." Her voice broke, just a little. "And I'll never tell a soul. Your secret stays with me. It always has."

After a long period of time, Calla finally stood, dragging her hands down the front of her skirt. "Well, you'll be staying here tonight. I won't hear any arguments."

She glanced toward the narrow hallway at the back of the house. "I've only got two rooms. One's mine, but the other's been empty a long time. Sheets are clean, though."

Before I could speak, Art was already moving. He dropped his pack by the door as if the decision had already been made. "I'll sleep out here by the fire. She gets the bed."

Calla opened her mouth as though to say something, but then just nodded. "All right, then. I've got one extra sheet I can bring you, and that fire's got a good burn left in it."

Art gave her a small smile.

I looked between them, guilt threading through me. "You don't have to do that."

"You'd kick me off halfway through the night anyway. Better to start on the floor than wake up there."

Calla snorted. "Stubborn, both of you." She started toward the back, pausing only to light a lantern off the hearth.

"There's water in the basin if you want to wash up," she called. "And I'll find you both something dry to sleep in."

I hesitated, then followed her down the short hallway. When she opened the door to the second bedroom, a thick silence wrapped around me. It wasn't much, just a narrow bed and a small woven rug. There was a small chest at the foot, and the room smelled faintly of dried lavender.

"You sure?" I asked.

Calla turned to me, hand still on the doorframe. "I wouldn't offer it if I wasn't." Something in me eased, just a little.

The fire had burned down to a gentle flicker by the time I returned from washing up. My skin still felt warm from the cloth, but the fatigue sat heavy behind my eyelids.

Art was already stretched out near the hearth, arms folded beneath his head, one leg crossed over the other like he was perfectly at ease on the hard floor. His sword was within reach.

Of course it was.

I hesitated near the doorway. "Comfortable?"

He cracked one eye open. "I've slept on rocks that gave more cushion."

A ghost of a smile tugged at my mouth. "You offered."

"Still do," he said, shutting his eyes again. "I like my sleep uncomfortable and full of regret."

For a time, neither of us said anything. The fire popped quietly, shadows stretching long across the walls. He didn't look at me, but I knew he wasn't asleep.

"What's the longest you've stayed in one place?" I asked.

Art shifted slightly. "Define long."

I sat on the stool, tucking one leg up under me. "More than a week. Two, even."

He snorted. "I once got snowed in during a blizzard. Spent three days trapped in a small town with a widow and her very aggressive rooster."

I raised an eyebrow. "That sounds miserable."

"It was. The rooster hated me. The widow not so much." He cracked one eye open again, just long enough to gauge my reaction.

I rolled my eyes, but my smile stuck. "Charming. I'm sure you broke both their hearts when you left."

I glanced toward the door. "Calla's different from how I remember."

Art turned his head toward me. "How so?"

"She was always strong, but now it's like ... she's holding the whole village together with thread and grit. Like if she stopped moving, everything would fall apart."

"She probably is."

I looked down at my hands. "I feel like a ghost here."

Art didn't say anything at first. The fire cracked softly between us.

"You're not a ghost. Ghosts don't cause me this much trouble."

I huffed a quiet breath through my nose. "You'd just find someone else to vex you."

"Maybe. But you're not a ghost, Celeste. You're still fighting."

I looked at him, really looked, and for a moment the firelight caught in his pale gray eyes, softening the hard edges of his face.

"You belonged here once. But you're not the same girl who left. And this place ... It's not the same either."

I didn't answer right away. I couldn't. Because he was right.

Whatever part of me that used to fit here had been carved out, replaced with something harder. Less forgiving.

I wasn't sure there was room left for peace.

Art just watched me, solid as the earth beneath us.

"I keep thinking," I said finally, "if I just stayed a little longer ... maybe I'd start to feel like myself again."

"You think that's who you were before?"

I blinked. "What do you mean?"

He adjusted again, not quite sitting up, but closer than before. The firelight flickered along his jaw.

"You act like the girl before Ardor was the finished version. Maybe she was just the start."

My chest tightened. I hadn't realized how much I needed someone to say that. Not with pity. Not with apology. Just ... acceptance.

"What if I don't like who I've become?" I asked.

Art tilted his head. "Then change what needs changing. Keep what doesn't. But don't pretend you're broken just because you're different."

My throat felt too tight to speak.

"And for what it's worth," he added, his voice softer now, "I like this version of you. Even if you don't."

The fire crackled, and I looked at him again. This time, I didn't look away. "You don't pretend you don't care like you used to."

He smirked. "I was charming even then."

I snorted. "You were irritating."

"Admit it, you'd miss it if I stopped."

I shook my head, but my smile lingered. The space between us felt smaller somehow. Not just in distance, but in something warmer. Like maybe I didn't want to pull away this time.

"Goodnight, Art."

"Night, Celeste."

I stood, carrying the last of the fire's warmth with me as I stepped into the hall. But before I disappeared into the dark, I glanced back.

His eyes stayed on me, and this time … I wanted them to.

The fire whispered behind me as the house drifted into silence.

15

The morning came quiet, pale light slipping through the shutters. I'd been awake long before it reached me, staring at the ceiling beams. The house creaked as it settled, the faint scent of smoke from last night's fire still clinging to the air.

Sleep hadn't stayed with me.

Every time I drifted off, I saw my mother's face, blood-streaked, her voice breaking as she tried to call my name. The memory clung like frost.

I pushed myself upright, the blanket falling from my shoulder, and sat there a moment just to steady my breath. My throat ached; my chest felt hollow.

I knew the question was coming, and I wasn't sure I was strong enough to ask it.

When I entered the main room, Art was already awake. He sat near the hearth with his back against the wall, honing his sword with a whetstone, as if he'd kept vigil the whole night. He glanced up once, offering me the mercy of silence.

Calla was in the kitchen, humming softly as she stirred something over the stove. Her shoulders were thinner than I remembered, her braid streaked with gray, yet she moved with the same patient resolve I remembered.

I stood there longer than I meant to, hands tight at my sides. At last, the words broke free.

"Calla."

She turned, wooden spoon in hand. "Mm?"

I swallowed. My voice came out softer than I wanted. "Did you bury her?"

The humming stopped and the house went still. Then Calla set the spoon down, wiping her hands on her apron. Her gaze met mine, searching. "We did," she said gently. "The morning after they took you."

I'd braced for the answer, but it still cut deeper than I expected. "Show me," I whispered.

Calla didn't ask if I was sure. She just nodded and untied her apron.

"Come," she said, motioning for us to follow.

I hesitated, then glanced back.

Art paused, one brow lifting slightly in question.

I gave a small nod.

The morning air bit harder than I expected. The village was just stirring, thin smoke rising from chimneys. Doors creaked as people stepped out to start their day. Heads turned as we passed, whispers trailing behind like shadows. Faces I knew, older now, wearier, watched us go. It had only been months since I'd left, yet it felt like years.

Art followed a step behind, saying nothing. I sensed him more than I heard him, a shadow that never strayed far.

Calla led us past the square and down a narrow path between the last of the houses. The packed dirt gave way to thin grass, dotted with withered wildflowers that had bloomed despite the neglect elsewhere. My stomach knotted with every step.

It didn't take long before I knew where we were headed.

The path ended in a small clearing on the hillside, the only place that looked cared for. The ground was uneven but carefully tended, the grass trimmed low around a cluster of markers. Some were carved, others no more than smoothed stones pressed into the earth.

An old willow stood at the edges of the clearing, its trunk split by a long black scar. I remembered when lightning had struck it, years ago, burning it from the inside out, smoke curling from the bark while the rain poured down. Everyone had thought it would fall.

It never did.

I had played here as a child, running between the trees. I never imagined I'd return like this.

Calla stopped before one of the markers. A flat stone, its edges chipped, a single name carved across the surface. The letters were uneven, but clear enough.

I froze. My knees went weak.

Calla's hand brushed my arm, steadying me. She didn't speak.

I drew a slow breath and knelt, tracing my fingers across the cool stone. My name was carved beneath my mother's, the letters shallow, as if someone had tried to mark that I had died too.

I couldn't seem to draw enough air. "I should've been there," I whispered, but my voice broke before the words could carry.

Calla lingered near me for a moment longer, then gave my arm a gentle squeeze. She turned back down the path, her footsteps fading into the hush of the clearing until only Art and I remained. He didn't come closer. Just waited, as though his presence might disturb the air around me.

The words I wanted to say tangled in my chest until all I could do was bow my head and let the silence hold them. The ground smelled of earth and moss, and the carved name blurred as my eyes stung and my tears fell to the soil.

I brushed my fingers once more across the cool stone before rising, my legs unsteady. "Forgive me," I whispered, but the wind swallowed it.

I turned toward the slope.

Behind me, I heard Art move.

I looked back. He stood before the grave now, head lowered. For a long breath he was still. Then he knelt and placed one palm flat against the ground.

A faint shimmer rippled outward, subtle as heat over stone. The brittle grass softened, color bleeding back into its blades. Wildflowers at the edge of the marker lifted their heads, petals opening to catch the light.

It wasn't loud or bright or meant for anyone but her. Just enough to make the place look cared for.

Alive.

I stopped halfway down the path, my throat tightening all over again.

I hadn't known Healing could work that way.

I didn't call out to him. Didn't even let him know I'd seen. I just stood there a moment longer before turning back toward the village.

Art caught up without a word. His boots crunched the grass, his steps keeping time with mine, and for a while, we walked side by side without speaking.

The path wound downhill through the thinning trees. I knew these slopes well; I'd raced through them as a child, chasing laughter and summer winds. Now the air carried only the stillness of morning, broken by the crow's call somewhere distant.

Everything felt different. Smaller. Duller. Or maybe it was just the way it felt to me now.

Calla waited where the trail met the edge of the village, hands folded, eyes searching my face. She didn't ask what had passed. She only gave me a small nod, the kind that said she understood, and then turned to lead us back.

We entered the village, villagers stealing glances as we passed. Their stares gathered around us, inescapable.

Beside me, Art remained quiet, his expression unreadable. Still, his presence anchored me. Like a shadow that never strayed far.

We had barely stepped back into the square when the first of them came forward. An older woman, Marta, whose face was carved deep with wrinkles, clutched her shawl tight as she looked me over.

"Celeste?" Her voice cracked. "By the gods ... is it really you?"

I forced a smile, though it didn't hold. "It's me."

Another villager—a man I half remembered from childhood—stepped closer, wringing his hands. "We thought ... we thought you were gone. All this time. Where have you—" He stopped, words faltering, as though the rest of the sentence was too heavy to finish.

The air around us thickened with their whispers. Faces peered out from doorways and behind low stone walls. Curious, cautious, their eyes clung to me like burrs.

"I'm here now," I said softly. It was all I could give.

For a moment, the air lightened, but then another voice cut through the murmur. "You say that like it explains anything."

The crowd parted for a stocky man.

Hugh. We'd rarely spoken. His jaw was tight, his gaze narrowed. He crossed his arms, studying me, his suspicion sharpened with hostility.

"How?" he asked. "How did you escape?"

The question dropped like a stone. Even the whispers hushed, everyone waiting, hungry for an answer.

My throat tightened. I could feel Art behind me, steady as a wall, but he didn't speak. He let the quiet stretch, let it belong to me.

"I survived long enough for the chance to come. That's it," I said at last, forcing the words past my teeth.

A murmur ran through the square, a ripple of relief mixed with doubt. Some lowered their eyes, as if ashamed they had wondered. Others studied me longer, doubt etched plainly across their face, like they wanted more than I was willing to give.

Calla moved closer, her arm brushing mine. "That's enough," she said, her voice cutting across the crowd.

But Hugh didn't step back. His eyes slid past me to Art, silent and steady at my shoulder.

"And him?" Hugh asked, his voice carrying louder than it needed to. "Who is he? Did he help you escape?"

The crowd's attention shifted toward Art.

"He—" I started, ready to tell them he wasn't the enemy. That without him, I wouldn't have made it back at all.

But Art's voice cut in before I could finish. Calm. Even. "I came across her by chance," he said, his whetstone-smooth tone carrying through the square. "She needed help, and I couldn't just walk on. So I made sure she got home."

The words fell over the square like water poured on a flame. Some of the tension bled out of the air. A few villagers nodded.

Art let that hang for a moment before adding, easy and almost conversational, "Truth is, I could use a few things myself. Supplies for the road. I've enough coin to pay fair."

That seemed to have got their attention. Suspicion drained into calculation almost immediately.

A man at the back cleared his throat. "Supplies we can manage."

I glanced at Art, but his face gave nothing away. He made it look effort-less, turning wary stares into nods of approval with a few calm words and the offer of coin. I couldn't tell if that was who he truly was, or just another mask he wore.

"We've got some dried grain left!" one man called out.

"I can spare cloth," another offered, clutching at the threadbare bundle in her arms as if second-guessing herself.

Someone else muttered about salted fish, though the look in his eyes said he needed it as much as he wanted to sell it.

The eagerness in their voices hit me harder than their suspicion had. These were people I'd grown up with, faces I'd known since I could walk, and now they scrambled to trade scraps for coin. Desperation had worn them thin, hollowed them out in ways I hadn't expected.

Art inclined his head politely to the offers. "I'll come by shortly," he said, as though the whole exchange was perfectly ordinary. He looked back toward me and Calla, his tone as even as ever. "I'll see what I can gather. In the meantime, you should rest."

And with that, he excused himself into the crowd, heading for the voices that had promised supplies.

Calla walked me back toward her house, her arm brushing mine every so often like she was afraid I might vanish. Inside, she fired up the stove. The smell of simmering broth and herbs soon filled the air. She set bowls on the table, motioning for me to sit, the warmth of the fire wrapping around us like a blanket.

I sat stiffly at first, staring into my bowl of untouched food, but Calla filled the silence the way she always did.

"Your home's still standing, you know," she said, careful, as if hoping the words might anchor me here. "They broke some things during the raid. The doorframe's split, and a few shutters are gone. But it's there." She gave me a small smile that didn't quite reach her eyes. "Some of the women gathered what they could afterward. A few ... assumed you weren't coming back. Took bits and pieces. Dishes, linens. Clothes."

Her voice carried a quiet warmth. "But if you want them back, I'll help you gather what's yours. The women who took them thought you were gone for good. They'd give it up if they knew you were here. I'm sure of it."

I tightened my grip on the spoon. The thought of stepping back into that house, of trying to live among what was left, turned my stomach. "I ..." The word stuck, heavy on my tongue.

Calla looked at me, patiently waiting.

"I'm not staying." The words came out harder than I meant, but once spoken, I couldn't take them back.

Her smile faded, brows drawing in. "Not staying?" she echoed softly. "Then where will you go? What do you plan to do?"

I stirred the broth without tasting it, watching the surface ripple. "I don't know yet," I said finally. "But I can't stay here. Not like this."

"Celeste ..." Calla's voice held a plea I hadn't heard since I was a child. "You've been through enough. This is your home. You'd have people here. A roof, food, safety."

I shook my head, still not looking at her. "It doesn't feel like home anymore."

She was quiet, as if deciding what to say next. When she spoke, her voice was low and cutting. "And your brother? What about him? When he comes back from the war and learns your mother is ... Do you mean for him to find the house empty? To come back to nothing?"

The spoon slipped from my hand, clattering against the bowl. I swallowed hard, forcing my voice steady. "He won't find anything. He'll find the truth, same as I did."

Calla leaned forward, her hand brushing mine. "And if the truth breaks him? If he comes back and you're not here either? Don't you think he deserves at least the one piece of his remaining family?"

I pulled my hand back, throat tight. "He deserves more than this place can give. And I can't be what he needs, not anymore."

Her eyes searched mine, the hurt plain in them, but I couldn't hold her gaze. The moment swelled, filling every corner of the little house. We finished the meal in silence, the taste of broth long forgotten beneath the weight of our words.

A knock at the door broke the stillness. Calla rose, wiping her hands on her apron before opening it.

A villager stood in the doorway. Jerrin, a middle-aged man with a patchy beard. He twisted his hat in his hands. "Calla," he said, his voice low and uneasy. "There are riders. Spotted them from the south road, just past the ridge. Not coming in, but ... watching, maybe. Hard to tell from this distance."

He glanced past her shoulder, and his eyes landed on me for a fraction too long. My skin prickled.

Calla didn't miss it either. She squared her shoulders.

For as long as I could remember, the villagers had looked to her in times of trouble. Not because she held any title, but because she carried herself as if she already did.

"How many?" she asked.

"Half a dozen at least. Maybe more. Some of the men think it could be scouts for another raid." He hesitated, shifting from one foot to the other. "We thought you should know first."

Calla's jaw tightened, and though her voice stayed even, I heard the strain beneath it. "Stay sharp, then. Keep the children close, and don't stray beyond the square. I'll speak with the others."

Jerrin gave a short nod, but his eyes flicked toward me again before he left. The intent behind that look lingered long after the door shut, like a shadow crawling over the room.

The latch had barely clicked before the door opened again. Art stepped through, a small bundle slung under one arm. Supplies, neatly wrapped in cloth. His eyes swept the room once before settling on me.

"They're coming," he said simply.

Calla's face hardened. "How close?"

"Close enough the ground shakes when they move," Art replied, setting the bundle down.

We stepped outside, and the air felt different. Tight, expectant.

Villagers had already gathered at the edge of the square, clutching pitchforks, rusted blades, and even kitchen knives in their trembling hands. Their faces were pale but set, with the kind of fear swallowed down too many times to count.

Down the north road, dust plumed in the morning light. Hooves pounded in rhythm, drawing nearer.

Calla straightened beside me, though I caught the faint hitch in her breath. She leaned closer, her voice low and grim. "The only Casters left are Merel and Garron."

I followed her gaze to an older woman clutching a staff, her braid streaked white, and a gray-bearded man standing stiff with a hand on his belt.

"Merel's Water," Calla said to Art. "And Garron's Wind. They weren't conscripted because of their age, and thank the saints for it, but" —she shook her head —"they're not what they once were. If it comes to a fight, they won't hold long."

The riders crested the hill, a line of dark figures stark against the sky. Sunlight glinted off steel. Their numbers doubled what had been reported, closer to a dozen now, not half.

Around me, villagers moved uneasily, gripping their makeshift weapons tighter. The square felt too small, too fragile to bear what was coming.

Art stepped forward, one hand resting on the hilt of the sword, calm as ever. "Then it's not their fight to win," he said.

The horses slowed to a steady trot, then fanned out as the riders reined in at the village entrance. Dust drifted around them, curling in the morning air. The villagers pressed closer together, fear thick as smoke.

Two riders pulled ahead, and my stomach dropped.

I knew their faces. The gray-bearded one and his younger companion. The same men who'd cornered me at the stables. Their eyes found me now without hesitation, the recognition flashing between us.

The older one leaned forward in his saddle, scanning the crowd before fixing his gaze squarely on me.

His lips twitched. "We're looking for a girl," he said, his voice carrying easily across the square. "Name of Celeste. There's a fine bounty on her head."

Murmurs rippled through the villagers. A few heads turned my way. Their eyes dug into my skin like knives.

The younger rider smirked, raising a hand. A small flame flickered to life in his palm, lazy at first, then flaring higher until the Fire reached even the front line of villagers. He let it fall into the dirt, where it flared and died, leaving a blackened scar. "Best make this easy," he drawled. "Hand her over, and no one gets burned."

The silence that followed felt worse than his threat. Calla stiffened at my side, but she didn't speak. The villagers shifted again, some edging back, others staring at me.

And for the first time since I'd returned, I felt every ounce of the danger I had brought with me.

16

rtemis

They weren't strangers.

As the riders fanned out at the edge of the square, I recognized the gray-bearded one and the younger man beside him. The same pair who'd cornered Celeste at the stables, pretending at idle talk. Back then their smiles had been too rehearsed, their questions too pointed. I'd felt their eyes on our backs long after we left that town.

Now I knew why.

I stepped just enough to place myself between Celeste and their line, my hand resting easy on the hilt of my sword. The villagers pressed together behind us, their pitchforks and rusted blades a thin barrier against mounted steel.

Garron and Merel stepped forward, but even from here I could see the strain in their faces. Age and years without practice dulled the edge of their Casting. They wouldn't last long in this fight.

The gray-bearded rider's eyes swept the crowd, landing squarely on Celeste. He didn't bother to hide the satisfaction in his smirk. His companion lit a flame in his palm and tossed it into the dirt, the hiss of burning earth loud in the morning hush. The villagers flinched as one.

"Best make this easy," the younger one said. "Hand her over, and no one gets burned."

I measured the distance. Twelve riders. Two Casters among them, maybe three if the younger one wasn't their only trick. Their formation was tight enough to break through the village line in a single charge, but the square would work against them if I could force them to bottleneck.

Behind me, I heard Celeste's breath catch. The villager's whispers thickened, spreading through the air.

If they wanted her, they'd have to go through me first.

Graybeard let his gaze sweep the crowd again, his grin widening. "There's good coin for anyone with enough sense to hand her over," he said, his voice smooth as polished steel.

The words dropped like a blade into the square. The villagers faltered, eyes flicking sideways, catching on Celeste just long enough for me to notice.

I tightened my grip on the hilt of my sword.

This was the danger I'd expected. Not the dozen men at the gate, but the fear already here inside the walls. Fear that could make neighbors point—or worse, step aside and let them through.

The moment stretched, brittle as glass.

Then Calla stepped forward, her chin lifted, her voice carrying clear. "There is no one here by that name."

A murmur rippled through the villagers, but no one contradicted her. Not one person.

Their faces stayed grim, their silence unbroken.

Interesting. I hadn't expected that. For all their fear, they hadn't turned Celeste over.

At least not yet.

The younger rider let Fire dance in his palm, brighter this time. He dropped it into the dirt again, the new scorch biting nearer than the last. "Try again."

I took one step forward, the square's dirt thudding under my boots. I rolled my shoulders once, loosening the tension.

Sword. Wind. I'd use nothing more.

Not while there were so many eyes.

Graybeard leaned on his saddle horn. "Then I suppose we'll have to search for ourselves."

He flicked his hand, and three of the mounted men spurred their horses forward. The crowd broke, villagers stumbling back with startled cries, their thin line of pitchforks and knives wavering like grass before a storm.

As I turned my head to look back, Celeste tensed. I caught the way she braced, the spark in her. She was ready to step forward. To meet them head-on.

Not yet.

I moved before she could, stepping right in front of her, cutting off her path.

Steel rasped as I drew my sword. The sound snapped through the square like a challenge, and the horses slowed to a prance, nostrils flaring, sensing the change.

Behind me, I felt Celeste, her frustration burning at my back. But this wasn't her fight to bleed for.

Not here. Not now.

The younger rider swung down from his horse with easy confidence, whistling a tune as he moved closer. He didn't bother to draw a weapon.

Flames licked over his knuckles as he flexed his hand, the glow painting his grin.

Two others dismounted with him, steel rasping as they drew their swords. They flanked him, their blades catching the light as they advanced on the square.

"See?" the younger Caster said, his tone loud and mocking. "We already know she's right there, hiding among you. And now we'll make an example of what happens to those who think they can shield her."

Behind me, the villagers stirred, fear breaking through in sharp breaths, a murmur threatening to spread. Calla hushed them, but their line wavered all the same.

I adjusted my grip on my sword, grounding myself. One Caster, two swordsmen, all young and cocky enough to think numbers were all they needed. The rest stayed mounted, watching and waiting to see how easily their advance would break us.

I let the air stir faintly around me, silent, unseen. Just enough to feel the current in my bones.

If the boy wanted to prove himself, I'd be happy to oblige.

The three of them closed in, boots grinding against the dirt, the Fire Caster leading the way with his hand wreathed in flame.

From the corner of my eyes, I saw the villagers draw back, the scrape of their boots betraying them.

Celeste stood behind me, taut as a bowstring.

I could feel every eye on me, waiting to see if I'd break.

I didn't move.

The Caster's grin widened. He raised his hand, flame swelling, heat prickling against my face. He thought he already had me.

That was when I struck.

A surge of Wind rushed forward with my step, tearing the Fire from his grasp and scattering it into sparks that died on the dirt. His eyes went wide, forming a curse.

Too late.

My blade slid through his ribs, the edge hissing as the gust carried it deeper. He gagged, blood bubbling from his lips, and collapsed in a heap.

I turned with the motion, catching the first swordsman mid-step. He had barely lifted his sword when mine swept across his throat. The strike was clean, the Wind carrying it faster than his eyes could track. His head snapped back, crimson drops spraying across the dirt in an arc. He stumbled, both hands clawing at the wound, then toppled sideways, choking until he went still.

The second swordsman panicked, swinging wildly. I slid past him with a burst of Wind, his blade cutting nothing but air. My sword drove into his gut, angled up behind his ribs. His breath left him in a wet gasp, eyes wide with disbelief as he slid off the steel. His blood spilled dark red across the square, soaking into the earth at my feet.

Three bodies lay motionless in the dirt.

I stood over them, sword low at my side, the air still humming faintly around me. The rest of the riders hadn't moved. Their horses stamped nervously, nostrils flaring, ears twitching.

Behind me, the villagers went quiet as the grave. Celeste's breath hitched, but she didn't speak.

I closed my eyes for a moment and took a deep breath.

After spending a lifetime of fighting men stronger than these—and even more who were not—I already knew how this would end.

A brief, one-sided lesson carved in blood.

I almost pitied them.

Almost.

I opened my eyes and lifted my gaze to the riders still mounted. "Who's next?"

The twang rang sharp, like an answer to my question.

Two bowmen had dismounted, strings already raised, and twin arrows hissed through the morning air straight toward me.

I didn't bother to raise my sword.

A flick of thought, a twist of the wrist, and air snapped the current to life around me. The arrows veered off course with a sharp whistle, one clattering against the stone rim of the village well, the other skidding across the dirt.

The bowmen froze, staring in disbelief. They had expected me to dodge. To bleed.

Not to turn aside their shots like gnats swatted in midair. Especially with no real movement that they could see.

I let the Wind die back down to a whisper, my grip tightening on my sword. My eyes fixed on them, their fingers shaking against the strings.

"Your turn," I muttered, and took one step forward.

The two bowmen stared, their first volley useless at my feet. One cursed under his breath, teeth bared as he yanked another arrow from his quiver. The other already had his string drawn, desperate to prove the first shot was no fluke.

I didn't move.

The air stirred around me, faint at first, then building into a low current that ruffled my cloak. The bowmen loosed their arrows together, aiming for my chest.

Another flick of the wrist and turn of Wind. Both shafts bent mid-flight, one spinning off into the dirt, the other snapping against the stone wall of the square. Splinters of wood rained toward the ground.

The bowmen's confidence faltered. I saw it in the tremor of their fingers as they nocked again, the frantic catch of their breaths.

"Go on," I said. "Empty them."

They did.

Arrow after arrow flew through the air, each one turned aside with nothing more than a bit of Wind. Some snapped in half, some dropped to the ground; a few even whipped back in wild arcs that nearly clipped their own mounts.

The villagers watched, wide-eyed, as the impossible became routine. Steel and wood undone like they were nothing more than twigs in a storm.

By the time the last arrow clattered to the dirt, both men stood panting, their quivers nearly bare, hands shaking as they lowered their bows.

I let the silence stretch, then took one slow step forward. The bowmen stumbled back in unison, pale and sweating. Their horses stamped nervously, ears pinned flat.

The rest of the riders hadn't moved, still mounted, still watching. They had two Casters among them, but neither had stirred. Not yet.

It was just me, the blade in my hand, and two bowmen who finally understood they had nothing left to stand behind.

One of the bowmen fumbled another arrow from his quiver, fingers shaking as he tried to nock it. Desperation made him clumsy.

At my feet, another shaft lay half buried in the dirt. I picked it up and weighed it once in my hand like a spear.

His eyes flicked up just in time to see me draw back my arm.

"Here. You can have this one back."

I threw.

The gust snapped into place as the arrow left my grip, catching it mid-flight and hurling it faster than any bowstring could. It screamed across the square and buried itself through the man's eye with a sickening crunch.

His head snapped back, the force driving him off his feet, his bow falling from limp fingers as he staggered, legs buckling. The arrow jutted grotesquely from his skull, blood sluicing down his face in a crimson stream.

He didn't fall immediately. He thrashed, hands clawing at the shaft jutting from his face, boots scraping furrows into the ground as if trying to run from death itself.

A wet, bubbling cry escaped him, more animal than human, before his knees finally gave way.

He collapsed, twitching once.

The other bowman froze, the half-nocked arrow slipping from his hand. His mouth hung open, eyes wide and white, locked on me in raw terror.

The square was silent again, save for the faint howl of Wind still curling around my shoulders.

I lowered my arm, sword still steady in my other hand. "Next," I said, voice flat.

Graybeard's grin was completely gone. He yanked his sword free and bellowed, "Ride him down!"

Four riders spurred their mounts forward, hooves thundering against the packed earth. The square shook under the weight of them, villagers scattering back, shouts breaking out as the charge bore down on me.

I exhaled once.

So it begins.

Wind surged underfoot, lifting me in a sudden burst that carried me clear of the first rider's sword. My blade flashed downward, splitting his collarbone as I soared past. He crumpled in the saddle, eyes glassing over as his horse screamed and bolted through the square.

The second came fast behind him. I twisted in the air, the current snapping around me, and tore a razor edge of Wind across his throat. Blood sprayed in a crimson arc as he clawed at his neck, his body pitching sideways out of the saddle.

I landed light, dirt scattering beneath my boots. The third rider's sword swept low, meant to take me as I touched ground. Too slow. My own blade met his mid-swing, the gust carrying it deeper, harder, severing his arm clean at the elbow. His weapon dropped as the follow-through ripped across his chest. He toppled backward, dead before he hit the ground.

The last came roaring down on me, lance leveled. I waited until the point was nearly at my chest, then snapped another burst beneath my feet. The Wind hurled me upward, higher than his reach. I plunged my sword down as I passed, punching through helm and skull in a single brutal stroke. The man sagged in the saddle, then slid free, reins tearing from his fingers as the horse barreled on, dragging him across the square.

Four bodies fell in the span of breaths. The horses screamed and scattered, kicking up dust and blood as they stamped through the fallen.

I stood in the clearing haze, sword dripping, the air still whispering at my shoulders.

I drew a slow breath. It came easily.

My core remained firm, untouched by strain.

The bounty hunters had driven me to the brink. These men hadn't even come close.

The last four dismounted and advanced side by side. The archer-turned-swordsman lowered his blade, teeth bared. Beside him, a brute held his greatsword high, winding his swing for the kill.

Behind them, Graybeard thrust out his hand, Fire roaring to life, the heat scorching the air. The other Caster—a lean man with a scar down his cheek—raised both his arms, Wind swirling tight into crude, jagged blades that shrieked through the air ahead of the charge.

Four against one. Steel, flame, and storm.

I didn't retreat.

The first Wind blade screamed toward me, fast but uneven, its shape betrayed by spiraling grit and leaves, edges fraying in the current. I cut through it with a snap of my own, my Wind crashing into it and shredding the blade into a harmless breeze. The Fire Caster's flame followed a heartbeat later, a gout of heat and light that seared the dirt. I side-stepped with a burst, Wind snapping at my heels, the Fire licking only dust.

The swordsmen reached me next. The smaller one swung wildly, all speed and no control. My blade met his, a gust carrying my strike wide, opening his chest for the follow-through. Steel bit deep into his ribs, tearing through lung and bone. He coughed blood and sagged against me before crumpling to the ground.

The brute barreled toward me, his strength slamming down in a crushing arc. I leapt into my Wind, rising above it, the blade cleaving only air. As I dropped, I twisted, the current snapping behind me, driving my sword clean through his neck. His head lolled on ruined sinew as he crashed back into the dirt.

That left the Casters.

Graybeard roared, Fire bursting from his palm in a wide arc meant to swallow me whole. At the same time, the other slashed the air, a dozen jagged Wind blades shrieking toward me, their form crude and impractical.

Too much. Too fast.

For anyone else.

I dropped low, wrapping myself in a light stream of Water that blunted the heat above.

So much for keeping it to Wind and steel. I was fortunate I hadn't made that promise aloud. Celste would have enjoyed pointing that out.

Their attacks clashed midair—flame and storm colliding in a burst of smoke. I was already moving through it, sword severing the haze.

The scarred Wind Caster saw me too late. He opened his mouth, but my blade was already across his throat. He fell to his knees, hands clutching uselessly at the spray pouring from his neck.

Only Graybeard remained. Fire still burned in his palm, his eyes wide now with something that wasn't just rage.

Fear.

He bellowed, flames bursting from his hands in a wide, desperate sweep. Heat shimmered across the square, but my Wind tore it apart as fast as it came, scattering embers harmlessly in the air.

I didn't slow. Step by step, I closed the distance.

"You should've let her go," I said.

The Fire Caster snarled and Cast again, another surge of heat bursting forward. Uselessly blown apart as quickly as it came.

"Keep Casting," I told him, snapping each spit of flame into nothing. My gaze didn't leave his. "Every scar she carries is because of men like you. You've had your share of her pain." I raised my blade.

"Now you'll have mine."

The current surged with it.

Steel and air became one stroke, cutting straight through fire and bone.

For a moment he stood frozen, eyes wide, mouth opening as if to curse me one last time. Then the blood came—a thin red line spilling down his chest, widening, breaking him open.

He slid sideways, hitting the dirt with a heavy thud. The Fire in his hand guttered out.

And then there was no one left standing.

17

A*rtemis*

The square was quiet now. The kind of silence that only followed slaughter. When even the wind held its breath.

I kept my blade up all the same, smoke still curling in ragged streams across the dirt. In my experience, bodies didn't always mean the fight was done.

The heat lingered, radiating from the ground where fire had kissed it. Ash floated down in lazy spirals, clinging to my clothes, to the hilt of my sword. Blood still dripped from the blade.

I drew a slow breath, stilling the current inside me.

Graybeard lay sprawled at my feet, eyes still open, glassy in death. Fear had frozen there, etched into him. I forced myself to look past it. What mattered was whether anyone else was waiting. Whether more of them would come.

My gaze swept the edges of the square, through smoke, across shuttered windows. The surrounding area rang with crackle of dying flame; the ragged breaths of the villagers pressed in around me. Some clutched their pitchforks and knives like they weren't sure whether to hold them tighter or let them drop. Others had fled into doorways, peering out from the shadows.

My gaze found Celeste in the swarm of faces. She hadn't run. Her eyes stayed on me, wide and searching. She didn't look away. Not even when the others did.

Her copper hair caught the dim light through the smoke, the color almost too bright for a place like this. Nearly two months of dust and road hadn't dulled it. If anything, the wildness suited her.

The freckles across her nose stood out against skin gone pale from the smoke. Her mouth was set tight, stubborn as ever. She looked small among the villagers, but there was nothing fragile in the way she held my gaze.

I exhaled once, slowly, but kept my blade raised. Habit keeping it there longer than reason.

Movement stirred at the edge of the crowd. Celeste broke from the press of bodies, her steps light but steady across the blood-spattered floor. The smoke parted around her, strands of red hair catching in the dim light as she came closer.

She didn't flinch at the corpses. Didn't look away from me. Whatever fear lived in the others, she held it differently. Like she was weighing me against what she'd already endured and found me the lesser of two terrors.

Her voice was low, meant for me and no one else. "It's done."

I let the words hang between us. She said it was over. For me, it never was. Not until every loose end was tied off. My grip eased just enough that I could rest the blade at my side, but I didn't sheath it. A drawn weapon spoke louder than any promise of peace.

Smoke parted at the edge of the crowd. Calla emerged, shawl pulled close, her eyes flicking from the bodies to me. She didn't seem like a woman easily cowed, but her steps slowed the nearer she came. Behind her, a handful of villagers followed, weapons still clutched in white-knuckled hands.

I didn't move. Let them come. The dead told their own story, and the living would be weighing it against what they thought of me.

Calla stopped just short of the blood-stained dirt, the others fanning out behind her.

When I finally broke the silence, my voice was calm, carrying just enough to reach every ear. "These men won't be needing their coin. Or their weapons. The horses are still nearby. All of it is yours."

A ripple went through the crowd. The faintest stir of hunger in desperate faces. Hands tightened on pitchforks, not in threat but in the reflex of men and women imagining what they could trade.

I let the sound of it build, let them taste the thought before I added, softer now, almost conversational. "All I ask is that you see these men to rest. They came here with Fire in their hands, and they fell standing. Leave them for the crows and you invite talk. Give them graves, and the night can end cleanly."

I let the words hang and raised my eyes to the people, meeting their gazes one by one. Not hard, not demanding, just open—almost imploring. A soldier asking neighbors to share in a burden he couldn't carry alone.

"And as for their shame ... Let it stay buried with them. No good comes from repeating how a dozen men and their Casters fell to one man. Best we let the dead keep their dignity."

A murmur rippled through them, low and uneven. Someone exhaled, another changed their grip until the haft of a pitchfork scraped against the dirt. A few of the younger men exchanged glances, as if to test whether anyone would speak, but no words came. The promise of coin and horses tugged at them, stronger than fear, and stronger than the urge to question me.

One by one, weapons dipped, low enough to show where their thoughts had gone. Toward hunger. Toward survival.

When Calla spoke, her voice carried the weight of someone with influence. "We'll see them buried. Properly." She pulled the shawl tighter around her shoulders, her gaze directly on me. "And the rest ... Best left in the earth where they belong."

It wasn't quite agreement. Not entirely. But it was close enough that the others relaxed by degrees, their fear easing into wariness, touched by a flicker of relief.

I gave the smallest nod, my bloodied sword still resting at my side.

Celeste stood only a step from me now, her presence quiet but unshaken, and I saw the way Calla's gaze softened when it found her. That single look said more than words. History, loyalty, and a promise already kept once today.

The square was heavy with the smell of smoke and blood, but the tension had loosened as villagers began to move again.

The fight was over. What remained was only the burying.

The spell of stillness broke in pieces. A few men edged forward, eyes darting between the bodies and me, before stooping to drag the dead toward the edge of the square. Others slipped past, heading for the horses or rifling through packs with the sharp, guilty hunger of those who hadn't seen coin in too long.

Calla stayed where she was, watching, until a man and woman came up behind her. One leaned in, whispering quick into her ear. Calla's jaw tightened, her hand flexing around her shawl before she turned back to us.

"I'll be holding a meeting," she said, her voice pitched to reach the crowd. "We've matters to settle after ... this." She didn't look at the corpses when she said it. Didn't look at Celeste either, though I saw the weight of her glance linger there a moment too long before it came back to me. "If you'll excuse me."

A few of the villagers fell in at her side, following her toward the hall at the square's far end, her steps brisk, shoulders hunched from age.

As I slid my blade into its sheath, a man stepped forward from the edge of the crowd. Middle-aged, with dirt still clinging to his work clothes. He hesitated, then gave a small nod. "Didn't reckon you would have been able to stand against that, but you showed me different," he said. "You saved more than a few lives here today."

I held his gaze, then gave the smallest nod. Gratitude was harder to meet than suspicion, and I wasn't about to linger in it.

The man dipped his head once more and backed away, melting into the crowd as if the words had cost him more than the fight itself. Others hesitated, torn between following his example and keeping their distance.

Only Celeste stayed close, her eyes still on me. She hadn't spoken again since the fight ended, and her silence was harder to bear than the villagers' stares. Finally, her voice broke through it, soft but resolute. "We should head back to Calla's. Get out from under all these eyes. Maybe even have something to eat. It's not really breakfast anymore. Maybe ... *latefast*?"

The corner of my mouth twitched, and before I could stop, a short laugh escaped me. "It's brunch."

She wrinkled her nose. "That just sounds silly. Latefast sounded better."

In that moment, the smoke, the blood, the corpses—none of it mattered. Just her, trying to pull me out of the weight of it all, and me letting her.

We slipped away from the square together, the crowd parting as we passed. Their whispers followed us, but no one stepped in our way. Celeste kept close, her shoulder brushing mine once before she caught herself and gave a small, nervous smile.

Once we arrived at Calla's and the door shut behind us, for the first time all morning, the noise of the village fell away.

"I'll get the fire going," Celeste said quickly, already moving toward the hearth. Her hands were stable, but I could hear the edge in her voice.

I didn't argue. The stink of smoke and blood clung to me like a second skin. "I'll wash up."

The basin held only cold water, but Fire Casting soon brought it to a tolerable warmth, and by the time I'd scrubbed the fight from my skin and pulled on my clean clothes, the smell of eggs and bread had filled the house.

Celeste was bent over the table when I stepped back into the main room, hair falling across her face as she laid out two bowls. She glanced up, and the small smile that tugged at her lips was different from the one she'd worn in the square. Softer, freer.

"Here, enjoy your latefast," she said, sliding a bowl toward me. "And I don't care what you call it."

I shook my head, the ghost of that earlier laugh still lingering. "Brunch," I said again, just to see her roll her eyes.

The chair creaked as I leaned forward, spoon in hand. For the first time since the square, the world felt still. No blades, no fire, no stares closing in from every side. Just the clatter of dishes and the sound of her breath across the table from me.

It stirred the shape of an old memory—quiet meals, a smaller table, someone sitting where she was now. Long enough ago it barely felt real anymore.

Celeste set her spoon down, her eyes narrowing in mock seriousness. "Well, at least you don't smell anymore. That's an improvement."

I took a slow sip from my cup before answering. "Suppose you'll be telling me to bathe every day now."

She smirked faintly. "Wouldn't hurt."

I shook my head, but a chuckle escaped free all the same.

The warmth of it didn't last long. Her smile faded, replaced by something more serious. "I recognized them. Back in the square. They were the same men who questioned me in Dunwade. They followed us here to my village."

Her spoon toyed at the edge of the bowl, pushing crumbs into the egg. "What if there are more? What if others come looking and someone speaks?"

"They won't." My voice was calm, matter-of-fact.

Her gaze flicked up, searching. "Why do you sound so certain?"

I leaned back, letting the question hang before answering. "They'll keep quiet," I said. "I gave them something better to talk about. Coin. Horses. Steel."

Her brow furrowed. "And their silence?"

I set my spoon down, meeting her eyes. "The villagers won't speak of it. They'll bury the dead and let the shame of those riders die with them."

Her lips quirked faintly, though her eyes stayed serious. "You make it sound so simple. Like buying bread at market."

"Bread costs less," I joked.

She propped her chin on her hand, watching me across the table. "You think you're very clever, don't you?"

"Most days, yes."

The door cracked open as we finished the last of the bread. Calla stepped inside, pulling her shawl loose as she set her basket down by the door. She regarded the empty bowls.

"Well," she said, one brow lifting, "looks like the two of you managed your own noonmeal just fine."

Celeste glanced at me, the faintest spark of amusement tugging at her lips. I let out a breath through my nose.

Calla hung her shawl, then crossed the room and lowered herself into a chair. Her hands rested on the wood for a long moment before she spoke.

"The meeting ran longer than it should have. Plenty of words, not much worth in most of them." She glanced at the two of us, her eyes softer than her tone. "Some argued we shouldn't have taken their coin or their horses. Said it wasn't right."

Celeste's brow furrowed. "After what they did?"

Calla shook her head. "Others said the same. That those men would've bled us dry if you hadn't stopped them. And most agreed by the end." She drew a slow breath. "But the real fear wasn't the bodies or the spoils."

Her gaze flicked between us, lingering a heartbeat longer on Celeste. "It was you, girl. Word is out. They know there's a price on your head. That was at the heart of it—the bounty. They're concerned more will come for you. I told them they were cowards. Then I told them you had no plans to stay. That settled most of it."

Celeste's shoulders dipped, her hand tightening on the rim of her bowl.

Calla exhaled through her nose, then continued. "Most, not all." Her gaze turned to me. "And then there was talk of *you*. Plenty want you to stay. To keep the village safe. Of what it would mean to have a blade like yours close at hand."

She didn't say Celeste's name again. I felt the omission unsettling. They were ready to open their doors to me and let the girl who'd grown up here walk away.

Celeste's gaze dropped to the table, unreadable.

"I'm not staying," I said, evenly.

Calla studied me for a moment, then gave the smallest nod. "That's what I told them you might say. They asked me to persuade you. I told them where they could put the idea."

She drummed her fingers once against the table, slow and thoughtful. "They'll keep the bargain. Bury the bodies, take the coin and the horses, and hold their tongues. Fear will do the rest."

Celeste looked up, searching Calla's face. "And if more come?"

"Then we'll deal with it if they do." Calla's tone was firm, but her eyes softened as they fell on Celeste. "But for now, you've done enough. Both of you."

Celeste leaned back, her fingers tracing the rim of her bowl. "We should be leaving soon."

Calla sighed. "I won't pretend there's no risk. Word travels, and trouble follows." Her eyes flicked to me, amused. "Still, I'd wager we'd survive a second visit." She looked back at Celeste. "Stay a little longer. The road isn't going anywhere."

Celeste didn't answer. She stared down at her hands, shoulders drawn tight. I recognized the look as exhaustion. She wouldn't admit she was worn down, but it clung to her all the same.

She breathed out slowly, almost a sigh. "We'll stay," she said at last, voice low. "No more than a few days. Long enough to sleep without flinching every time the wind blows."

Calla looked surprised, then her shoulders eased with relief. She nodded, wrapping her arms around herself. "Good. Then rest while you can. I'm going to prepare myself a meal; I haven't had anything yet to eat."

"I'll help," Celeste said, rising before Calla could wave her off. She took up a knife from the counter, setting to work with an eager, if clumsy, determination.

Calla arched a brow, watching the first uneven slice of carrot fall away. "If you swing that knife like you chop, I pity the poor fool who stands in front of you."

Celeste smirked, brushing the hair back from her face. "Guess I'm better at mending than cutting."

"And if you mend as slow as you chop, I'd hate to be your patient."

Celeste chuckled, shaking her head as she attacked the next slice with exaggerated care. "Don't you worry, I only take this long when no one's dying."

Calla gave her a sidelong look, lips tugging into something between amusement and fondness. "Don't think I won't make you eat those crooked pieces when the pot's done."

"That hardly seems fair," Celeste said, grinning.

"Life's not fair, sometimes," Calla retorted, dropping another handful of chopped greens into the pot. Her words were sharp, but her tone wasn't.

I stood, collected my sword and gear, and moved a few paces back before sitting, the blade across my lap, cloth rasping softly against steel in time with their chatter. The blood had long been scrubbed from my skin, but the blade remembered, and I worked until the metal gleamed.

The scent of stew soon filled the room, pushing back the memory of fire and ash from the morning's fight. Their voices wove through the small house with Calla's dry wit, and Celeste's laughter, and for a little while, it was almost peaceful.

After a time, I rose, sliding the cleaned blade back into its sheath. "I'll see to the horses," I said, more to the air than to either of them.

Celeste glanced up from the pot she was stirring, lips parting like she meant to offer help, but Calla nudged her shoulder with the back of her hand. "Let him go. You'll only get in the way."

I stepped outside, the air colder now without the fire's warmth. The horses stirred as I approached, ears flicking, hooves shifting restlessly in the dirt. I set to work in silence, tossing hay into the trough, checking straps, running a hand down their flanks until their breathing slowed.

That was when I felt it. Eyes on me.

Two villagers hovered a short distance off, their hands empty, their shoulders tight. One carried a bundle of carrots tucked under his arm, the other stood with nothing but the look of a man torn between gratitude and unease.

They edged closer, the braver of the two clearing his throat. "For the horses," he muttered, holding out the bundle.

I took it without a word, setting it by the trough.

The man rocked back on his heels, then forward again. "If more come …" His voice cracked, then steadied. "If more come, you'll cut them down the same, won't you?"

I kept my eyes on the horse as I ran a hand along its bridle. "If they force me to."

The villager gave a quick nod, almost a bow, then turned back toward the town's center. His companion followed, still unable to meet my gaze.

I stayed by the horses a while longer, running my hand down their withers until the steady rhythm of their breathing was all I heard. The bundle of carrots lay untouched in the trough.

The door creaked behind me, and I didn't have to look to know who it was.

"I've come to help," Celeste said, her sleeves rolled up.

I gave the faintest shake of my head, but I didn't stop her. Together we moved through the packs, opening satchels, dropping supplies onto the ground. We counted the coin first. Heavy still, more than enough to keep us moving toward our next destination. She stacked the silver neatly, her fingers quick, her brow drawn in concentration.

Next came the weapons. I drew out a crossbow I had purchased earlier in the day before the fight broke out, laying it across my knee to check the quality. The bolts were good, and the string frayed but serviceable.

Celeste's laugh broke the quiet, bright and sudden. "Why do you even need that? You could just throw arrows like spears. Like you did before."

I glanced up at her. "Strange to carry arrows but no bow."

Her smile widened. "You planning to use both at once? Cast with one hand, shoot with the other?"

"Wouldn't be the first time."

She shook her head, laughing again. "You're worse than a magpie, hoarding shiny things."

I laughed. "Hoarding's fine, as long as you win with it." I set the crossbow aside and drew the bolts together in a neat bundle.

We finished sorting the packs, then walked the village for a while, keeping to the quieter streets. Celeste carried water for Calla, and I bartered a few coins for bread and oil. Villagers watched us, the fear slow to fade, the gratitude slower still.

By the time the shadows stretched long, we'd seen all we needed of the place, and Calla was calling us back to the table.

The stew Calla and Celeste made was simple but filling, heavy with root vegetables and the kind of seasoning born of necessity rather than choice. We ate without hurry, the warmth of the food easing the edge of the long day.

When the bowls were empty, Calla gathered them into the basin, wiped her hands on her apron, and gave us both a look that landed somewhere between stern and weary. "You've done enough for one day. Get some rest. Tomorrow will come fast."

She didn't wait for an answer before retreating to her room. The sound of her door shutting left the house in a hush broken only by the crackle of the hearth.

As Celeste headed to her room, I settled back onto the floor where I'd left my gear, sword propped within reach, the warmth of the flames casting long shadows up the walls.

The door to Celeste's room opened a moment later. She stepped out with her bedroll tucked under her arm.

I frowned. "There's a bed in there, you know."

She knelt beside the hearth, spreading the blanket across the floor. "I'd rather sleep near the fire."

"You'll get a better night's rest on a mattress."

Her hands smoothed the fabric flat, her voice calm but firm. "The fire's warmer. Besides ..." She glanced at me. "I don't mind the company."

I watched her for a moment, then shook my head with a faint huff. "Stubborn as ever."

She only smiled and eased onto the blanket, turning toward the fire. The room felt softer now.

I lay back on the floorboards, the day lingering in my muscles. Her breathing evened beside me, until the house itself seemed to match it.

For once, I didn't mind the company either.

18

The mornings always came too soon.

The fire in the hearth had burned to embers, casting only a dull glow, and the floorboards felt harder than they had the nights before. For a long while I stayed still, listening to the rhythm of Art's breathing, steady as the slow rise of dawn. My chest felt tight, caught somewhere between rest and whatever waited beyond the door.

The smell of bread pulled me up first, followed by the scrape of Calla's kitchen chair legs.

By the time I sat at the table, she was already setting out bowls, her shawl pulled close against the morning chill. It had been five days since we told Calla we'd stay a while. Long enough for this to begin feeling almost normal. And part of me wished I could hold onto it longer.

"Eat before you go," she said, brisk, though her eyes softened when they landed on me.

Art joined a moment later, quiet as always. He tore the bread in half and slid a piece my way. The three of us ate without much talk. Calla with her patience, Art with the calm precision of someone who never wasted a bite, and me trying not to let the food catch in my throat.

Leaving was the right choice. I knew that.

Still, each glance at Calla's hands as she folded the cloth napkin, each note of her voice as she reminded me to keep to the main roads, hit harder than I expected. I wasn't family here, not truly, but she had given me shelter and warmth when I needed it most.

When we emptied our bowls, the quiet crept back in. Calla only shook her head when I tried to help with the washing, and instead she gripped my hand tight in both of hers. "Keep your promise, girl. But don't lose yourself to it."

I swallowed hard and nodded. Words would've broken something I wanted to leave whole.

Outside, the air was damp with dew. Our horses restless at the posts, snorting clouds of white into the chill. I ran my hand down the flank, grounding myself in the solid warmth before swinging up onto the saddle. Art was already mounted, reins in his hands.

Calla lingered in the doorway, her shawl drawn tight, the lines on her face deepened by the pale morning light. I lifted my reins. "We'll come back," I said, though I wasn't sure if it was true.

Beside me, Art straightened in his saddle. His voice carried low across the yard. "You gave us a place to rest when we had no right to ask. I won't forget it."

Something softened in Calla's eyes. Then she nodded, arms folded close as if to hold herself together.

The road stretched ahead, damp with morning mist. Our horses' hooves clopped in a slow rhythm, the sound carrying across fields still heavy with dew. For a while, neither of us spoke. Avriel fell away behind us, its smoke rising faint against the gray horizon, until even that was gone.

I kept my eyes forward, though a part of me wanted to look back again. With every league, the past fell further behind us. We had rested, slept, eaten hot meals. Meanwhile, Faylen had none of it. Her voice was still a whisper in my ear, our promise of escape still unfulfilled.

The reins creaked in my grip as I urged my horse faster.

Art rode at pace beside me. His shoulders were relaxed, but his gaze drifted over the rise and fall of the hills, always watchful. Time seemed to slip into the rhythm of hooves, the creak of leather, and the occasional call of a bird overhead.

When the sun climbed higher, spilling light over the open fields, Art finally broke the silence. "We've a long road still before Rodin." He glanced my way, his expression unreadable. "That makes it the perfect time for lessons."

I straightened in the saddle, my pulse quickening. Lessons. I had hoped for it, expected it even, but hearing the words sent both nerves and anticipation rushing through me. We couldn't have any lessons while back in the village for risk of exposure.

Then he said, almost offhand, "Before we get to the practical, we should start with a little history. Casting's young. You know that, don't you?"

"I know it's only been a century or so. But has anyone ever pinned down the exact date?" I asked.

He gathered the reins in one hand, gaze never leaving the road. "Less than a hundred and forty years. Before then, no one drew flame from their own body, or bent Ardor from their hands. No records, no stories. Just … nothing.

"Then, slowly, people began to change. A spark here. A whisper of Wind there. At first, it was only the four pillars—Earth, Wind, Fire, and Water.

But it spread. Not fast and not all at once. Just a few more with each generation, like something was waking up. The others came decades later."

He held out his hand, and an Ice shard formed in his palm. "The first Variant was Ice," he said. "A branch of Water Casting. Those with larger cores—and the right spark—began to shape Water differently. Not just moving it but freezing it." He turned the shard slightly, light catching along its edge.

"They were the first to step outside the four pillars. Because they came first, Ice remains the most common Variant. Once it appeared, the classification followed. The four pillars stayed the foundation. Everything beyond them became known as Variant."

"So if Ice split from Water, what stops one of the other pillars from splitting again?" I asked.

He let the shard of Ice linger a moment longer, then loosened his fingers. The edges dulled first, then the structure softened. Water slipped between his knuckles in a thin stream.

"The truth?" He wiped his hand against his thigh. "There's nothing stopping it. Ice was only the first split we recognized. That doesn't mean it was the last. Healing. Lightning. Those could be branches from one of the pillars in ways we don't fully understand." He gave a small shrug. "But I wouldn't know, I'm not a scholar. What I do know is that Casting isn't stagnant. It continues to grow with us."

A question I'd been carrying rose to the surface. If I let him move on, it would slip away again. "How fast does a core fill?" I asked.

"Slowly," he said simply. "Like a natural spring. Sleep and food help. But there's no shortcut. That's why most Casters guard every drop carefully."

He glanced at me then, catching the edge of my smirk. His mouth twitched in return. "You've noticed something, haven't you?"

"Yeah," I said. "I recover faster than I should."

He laughed. "Healers are different. We replenish quicker and mend ourselves without realizing it. Repairing small fractures in our core the same way we knit flesh back together. We regain strength and stamina faster than any other Caster."

"It doesn't mean we're endless," he added. "Just harder to empty."

I let that sink in. Before I could speak, he went on. "You remember what I told you about Enervation? About crossing that line."

My stomach tightened.

"If you want to grow strong, you'll have to do what most Casters won't. You'll have to cross it on purpose."

I snapped my head toward him. "On purpose?"

His gaze never left the horizon. His voice was calm, matter-of-fact. "A core doesn't grow from comfort. It grows from being torn and mended, again and again. You survived it once. You'll survive it again. If your core can stretch, this is how we'll find out."

He didn't let me linger in doubt.

"We'll start small. And if you're not comfortable with it, we'll find another way. But ride in front of me. That way, when you fall, I can catch you."

The words hit me unexpectedly. The idea of sitting in front of him. I'd pictured lessons, yes—straining myself, maybe collapsing—but not pressed that close, not with his arms braced around me.

My stomach tightened, heat creeping up the back of my neck.

I shifted in my saddle, focusing on the reins in my hands as if they might steady me. The thought of falling unconscious while he held me should have been a comfort. Instead, it sparked something else. Not fear, but a tight, uncomfortable awareness of how close he would be. Nerves that had nothing to do with Enervation.

I forced the tremor from my voice. "That sounds ... dangerous."

His expression didn't change. "It is. But it's the only way forward." His mouth twitched faintly. "Don't worry, I won't drop you. I'd never hear the end of it."

He said it like it was nothing, like my slumping half dead against him was just another step in a lesson.

I needed something else to think about.

I cleared my throat. "As an Aberration, can you Cast two elements at once?"

His mouth tugged faintly, like he knew exactly what I was doing, but he didn't push. "Yes. But not through the same hand."

He lifted his hands.

Flame bloomed in his palm, heat rolling outward in a slow breath. It flickered once—then the Fire guttered out. Cold swallowed it.

Ice surged over the same space, forming where the flame had been, climbing in jagged lines from his fingers until a shard rested there instead. The heat vanished as if it had never existed.

"Doesn't matter how many sit in the core. The body can only shape one through a single path."

The Ice thinned, cracked, and dissolved into droplets that fell away. "Switching becomes easy. Blending doesn't."

I blinked, surprised. "What's the difference?"

"For most Casters, channeling the same element in both hands at the same time is already considered skilled Casting. It takes control that few ever master."

He lifted both hands this time.

Fire bloomed in his right palm—bright and alive. In his left, frost gathered along his fingers, gathering into a swirl of Ice flurries. Heat shimmered on one side, cold bit on the other, two opposing forces held in perfect balance.

"But Aberrations can do more. We can channel different elements at the same time. One in each hand. But it's harder still, demanding separation in the mind—two paths, two currents."

The flame climbed higher while the frost grew in strength, spreading across his knuckles. Then he closed his fingers. Both vanished with a faint hiss.

I stared at his hands, then at him. "Now you're just showing off."

A faint curve touched his mouth. "You asked."

I hesitated, then frowned. "But ... when I used Ardor in the forest, I split it. I Cast Ardor in each hand."

He looked back at me. "You Cast the same element in two different directions. That kind of split is rare. Some Casters train for years and never manage it. You did it on instinct."

I blinked. "I thought anyone could, honestly."

A faint breath escaped him. "No. Not anyone. Though I suppose I should commend you for not setting yourself on fire in the process."

I rolled my eyes. "You could've stopped at 'commend you.'"

"And compromise my integrity?" he asked in mock offense.

The faint amusement faded from his expression. "You do have talent, Celeste. Real talent. But talent without control is a liability. If you split your Casting without knowing exactly how to guide it, it won't just drain you—it'll leave you exposed. If you lean on instinct alone, it will turn on you when you least expect it."

The praise sent a slow, thick heat through my veins.

A small, reluctant smile tugged at my mouth before I could stop it. "You could've stopped there."

His brow lifted slightly. "At the first 'talent'?"

"Yes. You seem incapable of ending on a compliment."

He huffed a laugh. "Honesty is a heavy burden, I suppose."

I gave him my most menacing scowl, which he ignored entirely.

"All right," he said after a moment. "Before you grow too fond of praise, there's something else you need to understand. Ignition."

I frowned. "Ignition?"

He nodded. "The moment a Caster first awakens their element. It can happen at any stage of life, but it's most common in the younger years, when a core is still growing. Young adults, usually. Children sometimes. Rarely adults. But no one knows why some are born with the spark while others live and die without it."

His gaze lingered on the horizon. "Most believe everyone carries the potential for one element. But potential alone isn't enough. To ignite it, something has to strike—an experience sharp enough to tear the core open. Fire Casters often awaken to anger or fear. But that same fury won't stir Wind. Every element answers to a different key."

A chill ran down my spine. "And Ardor?" I asked quietly.

At first, he didn't answer. Then his voice dropped lower. "I told you I once met an Ardor Caster. They told me it came to them in terror. In resisting something meant to break them."

The words sank and my throat tightened, but I forced my eyes forward.

After a moment, his voice softened, almost like a reprieve. "Ignition's never easy. But once it happens, it changes everything. It shapes the element you carry, and the way you'll wield it."

The road carried us onward in quiet hills that rolled out in every direction, the sky wide and endless above them. We passed the hours in pieces—small talk about nothing, then sudden lessons on Casting. He'd explain a principle. I'd test it. Then he'd make a joke when I'd fail.

The rest of the time, we let the road speak for us.

The ache in my legs dulled by the steady rhythm of my horse beneath me. The sun climbed higher, the morning stretching thin into noon.

I found myself wondering what Calla would be doing at this hour. If she'd already set bread to rise. If she'd stepped outside to sweep the porch or trade gossip with a neighbor passing by. I could almost see her at the table, shawl gathered at her shoulders, humming to herself as she stirred something simple over the fire.

Time passed by with the rhythm of hooves. My thoughts turned over one after another until they finally returned to what I'd been avoiding since morning.

"When am I supposed to start?"

He tilted his head, the corner of his mouth tugging. "I was going to give you another league before you asked. But now works."

I let out a breath that might have been a laugh. Of course it did.

I slowed my horse as he did the same and swung down, boots hitting the dirt with more confidence than I felt. I tied my mount's lead rope to the steel ring at his saddle, giving myself exactly three seconds to reconsider.

Three seconds was enough.

"Right," I muttered to no one in particular.

Before I could talk myself out of it, I stepped into his stirrup and pulled myself up, settling in front of him. If I waited until camp, I'd waste half the afternoon unconscious—and I wasn't about to admit that was the real reason I'd stalled.

His hands came to the reins on either side of me.

I straightened a little too quickly. "This is fine," I said, mostly to myself.

He didn't say a word, but I felt the low vibration of a laugh against my back.

Art shifted behind me, gripping the reins in one hand. "You've been practicing in bursts all morning. Now you'll hold it."

I felt him lean just enough to be heard clearly.

"Keep using both hands like you've been doing. You've proven you can split it, now you'll sustain it—feeding it until your core runs dry. When it does, don't resist the edge. Don't panic. I'm right here."

I nodded, though my throat felt tight.

His voice stayed calm, almost detached, as if he were talking me through a simple drill. "Start with the basics. One hand, then the other. Then both together."

So I did. Pulse after pulse, until the strain crawled down into my core. I bit down on my lip and focused, sending the light in flickers. Some came too strong, others sputtered.

"Good. Keep it even. Control the flow, not the brightness."

The sun was climbing higher as we rode. He had me draw the Ardor light small and precise, no larger than a coin, then spread it wide across both hands until it blinded me. He made me shape it, compress it, release it, then call it back again.

At some point, with sweat sliding down my spine, I became aware of him behind me. His voice a constant at my back. Beneath it, the scent of leather and smoke—cleaner than I expected. It caught me off guard, how solid he felt. How easy it would've been to lean back.

I forced my attention back to the light in my palms before my mind wandered any further.

It felt endless, each new demand driving the core lower and lower. My breath grew shallow, my vision edging with black. Sweat stung my eyes, and still his voice came. "Not much longer. Let it drain slow. Keep shaping it. When it breaks, I'll catch you."

The glow faltered, flickering out between my fingers. My body ached with emptiness. The reins slipped from my grasp as the world blurred, weightless and distant.

Strong arms closed around my waist, firm and certain, drawing me back against him.

"Easy," Art murmured, his breath warm at my ear. "I've got you."

Then darkness took me.

19

Celeste

When I stirred, the first thing I heard was water. A steady trickle, cool and constant, threading through the quiet. I blinked against the glare, branches overhead breaking the sunlight into soft patches. The ground was firm beneath me, grass damp with shade.

I moved, slow and clumsy, until the ache in my body reminded me of what I'd done. Hollow, drained, like I'd been wrung out to the bone.

"You're awake."

Art sat not far off, back against a tree trunk, with a pan balanced over a small fire. The smell of cooked meat and herbs drifted toward me, strong enough to make my stomach tighten. Two waterskins rested on a rock nearby, darkened where the water had touched it.

He didn't move right away, just studied me with that unreadable calm. "You were out longer than I expected. A good stretch of daylight."

I pushed up onto my elbows, breath labored. "By the creek?"

"I carried you down from the saddle." He said it as if my weight, my limp body, hadn't been a burden at all. "Figured water and shade couldn't hurt."

I lowered my gaze, heat prickling my cheeks despite the cool air. My mouth was dry, my body still heavy, but the scent of food pulled me forward. He reached for one of the waterskins and passed it over without a word.

The water was cool, clean, and it steadied the tremor in my hands.

"You cooked?" I asked him.

His mouth tugged at one corner. "Didn't want you waking to nothing."

The simple words sank deeper than they should have. I looked down, brushing grass from my palms, hoping he couldn't read the warmth rising in my face.

I drank deep again, the water soothing the rawness in my throat, but I couldn't wash away the ache in my body. The memory of losing consciousness lingered raw and humiliating.

"I don't know how I'm supposed to keep doing that," I muttered. "Over and over. I hate it. The way it feels, going under like that. Like I've lost everything."

Art stirred the pan, not looking at me right away. "That's because you did. That's what it means to drain your core."

I shot him a glare. "That's not helpful."

His mouth twitched, the faintest hint of a smile. "Didn't say it was meant to be."

"If I'm supposed to collapse like that every day, I hope you don't mind being my cushion every time I pass out."

He finally glanced over, one brow lifting. "At least you don't snore."

A laugh escaped me. "You're insufferable."

"And you're stubborn," he countered, calm as ever. "Makes us even."

The food was simple but better than what we'd been eating—fish pulled from the creek, cooked crisp over the pan with a few wild herbs he must've gathered nearby. But after waking hollow, it tasted better than a feast.

I ate slowly, each bite easing the ache in my stomach, washing it down with the cool water from the creek. Art didn't say much, just kept watch on the stretch of hills while the fire crackled low between us.

When I finally set the skin aside, I drew a breath. "How often do you plan on putting me through that?"

His answer came without hesitation. "Again. In a few hours."

I nearly choked. "A few hours? You can't be serious."

He looked at me then. "We don't have the time, unfortunately. Best to push while you're with me. Out here, I can protect you while you recover. Once we're there, you won't have that luxury."

My mouth fell open, but no argument came. The logic was sound, infuriatingly so.

A faint glint of amusement tugged at the corner of his mouth. "Besides, it'll make the trip seem quicker."

I narrowed my eyes and crossed my arms. "At this point, I think you just enjoy making me miserable."

He didn't deny it. Just gave the smallest huff of breath before turning back to the fire.

When the last of the fish was gone and the fire was nothing more than a scatter of gray ash, Art rose without a word. He poured the dregs of the creek water over the stones, then kicked dirt across the embers until the ground looked as though no one had rested there at all. His movements were efficient, not a motion wasted.

I gathered myself more slowly, still stiff from the hollow ache Enervation left behind. My fingers fumbled with the cinch on my saddle until Art's shadow fell over me. He checked the strap himself, giving it a firm tug before stepping back.

"Still weak?" he asked.

"I can manage." My voice came out thinner than I liked.

He studied me for a moment, then gave the faintest nod. "Mount up, then."

With more effort than I wanted him to notice, I swung onto the saddle. The leather creaked under my weight, and my horse shifted, ears flicking back. I smoothed a hand over her neck, steadying us both.

Art mounted his own in a single motion, his posture easy, as if he hadn't just carried me half the day.

The road stretched ahead in a long pale ribbon between the hills. He set the pace, calm and unhurried, the kind meant to last until evening. I fell in beside him, the creek fading behind us until all that remained was the taste of ash still clinging faintly to my tongue.

For a while I said nothing, content to let the silence carry us forward. But the question pushed in, insistent, until I finally broke it. "You've done this before. Trained someone like me?"

Art shook his head. "I've trained Casters, yes. But none like you."

I wasn't sure what unsettled me more. That he'd taught others, or that he was so certain I didn't belong among them.

I turned in the saddle. "You mean, no other Aberrations?"

His gaze stayed on the road ahead. "Aberrations aren't identical. From what I've seen, most are born with cores deeper than usual. Depth enough that, under the right conditions, they can ignite more than once."

He paused.

"That doesn't mean they will. Ignitions are fickle. Some Casters live their whole lives with the depth for it and never strike the right spark. They end up powerful in a single element instead. Stronger than most. But still just one."

I frowned, turning the thought over. I wasn't sure how that answered my question.

His mouth twitched faintly. "I've only fought beside a handful of other Aberrations. Once there was a man who carried three affinities. But I've never trained one before."

He glanced at me then, faint amusement in his eyes. "Consider yourself honored. You're my first."

I huffed. "You do enjoy turning everything into a lesson, don't you."

"If you're going to be my first Aberration student, I'd rather not have you embarrass me."

"I'll do my best not to disgrace the academy," I said dryly.

The humor lingered a moment longer, then thinned. "You think ..." I hesitated. "You think I could become like you? That I could learn more elements?"

Art's expression changed, but his tone carried the weight of certainty. "I don't just think it. I believe it. You're already walking the same path I was—a Healer with another affinity. You'll gain more than you realize."

I looked away, my pulse quickening, the road blurring as the thought sank in. More elements. More power. It should have thrilled me. Instead, my mind went to the compound—to the promise I'd made to Faylen—and whether even more affinities would be enough.

After a while, I found my voice again. "How many?" I asked, a little eagerly. "How many could I learn?"

Art adjusted the reins in his hands, the leather creaking. "Ambitious already?"

"That's not an answer."

A faint breath of amusement left him. "I can't give you a number."

"Then which ones? Do you at least have a guess?"

His gaze drifted to me. "No. I told you—ignition follows emotion. Each element listens for something different. And whatever lies in you will only wake when it's forced to."

"That's wildly unhelpful."

"It's honest."

I exhaled through my nose. "But if I'm like you ..."

"You'll have the chance," he said. "That's all I can tell you. More than most ever do. That's something."

The hills rolled on around us. The idea bloomed in my mind anyway—Fire, Wind, something stranger still. The thought was intoxicating. A smile tugged at my mouth. "So it's possible."

"It's possible."

I adjusted slightly, curiosity flaring brighter. "When did it happen for you? When did you start gaining yours?"

For the first time, something tightened at the corner of his jaw. "Not all at once," he said.

I leaned toward him, despite the ache in my body. "How long then? A year? Two?"

"Longer," he said, his tone firmer now. "It takes time. Training. Strain." He exhaled loudly. "More than you can imagine."

I tilted my head. "So you just woke up one day and there was another?"

His eyes flicked to mine. "Eventually. That's enough for now."

I sat back in my saddle, heat flooding my cheeks. He wasn't angry, but the edge in his tone told me not to press further.

Still, excitement coiled beneath my ribs, refusing to be put out. If it had taken him years to gain more, then maybe it was only a matter of time for me too.

The sky widened above us as the sun began its slow dip. The reins were damp from my sweat, my palms still raw from the earlier strain. The thought of doing it again made my stomach knot.

I glanced sideways at him. "What happens if I fail? If I push too far and ... don't come back?"

"Then I drag you back. Annoyingly alive," he said, a flicker of dry amusement in his voice. Then, more quietly, "That's why we're doing this together. If you go too far, I'll be there."

His gaze softened slightly. "I've done it alone. And I'm still here."

Something in me eased.

But I couldn't shake the image of him collapsed somewhere in the forest, waking with no one at his side. No one to be certain he would wake at all.

I looked forward again, watching the sun continue to descend.

"Do you ever regret it?" I asked.

He turned his head slightly, just enough to catch my meaning.

"Having more than one element. Being what you are."

He said nothing for a long while, and for a moment I thought he might ignore me. Then his gaze slid back to the horizon. "Power doesn't erase what you've lost. It just makes you live with it longer."

I didn't know what to say to that, so I said nothing at all.

The rhythm of the horses filled the space between us. My thoughts twisted tighter than the reins in my hands, but there was no more I could ask.

Not yet.

Art's voice broke the quiet again. "We'll begin once more before dusk. Call the Ardor and hold it. This time, you'll push further."

I groaned, loud enough for him to hear, but slowed my horse all the same. With stiff legs, I dismounted, tied off the reins, and climbed up in front of him again. The saddle felt even smaller than before, his presence close enough to remind me what was coming.

"Same as last time. One hand, then the other."

Time blurred into rhythm of calling and releasing light. My breath grew shallow, my vision dimmed, and still he pushed me forward with that unrelenting voice at my back.

"Not much longer," he whispered.

I gave a shaky laugh, the light trembling in my hands. "Better get ready. I don't get lighter the second time."

His arm tightened around my waist as the glow faltered. "At least this way I get some peace and quiet."

I meant to answer, to deny him the last word—but the dark rushed first. My body went limp, and his hold was the last thing I felt before the world slipped away.

***

It was dusk when I woke from the latest fall. The first time had nearly terrified me. By the ninth day, they all felt the same—no dreams, just darkness and then waking again as if no time had passed.

But this time, the world felt different. Louder. Brighter.

Hooves clattered against stone instead of dirt, and voices drifted on the evening air. Vendors calling out their wares, children laughing somewhere beyond the street. Narrow buildings lined the street, lanterns already being lit with the sun set.

We were in a town.

I cleared my throat, buying myself a moment as awareness settled in. I was still slumped against Art, his arm firm around me, guiding the reins as if it took no effort at all. And people were staring.

A pair of women paused at a stall, their conversation faltering as their eyes followed us. A group of boys leaned against a fence, pointing, whispers chasing after us as we passed.

I glanced back at Art.

I straightened, pulling myself upright in the saddle. My limbs felt heavy, sluggish, but I forced composure into them.

Art didn't seem to notice, or more likely didn't care. His expression stayed fixed as he guided the horse forward, eyes scanning the street like the stares weren't even there.

I tugged at my sleeves, wishing the ground would swallow me whole. "They're all looking."

"Let them," he said simply, not even glancing their way.

That was the end of it, at least for him. But my cheeks still burned as the town unfolded around us.

We'd ridden through smaller villages these past days—little more than crossroads with a small cluster of houses and maybe a single inn. But this was different. The place stretched further. Two-story buildings and a proper market square.

Larger than Dunwade. Larger than anywhere we'd stopped so far.

Greyfen, I realized, from the weathered name carved into the beam above an inn door.

Stalls lined the main street, the smell of baked bread and roasting meat mingling with the sharper tang of tanned leather. People wove between carts and shops, voices carrying with the clatter of hooves and wheels over stone.

I drew a slow breath, trying to hide the unease in my chest. Wherever we stopped, I only hoped I'd be able to walk on my own two feet again before anyone else decided to stare.

The main street bent toward a two-story building with a painted sign swinging over the door, displaying a faded image of a stag with antlers curling wide. Lanterns glowed in its windows; the sound of laughter and clinking mugs spilled out into the street.

Art slowed the horse as we drew up to the post outside. I slid down with more wobble than grace, my legs stiff from the ride and the remnants of strain clinging to me. He dismounted in one clean motion, tying off the reins before I had even found my footing.

A boy with straw clinging to his shirt hurried out. "Rooms for the night?" he asked, eyeing the horses more than us.

Art handed him a coin without hesitation. "Two nights. Feed and water them well."

The boy's face lit up with surprise, then he darted to the trough with reins in hand.

I gathered my satchel, following Art inside. The inn smelled of warm wood and spiced ale, a sharp contrast to the crisp air outside. The common room was busy, locals at tables, voices carrying in a low hum, tankards clattering against wood. Dunwade had been quiet, almost wary. Greyfen was something else entirely.

Art spoke briefly to the innkeeper, a broad woman wearing an apron dusted with flour, then passed me a key. "Upstairs. First on the left."

I turned it over in my hand. "You already paid?"

"Always easier," he said simply, then added, "Leave your things. We'll eat in town."

I climbed the narrow staircase, my boots echoing on the worn steps, and into a small room with two narrow beds, a table, and a basin. Simple, but clean.

I set my satchel down, running my hand over the wooden frame of the bed, trying to imagine sleeping in a place this bustling. My village had been nothing compared to this.

When I came back down, Art was waiting by the door. We headed out onto the street. Greyfen stretched wide around us. Stalls still lined the street, merchants calling out the last of their goods, and the press of people was more than I had ever seen in one place. It was overwhelming, but strangely thrilling too.

I slowed as we passed a baker's stall where flatbread was grilling fresh on the stone. The man behind the counter flipped one onto a board and brushed it with herbs, the smell making my stomach growl.

Art stopped just long enough to barter a coin for two pieces, handing one to me without a word. I tore into it while we walked, the crisp edges flaking on my fingers, the flavor rich with oil and garlic.

"This is incredible," I said around a mouthful.

Art gave a faint smile, though he was already scanning the next corner.

We passed smithies still glowing with fire, a fiddler playing at the edge of the square to a small applauding crowd. My eyes drank it in greedily, each sight a reminder of how much larger the world was than the corners I'd known.

By the time we reached the tavern, I felt dazed from it all. The sign over the door was painted with a fox mid-leap, and laughter spilled out the open shutters, rough and good-natured.

Inside, the heat and noise wrapped around me like a blanket. Tankards thudded against tables, voices rose in chorus to a song I didn't know, and the scent of roasted meat and spilled ale mingled thick in the air.

We found a seat near the back, Art taking the corner where he could keep the room in view. I sat across from him, my heart still racing from all of it.

A woman came to our table, a tray balanced on her palm. "What'll it be, handsome?" she asked.

Art ordered plainly. Some bread, a stew, and ale. When she glanced at me, I started to ask for water, but I faltered when a man at the next table raised his tankard in my direction.

"A pretty face!" he called, grinning. "That earns a drink!"

Laughter rippled through the room, light and harmless. Before I could protest, the woman set a tankard down in front of me, foam spilling over the rim.

My cheeks warmed as I met Art's gaze. He didn't move to stop it, just arched a brow and drank his ale. "You'll offend them if you don't."

I lifted the tankard with both hands, the wood cool and damp against my palms. The first sip was bitter, but warmth spread down my throat, loosening the tightness in my chest.

The men at the other table cheered, clapping the wood with approval, and I laughed along with them. Before long, more of them drifted over, pulling up benches and crowding around, their voices loud with ale and good cheer.

Their attention made me uneasy, and when one leaned too close, I rose and slid onto the bench beside Art instead.

The tavern filled up fast around us, voices rising with the ale. Somehow I'd ended up with a second tankard, then a third, each one pressed into my hand with cheers and laughter from the company that had gathered at our table. A pair of farmers made a contest of it, daring me to keep pace with them.

By the fourth round they were slumping forward while I was still upright, swaying but laughing. For each one I drank, I swore Art downed two, steady as ever.

"Didn't think you had it in you," one of the men mumbled before sliding off his bench.

The table roared with laughter, and someone clapped me on the back hard enough to send me stumbling against Art.

I shot out a hand to catch myself, fingers curling around his arm. The solidity of him startled me. Firm beneath my weight, warm under the coarse fabric of my sleeve.

"You're steadier than the floor," I said before I could think better of it, grinning up at him.

He looked at me with faint amusement. "Is that supposed to pass for a compliment?"

I laughed and let go, though it took me a moment longer than it should have. The others at the table didn't notice, too busy calling for another round, but I caught the faint twitch of his mouth.

By the time the night wore thin, I could barely stand. Art caught me as I swayed, pulling my arm over his shoulder without asking. The crowd parted for him as he steered me out the door, his grip firm.

At the inn, my legs felt boneless. Art guided me up the narrow stairs and into our room, steadying me with one hand at my arm until I flopped onto the edge of the bed.

I tipped my chin down, hair falling into my face, and squinted up at him through a haze of laughter and ale. "Don't look so serious. I don't bite … unless you ask."

His mouth twitched, half amused. "You'll regret saying that in the morning."

I meant to argue, to come up with something clever, but the weight of exhaustion pulled me under before I could. The last thing I felt was the brush of his hand against my shoulder, a quiet weight as the world went dark.

20

Celeste

I woke to my heartbeat hammering inside of my skull. My mouth was dry as dust, and when I tried to swallow, the taste of stale ale clung to the back of my throat. The light creeping through the shutters stabbed at my eyes like knives.

I groaned and dragged the blanket over my face, wishing the world away. It smelled faintly of soap and mildew. It was cleaner than anything I'd slept in for months, but it did nothing to ease the pounding in my head.

What happened?

I tried to piece the night together. Music, laughter, tankards slamming on tables. Someone clapped me on the back ... Art's arm under mine, holding me.

Heat flushed my cheeks even as the memory blurred into the haze of ale.

A floorboard creaked. I cracked one eye open, and peeled the blanket back, wincing at the light. Art was at the table, sitting with his back straight as always, sharpening his sword with slow, deliberate strokes. His sleeves were rolled to the elbow, the morning sun catching the tattoos across his forearm. He looked like he'd been awake for hours.

"You're alive," he said without looking up.

"Barely," I croaked. My voice scraped against my throat like gravel.

His mouth twitched. "You'll survive. First hangover's always the worst."

I pushed myself upright and immediately regretted it. The room tilted and I clutched the bedframe, muttering a curse.

"Slowly. Do you remember anything?" He set the whetstone aside and finally looked at me.

Heat crawled higher up my neck. Bits and pieces. Along with the most mortifying memory of all. My own voice, slurred and reckless.

I wished the floor would open and swallow me whole.

"I … remember enough," I muttered.

"Good," he said lightly, though the corner of his mouth betrayed the faintest smirk. He picked the sword back up and went on sharpening.

The calm of it only made my stomach twist harder. I pressed a hand to my forehead, groaning again. "Please tell me this goes away."

"In a few hours." He set the blade down, reached into his satchel, and slid a small flask across the table. "Water. Drink."

I shuffled over, each step heavier than the last, and took it. The water was cool, almost sweet, and it soothed the raw dryness in my throat. I drank deep, then lowered it with a gasp.

Art leaned back in his chair, folding his arms. "So," he said, voice as dry as the air outside, "still think you can outdrink farmers?"

I closed my eyes. "Never again."

Art's chuckle was low and quiet.

I cracked one eye at him. "Why aren't you miserable too? You drank even more than I did."

He shrugged, as if it were the simplest thing in the world. "I can hold my own. But it's more than that. My Healing gives me an edge. Makes it harder to get drunk, harder to stay drunk ... and harder to feel the price of it afterward."

I groaned and lifted my head, squinting at him. "Then why isn't mine like that? Shouldn't I be immune to this?"

The faintest smile tugged at his mouth. "You drank grown men under the table, Celeste. That's more than most can say. You just don't see it yet because you're new to all this."

My stomach twisted, though I wasn't sure if it was from the hangover or the reminder. "So what you're telling is I'll eventually be able to drink like you and not feel it?"

He raised a brow. "Among other things. Healing takes time to grow into. You're only scratching the surface."

I slumped back onto the bed with a groan, clutching the blanket. "That doesn't help me now."

He rose from the chair and crossed the short space between us. "Sit up," he murmured, the words more coaxing than firm. His hand slipped beneath my shoulder, steadying me as he eased me upright from where I'd collapsed against the blanket. The world spun for a moment, but he kept me anchored until I found balance again.

Then his hand found my face. His thumb brushed along my cheekbone while his other fingers rested warm against the hollow of my neck.

"What are you—"

"Hold still."

The words were plain enough, but his voice carried a softness that startled me. Heat pulsed beneath his hand, sinking deeper, like a heartbeat that was not my own. The pounding in my skull dulled with every breath, the queasiness in my stomach easing until all that remained was the solid weight of him there.

I exhaled, letting my eyes fall shut, too tired to question the closeness. "That ... actually helped."

His thumb moved, just slightly, almost a caress, almost nothing at all. "Good," he muttered.

I opened my eyes again, catching his for a fleeting moment. Up close, his pale gray eyes looked almost silver before he turned away. Still, he didn't move his hand. It lingered at my cheek as if the Healing wasn't quite finished, though the ache had already faded.

I could have pulled away.

I didn't want to.

I leaned into his touch instead, too worn down to care, and the warmth of him seeped into places the Healing couldn't touch.

When at last he drew his hand back, the air against my skin felt colder for the loss.

Almost without thinking, my own hand lifted to where his had been. My fingers brushed the spot, lingering there as if the warmth might still be caught in my skin.

Art cleared his throat and leaned away, reaching for his satchel by the table. "Drink more water," he said evenly, his tone sliding back into the practical.

I dropped my hand, embarrassed at being caught in the small gesture. "Right. Water."

He tightened the straps on his satchel, then glanced back at me with his usual expression. "We've got a full day ahead. Eat something, clear your head. I want to ask around, see if there are any whispers of bounties moving through town. The sooner I know who's watching the roads, the better our chances when we head toward Rodin."

I nodded, though the thought of food still made my stomach turn. He was already thinking ahead, composed as ever, while I was still trying to find my footing.

"Get dressed," he added, his voice quieter, though not unkind. "I'll meet you downstairs."

The door shut behind him with a soft click, leaving me alone in the room. My hand drifted to my cheek again before I could stop it, heat rising under my fingers at the memory of his touch.

I shook it off, forcing myself upright. There were bigger things to worry about than the way his hand had felt against my skin.

The morning air hit cool and crisp when I left the inn, though the streets were already alive with sound. Merchants barked their wares from beneath bright awnings, voices carrying over the hum of foot traffic. Horses clopped over cobblestones, children darted between stalls, and the scents of spices, smoke, and bread baking somewhere close by, layered so thick I almost couldn't sort one from the other.

Reluctantly, I drew the hood over my head, tucking my hair beneath the fabric as we stepped fully into the press of the market.

Greyfen's market was a world unto itself.

I slowed without meaning to, my eyes catching on everything at once.

Bolts of fabric hung in shimmering cascades of color I'd never imagined, bright as autumn leaves. A woman ground herbs with a stone pestle, the smell sharp and heady, while another stacked jars of honey so golden they caught the morning sun like glass lanterns. A cage of birds squawked as I passed, feathers flashing green and blue, nothing like the dull sparrows that haunted my village.

I must have lingered too long because Art's voice sounded at my shoulder. "Try not to look so wide-eyed."

I tore my gaze from the stall of trinkets I'd been staring at, cheeks warming. "I've never seen half of this before."

"Exactly," he said, tone dry as kindling. "Which is why you shouldn't gawk. Someone will see you coming a league away and charge double."

That earned him a frown, but I kept walking, only to falter again at the next stall. There was fruit I didn't recognize, oblong with a skin of mottled red and yellow that shone like polished stone. The vendor caught me staring and, with a practiced slice, split one open. Inside, the flesh gleamed a rich golden hue, clinging thick around a pale pit. Juice welled at the cut, sticky and fragrant, and he offered me a slice with a smile that suggested he already knew I'd never tasted anything like it.

I hesitated.

Art didn't. He plucked it neatly from the man's hand and passed it to me. "Taste."

The juice burst bright and sweet over my tongue, startling enough that I gasped. The vendor chuckled.

"Not everything here will bite you," Art said. There was the faintest twitch of a smile at the corner of his mouth.

I wiped my chin with the back of my hand, glaring at him even as I reached for another slice. "You could've warned me."

"And missed that face? Never."

The vendor leaned forward, smile widening when I reached for another piece. "A fine taste, eh? For you lovely girl, three coppers each."

I froze, the sweet juice still on my tongue. Three coppers? For fruit? My hand hovered near my pouch, uncertain.

Before I could speak, Art's hand closed over mine, setting it back at my side. He plucked the fruit the vendor had been offering and set two coppers at the table. His voice was calm, but hard enough to cut. "They're worth one each. No more."

The man's smile faltered. "Imported fruit, it's hard to come by. Worth every coin."

"Not today," Art said. His gaze didn't waver, and after a tense moment, the vendor snatched the coppers and muttered under his breath.

Art dropped the fruit into his satchel and steered me away from the stall.

I glanced up at him. "Was he really—"

"Trying to rob you blind? Naturally." His mouth twitched. "You looked ready to hand him your purse for fruit I could've plucked from a roadside orchard."

"If it's that easy, you're welcome to fetch one from the next orchard we pass," I said, eyeing him with open doubt.

"Of course. And I'll even give you the discounted rate." He winked.

I shoved at his arm, though I couldn't quite hide my grin.

The market swelled with voices and music. A songstress stood on a low wooden platform, skirts flourishing around her as she sang. Her voice rose above the crowd, clear and full, weaving through the bustle like silk.

The melody mirrored a river's mood, bright and quick one moment, then soft as a lullaby the next. A small drum kept time, struck by a boy no older than twelve, the rhythm steady beneath her soaring notes. People clapped in time, coins ringing as they hit the tin bowl placed at her feet.

I stopped without meaning to, pulled in as if her voice had caught me by the sleeve. The sound wrapped around me, tugging at something I couldn't name. A pair of children tried to mimic her, spinning in clumsy circles until they collapsed in a heap of laughter.

Beside me, Art stood with arms crossed, his gaze sweeping the crowd more than the performer. But when I glanced at him, I caught it, the faintest softening in his eyes, as though the song had brushed against him too before he forced the steel back into place.

I looked away quickly, pretending not to notice, and turned my attention to nearby stalls.

The last note of the song lingered in the air even after the crowd began to disperse, leaving only the soft rattle of coins in the singer's bowl. I lingered a little longer, unwilling to let the moment go.

Art was already moving again. I hurried to catch up, but my eyes caught on a small stall tucked between a potter and leatherworker.

Strings of pendants swayed in the breeze, polished stones bound in silver wire, small carvings of wolves, ravens, and foxes hanging from leather cords. Nothing grand, nothing costly, but all carefully made. I stopped short.

Art glanced back. "What is it?"

I shook my head. "Nothing. Just ... wait here a moment."

He frowned, but he didn't argue.

The stallkeeper was an older woman with kind eyes and roughened hands. My fingers hovered over the array before settling on a piece of iron etched with a wolf's head. Simple, sturdy. Exactly the sort of thing he might actually wear without complaint.

"This one," I said.

The woman followed my glance toward Art, who stood a little ways off, arms folded. She smiled as though she knew more than she let on. "A good choice."

I paid before my courage could falter and returned to him, pressing the pendant into his hand.

He looked down at it, then at me. "What's this?"

"A gift," I said, more firmly than I felt. "You buy things for me. It's only fair."

For a second, I thought he might hand it back. Instead, he slipped the cord over his wrist, tucking the wolf's head against his skin. "Practical enough," he said, his tone even, though something quieter lurked beneath it.

I tried not to smile too wide, but the warmth that spread though my chest felt almost giddy.

We walked on after that, weaving deeper into the market streets. Art veered toward a broad wooden board nailed against the wall near the square. Dozens of parchment sheets flapped in the breeze, tacked in messy layers.

Before we got too close, his hand brushed my arm. "I'm going to check the boards," he said quietly. "Best if you hang back."

I frowned. "Why?"

His gaze flicked over the square, then back to me. "Crowds remember faces. No sense giving them one to remember."

I stayed where I was, hood low, watching him scan the notices line by line. From where I stood, I could only catch pieces: the scrawled writing, the way his eyes scanned every line like each one carried a hidden answer.

He lingered, until a man waiting behind him cleared his throat impatiently. Only then did he step aside and move on.

It went on like that through the afternoon. At a smithy, he waved me toward a shaded wall before striking up a conversation with the craftsman. At a tavern doorway, he told me to wait across the street. At a wagon, while two men loaded crates, he angled his head for me to hang back, then went forward alone.

Each time, I obeyed, though irritation gnawed at me. To any passerby, I must have looked like a lost girl while he drifted from stranger to stranger.

All I caught were fragments. The smith shaking his head, muttering something I couldn't hear. The wagon men shrugging, pointing east. A barkeep leaning on the doorframe, lowering his voice until I couldn't make out a word. Every time Art returned, his shoulders seemed a little heavier, though his expression stayed the same.

By the time the sun dipped lower, he finally returned to me for good.

"Well?" I asked, tugging the hood back just enough to breathe in the cool air.

"Nothing worth worrying about," he said.

I let it go.

Still, I couldn't shake the sense that all this wandering, all those quiet conversations, hadn't given him what he'd been after. And that the silence weighed on him more than he let on.

We stopped at one last board on the far end of the square. The parchment here was newer, tacked up in neat rows, but Art studied them no differently than the others. I kept my hood drawn low, waiting where he'd told me, trying not to fidget under the gaze of passerby.

When he finally turned back, his expression hadn't changed, but I could feel the change in him. He walked to me, his eyes unreadable.

"That's enough," he said.

I searched his face. "You found something?"

His pause stretched a breath too long. "Not on the boards. Nothing posted. No bounties, no notices. Whoever wants you hasn't gone through the open channels. They're hiring directly." His gaze drifted briefly over the crowd, then settled back on me. "But I know who's behind it."

My stomach tightened. "Who?"

"They call themselves the Black Veil," he said flatly.

The name meant nothing to me, but something in his tone made my throat go dry.

"Well, they don't call themselves anything," he corrected himself, as though sensing my confusion. "That's what others call them. They've got a fairly large network, too large for anyone to pin down. Never in the same place twice. If you strike one nest, three more crop up somewhere else."

My chest constricted. I didn't need the name to know who he meant. I remembered the firelight flickering against wet stone, the stink of iron shackles.

I swallowed, cutting the thought short. "So it was them."

"It was." He adjusted the strap on his satchel, his gaze flicking across the crowd again before returning to me. "But ..." His words trailed off, his jaw working. "Something's still wrong. The men they've sent after you. They were too skilled, too clean. Not the kind I'd expect from their ranks. I can't place it yet."

The admission unsettled me more than anything else. Art was always so certain, so unshakable, never one to doubt himself out loud.

Art's eyes swept the square one last time before he exhaled through his nose. "That's enough for today."

I tilted my head. "That's it?"

"That's it," he said firmly. Then, softer, "We leave tomorrow. Which means we've got the rest of the day to enjoy ourselves while we still can."

The words surprised me.

We walked the markets again, but this time his pace wasn't as brisk, his eyes no longer searching. We paused to watch a juggler balancing knives while children shrieked with delight.

By the time we'd wound back toward the square, the lamps were being lit, warm light spilling across the cobblestones. I thought we were finished, but Art stopped at a jeweler's stall.

"Wait here," he said, already pulling a coin from his pouch.

I blinked. "Art—"

He ignored me, speaking quietly to the vendor. A moment later he turned and held out a small box. Inside lay a thin chain with a rectangular ruby pendant, its deep red color glowing in the lamplight.

"For me?" The words came out smaller than I meant.

He smiled. "You bought me something. Fair's fair." He lifted the necklace before I could protest and reached around to clasp it at the back of my neck, the stone settling cool against my collarbone. The stone gleamed brighter still against my hair, almost as if it had been chosen for that alone.

I grazed it with my fingers, not trusting my voice.

"Matches," he said simply, stepping back as if that explained everything.

It was more than enough.

The town felt different that evening. Where yesterday the market had been a crush of bartering and noise, tonight paper lanterns had been strung between posts and stalls, their warm glow spilling over shared fires and long tables set up in the square. Laughter spilled out of every open doorway, voice raised in song. It reminded me of what the older villagers back home used to say about festival nights, though ours had never been this large or this loud.

Art didn't steer us to the quiet inn we'd slept in before. Instead, he angled us toward a tavern with a painted sign of a stag's head, music already spilling from its windows. Inside, the air was warm and thick with the smell of ale, roasted pork, and pipe smoke. A fiddler played from atop a table, his tune swallowed by the chorus of voices shouting to keep time.

I expected Art to make for a shadowed corner, as he always did. Instead, he fetched us ale, took a seat closer to the center, and set two tankards down before I could blink.

"You're not usually this eager," I said, eyeing him over the foam.

"You wanted to prove it," he said evenly, a flicker of amusement in his eyes. "Tonight seems as good a night as any."

I flushed, remembering yesterday's words. "Oh? So you *do* want to keep up with me?"

His smirked. "We'll see who keeps up with who."

By the time we'd finished the first round, we were drawn into one of the games at the next table. A simple ring toss, iron hoops thrown toward pegs hammered into the floor. Losers drank. Winners pointed out the next victim.

They shoved a ring into Art's hand, laughing that he'd never make it with shoulders that broad. He said nothing, only narrowed his eyes at the target. The ring spun from his hand and landed dead on the center peg.

The table roared.

He played again, and again, never missing. By the third round the men were groaning, accusing him of sorcery, while Art only sipped his ale like it was the most natural thing in the world.

"You're a Caster, aren't you?" one of them called, half daring, half jeering. "I'll wager a silver it's Wind you're using!"

The crowd leaned in, eager for a spectacle.

Art set his tankard down and lifted his hand over it. At first, nothing happened. Then water beaded across his palm, gathering until he poured a steady stream straight into the tankard. Clear, cold, and unmistakably his Casting.

The tavern burst into laughter and applause, the man who'd accused him smacking the table in delight. "A Water Caster! Hah! Knew it was something!"

Art only raised his brows, calm as ever, before tossing the ring again. Dead center.

The others groaned and drank.

But I had seen the faint stir of air, the way the hoop curved just so.

"You're cheating," I said under my breath.

He slid me a look, mouth twitching as though he were fighting down a smile. "Then you'll just have to prove it."

The night blurred into flashes of music and laughter, each moment tumbling over the next.

But the heart of it all became the table where Art sat.

What started as a few rounds of ring toss turned into something louder, rowdier. A drinking contest that stretched the length of the hall. Two tankards were set out.

The rules were simple: Drink until one faltered, then another challenger took the loser's place.

Art never moved.

One man went down after five rounds, another after two, then a red-faced farmer after barely one. Each time, Art drained his tankard and set it down with the same calm finality before motioning for the next.

The crowd around the table grew until it seemed like half the tavern had gathered, cheering or jeering, coins changing hands with every new match.

I sat at Art's side, torn between amusement and disbelief. His cheeks had gone red, his eyes just a little too bright, but he never wavered. Tankard after tankard disappeared in front of him, his challengers staggering off to laughter and groans.

"You're actually enjoying this," I murmured.

His gaze flicked toward me. "Maybe I am."

I straightened, heart thudding louder than the tavern noise. "Then let's see how much."

His brow lifted, though the smile lingered. "See how much what?"

"How much you're enjoying yourself." I nudged one of the empty tankards toward him. "Drink against me."

A few men nearby overheard, and the challenge caught like fire. Fresh tankards slammed onto the table, the crowd cheering and laughing, eager for one more spectacle.

Art's eyes held mine, weighing me for a long moment. Then he reached for a tankard. "You'll regret that," he said, his voice low, but his amusement made my skin prickle.

I grinned, heat and ale warming my chest. "Prove it."

The crowd howled as we lifted our tankards.

The first round burned hot down my throat, but I slammed the tankard down with a grin, foam dripping over my fingers. Art matched me, the crowd banging their fists against the table.

Another pair of tankards appeared, then another. The noise swelled around us, clapping, cheering, voices chanting something that sounded like a name, even if none of them knew mine. My head felt light, the edges of the room softening, but I refused to falter.

Art stayed steady, but the flush along his cheekbones grew darker with each round. His hand lingered on the table a moment too long after the third tankard, his fingers curling against the wood. He raised the next, but when he set it down his other hand gripped the edge of the table, catching himself.

The crowd caught it before I did, shouting, laughing, and pounding the wood. He met my gaze, his smile slanting rueful this time. "That's enough," he admitted.

The tavern erupted into cheers, half of them celebrating the win. Music struck up again, faster now, strings and drum pounding together. The crowd surged toward the open space near the hearth, bodies spinning, boots stomping against the floorboards.

I caught Art before he could sink back into his chair, my hand locking around his wrist. "Not done yet."

He raised a brow, already shaking his head, but I tugged harder. The crowd swallowed us whole, pulling him from the table and into the crowd of bodies.

"Celeste—"

"Dance with me!"

For once, he didn't fight it.

The music spun around us, wild and loud, and for the first time since I'd met him, Art let himself be pulled into it. Art's hand moved to my waist, drawing me through the whirl of the crowd, warm even through the fabric. My own hand curled at his shoulder, the strength in him so certain it made the floor feel steady beneath my feet.

His eyes caught mine as we moved, brighter than I'd ever seen them, alive in a way I didn't think he could be.

The sound of the crowd blurred, the fiddler's song stretched thin. Heat spread through my chest as the music swelled, and before I could second-guess myself, I leaned in.

His lips met mine, warm and certain, and for a moment the rest of the world ceased to exist—no crowd, no music, no fighting to survive. Only the warmth of him against me, the faint taste of ale still on his breath. I lingered there, caught in the heat and the ache, wishing it could last.

Then he pulled back.

His breath brushed against my cheek as his hand lingered at my side, then slipped away. His voice was low, rougher than usual. "No ... we can't."

I froze, blinking at him. "Why not?"

His jaw tightened. I almost thought he might tell me. Something real, something that would explain everything he kept behind those guarded eyes. Instead, he shook his head once, the words falling flat. "It's just not right."

The music crashed around us, laughter and cheers filling the tavern as the dancers spun past. But between us, there was only silence.

Before I could reach for him, he stepped back, turning from the floor. The crowd parted without resistance, swallowing him in their movement as he walked away.

I stood in the middle of the room, the ruby at my throat heavy and cold against my skin, the warmth of his touch already fading.

21

The world spun when I opened my eyes, like it hadn't quite settled yet. Pressure throbbed somewhere behind them.

Wonderful.

With a groan, I sat up, and pressed my palm to my temple. Now that I knew it was possible, I let my Healing flare. Warmth spread through me, and the ache vanished in seconds.

I stared at my hand, flexing my fingers. If only everything else were that easy.

The other bed was empty, the blanket folded neatly at its foot.

Typical.

Art was already gone, probably off scouring for supplies or answers he'd never share.

I fell back against the mattress, staring at the ceiling beams. The ruby necklace felt cool against my skin, heavy where it rested at my collarbone. I touched it absently, wishing the memory of last night could vanish as easily as the hangover had.

But I pushed it aside. I'd survived worse. I'd keep moving, with or without his answers.

I pushed myself up again and got to work. The basin water was cold, but it cleared the last of the fog as I washed. My clothes smelled faintly of ale, but I pulled them on anyway, lacing them tight. By the time the shutters let in a full strip of daylight, I had packed what little we carried and set both satchels by the door.

The latch clicked not long after, and Art entered. He had a parcel of bread and cheese tucked under his arm, his expression carefully neutral.

"You're up," he said simply, setting the food on the table. "Good. We'll eat, then head out before the road fills up."

No mention of the tavern. Or the dance. Or the kiss.

I only nodded, twisting the necklace between my fingers without realizing I'd reached for it.

We ate without ceremony, the bread coarse but filling, the cheese strong on my tongue. Neither of us said much, but the silence wasn't strained. It was well-worn, like slipping into a cloak we both knew too well.

After clearing our plates, Art gathered up our things, and we made our way down to the busy common room. No one spared us more than a glance. By the time we reached the stables, the noise of Greyfen was already fading behind us.

Our horses stamped impatiently, their breath fogging in the cool air. I ran a hand along my mare's neck, the simple rhythm calming me. Art checked the tack with his usual care, then swung onto his saddle.

"Ready?" he asked.

I nodded, pulling my hood up against the wind before mounting.

We left the town with the morning light at our backs, the road stretching long and quiet ahead.

The ruts in the road were deep from wagon wheels, the trees thinning to our right where the wind combed through tall grass. My mare's gait was steady enough that I let the reins rest loose in my hand, the ruby at my throat tapping against my collarbone with each step.

Art rode a pace ahead, then slowed until we were side by side. "You should try Casting."

I blinked at him. "While riding?"

He gave a small nod, the corner of his mouth lifting like he was trying for encouragement. "Start simple. A stump, a rock. Just see if you can land a hit while the horse keeps moving."

I groaned, letting my head fall back. "Can't we just ride without turning everything into a lesson?"

"Suppose we can," he said after a moment.

He nudged his horse ahead a few steps, the smile already gone.

I bit back a smile, turning my gaze to the road. He wasn't wrong—but today, I didn't feel like letting him be right.

The silence stretched, broken only by the rhythmic thud of hooves and everything left unsaid between us.

Dust rose ahead, wagons, oxen, riders strung out in a loose line moving the opposite direction. A small caravan.

We slowed to let them pass, Art offering a nod to the lead rider. The man returned it, his eyes flicking briefly to me before he urged his horse on. Children peered out the back of one wagon, wide-eyed, while a pair of guards at the tail raised their hands in casual salute.

"Afternoon!" one called.

Art's reply was clipped. "Safe roads."

We moved past them without pause, gazes trailing in our wake. No one lingered, no questions asked.

Just travelers passing, carrying on with their lives.

I kept my gaze forward, jaw tight.

To them, I was just another face in the crowd. To Art, I was someone who needed hiding.

Dust from the caravan still clung in the air when a fork in the road came into view. A weathered post flagging under the weight of two signs. One pointed south, etched with letters I didn't need to read to know where it led, and the other northwest, toward a name I didn't recognize. Asholt.

Art slowed his horse. "We'll cut through this town."

"I thought you said Rodin was only a few days ride from here."

"It is. But I'd rather not be exhausted when we reach its walls." His tone left no room for debate.

I nodded, as we turned onto the northwest road.

The town soon came into view, nestled in the dip of a shallow valley. The roofs were clustered tight as though bracing against the wind. Smaller than Greyfen, quieter too, but still alive with the rhythm of people moving about.

A few stalls remained open in the square, though most merchants were already shuttering for the night. A boy darted between them with a bundle of kindling; a woman swept her front doorstep.

It smelled of bread, woodsmoke, and damp earth.

Art guided us past the last of the market stalls, his gaze sweeping the square with that same sharpness he never set down. But no one looked twice at us. No bounties, no whispers. Just another evening in another town.

He dismounted at the inn's post and handed off his reins to a waiting stablehand. I slid down after him, my legs stiff from the road, the ruby thudding against my chest as if reminding me it was still there.

The stablehand led our horses away, and Art paused only long enough to run a hand down the straps of his satchel, eyes already scanning the square.

I lingered at the inn's steps, breathing in the night air. Asholt felt different from Greyfen. There was no wild laughter spilling from every doorway, no music rising above the rooftops. Just the muted thrum of people settling into their lives.

A rhythm I didn't belong to.

"We'll take a room," Art said, nodding toward the inn.

I crossed my arms. "You can. I want to look around first."

He didn't argue, not out loud, but the way he fell into step a pace behind told me I wouldn't be left to wander alone.

The square opened ahead of us, lanterns strung from post to post, their glow soft against the cobbles. A row of rough tables had been set near the fountain, tankards clutched in hands, bowls steaming with stew. Laughter rose from one corner when a fiddler played a quick, crooked tune, the bowstrings squealing at the edges, but no one seemed to mind.

I slowed, letting the hum of it wash over me. Not a festival like Greyfen's, but enough to feel like celebration. A painted banner stretched between two poles, its lettering faded but legible: *Festival of the First Frost.*

The wind felt colder, the air already carrying the bite of winter. The townsfolk had gathered to face it with drink and song, as though the cold itself could be warded off by cheer.

At some point, I lost track of Art behind me.

Voices rose and fell like waves against the edges of the lantern light. Tables clustered in uneven lines, their benches worn smooth by years of use. Smoke from the spits curled thick and savory.

Art came back from the ale casks with two tankards in hand. He didn't look at me as he set them down on a bench near the edge of the crowd, taking his seat with the same calm resolve he carried everywhere.

One tankard he lifted. The other he left waiting, foam spilling over the rim.

I lingered for a second before turning away, sliding onto a bench of my own across the square. My hood slipped back as I sat. Even from here, I could feel the noise closing in, voices bleeding into one another until they blurred.

I wasn't angry at him.

I kept repeating that to myself, as if the words could smooth the ache in my chest. He'd done nothing wrong. If anything, he'd shown more sense than I had.

But the space between us felt raw all the same, tender in a way I wasn't ready to face. I just needed a moment alone.

A barmaid passed by not long after, balancing a tray filled with tankards. She paused when she saw me, head tilting as if to mark the stranger among the crowd. "Ale?" she offered, her smile easy, trained.

I shook my head at first, then caught the cool weight of Art's gaze across the square. He hadn't moved, hadn't touched the second tankard. Just watching, silent as ever.

My chin lifted a fraction. "Yes," I said, reaching for the tankard she offered.

The barmaid's smile widened. "On the house, sweetie. Happy festival night." She moved on before I could answer.

The froth was cold against my fingers. I took a slow sip. The bite of it wasn't unpleasant. Stronger than Greyfen's, though.

The bench creaked a while later as someone else sat down beside me.

"Well now," a voice said, rough with drink but softened by a grin. I turned to find a man built like a wall, two tankards clutched in his hands. His hair was sun-bleached, his shirt unlaced at the collar, and he smelled faintly of hay and ale.

"Didn't think Asholt had enough luck to host a face this fine tonight." He slid one tankard toward me. "What do you say?"

I raised a brow. "That depends on what I'm saying yes to."

He chuckled, low and easy, before lifting his own tankard for a long pull. When he came up for air, foam streaked his lip. He wiped it away with the back of his hand.

"Henry," he said, grin tugging wide as though we'd known each other longer than a breath. "AurenVale's got me posted here. Keeping the roads clear while the real fighting drags on elsewhere. Not much glory in keeping sheep safe, but it pays the same as bleeding on some field. And at least Asholt knows how to keep a man well supplied with ale."

The tankard sat between us, still frothing. He nudged it closer with two fingers, eyes bright under the lamplight. "So what do you say? Share a drink with me, festival girl?"

I traced the rim of my own ale, letting the sharp bite of it linger on my tongue before setting it down again. Across the square, Art's figure was still visible through the crowd, unmoving at his own bench. His second tankard sat untouched, froth long since dulled.

Henry's grin lingered, bold as if I'd already agreed.

I let my fingers brush the side but I didn't take it. "Generous," I said lightly, "but I don't accept drinks from strangers."

His brows lifted in mock offense, mouth already opening to argue.

Before he could, a barmaid drifted past with a tray of fresh ales. I raised a hand, and she slid one toward me without breaking stride.

I lifted it in a small toast, letting the lanternlight catch on the rim. "I don't accept drinks from strangers," I repeated, meeting his gaze over the tankard. "But I'll raise my own with them. The name's Anna."

The lie slipped from my lips, a name Art and I agreed upon during our time on the road.

Henry barked a laugh and swept his own ale back toward himself. "Fair enough." He tipped it back in a long pull, foam running down his chin. The second tankard still waited by his elbow, patient as a promise.

He downed his drink and set it down with a thud. "So, Anna. Don't think I've seen you here before. Passing through?"

"Something like that." I took another sip of my own ale, cool foam brushing my lip.

He leaned in, elbows on the table, his grin easy. "Well, Asholt's not much, but it's got good ale and a soldier or two to keep the road clear. Good enough for a festival, anyway. And good enough company, if I say so myself."

I tilted my head, studying him. "Confident, aren't you?"

"Earned it." He brushed the thumb across the badge at his shoulder, more gesture than proof. "AurenVale says guard the roads, so I guard the roads. Not much to it. But I figure the trick's knowing where to sit once the work's done." His grin tilted, eyes glinting as though he meant this bench and nowhere else.

I arched a brow. "And if I prefer quiet company?"

"Then I'll just have to convince you I can be quiet too."

I snorted softly into my ale. "You're already failing at that."

He laughed, loud enough to turn a few heads nearby. "Fair. But you're still sitting here."

I drained the last of my tankard and rose, the wood creaking beneath me. "Not for long," I said, then tipped the empty cup in his direction. "Your turn. I'll get this one."

His brows lifted in pleased surprise. "Now that's a proper festival spirit." He pushed his tankard across the table without hesitation.

The crowd swelled near the fountain where the casks were lined, lanterns hanging low above the barrels. A man stood behind them, apron stained, arms like corded rope. A faint rime clung to the iron hoops of the casks, thin curls of chilled mist drifting where his hand rested against the wood.

He traded empty tankards for coins with quick efficiency, tapping the spigot and sliding foam-topped drinks across the table without a word wasted.

I shouldered in, set both tankards down, and fished a coin from the pouch Art had handed me weeks ago. The man gave me a curt nod and pulled the lever. As the amber liquid filled the tankards, he brushed two fingers along the rim. A tiny shard of Ice formed and slipped into the foam.

I reached to take them, only to find Art already there, one hand steadying a tankard before it could topple. His voice was quiet enough to slip beneath the din. "He's not worth your time."

The weight of his words hit harder than the ale's bite. I tightened my grip on the tankard's handle, met his gaze head-on. "You didn't seem to care until he was."

At that moment, the square fell away. The noise, the heat of bodies, even the glow of lanterns. Just his eyes on mine, unreadable as ever.

"Be careful," he said at last. Then he released the tankard, turned, and slipped back through the crowd, vanishing into the darker edge of the square.

I stood a while longer, the two brimming ales heavy in my hands, my pulse louder than the fiddler's tune. Then the tapster barked at the next in line, and I forced myself to step aside.

Henry looked up as I wove back through the crowd, tankards in hand. His grin spread wide, and he swept an arm across the table with theatrical flourish.

"Well, look at that. Thought you'd ditched me."

Two fresh ales already sat in front of him, freshly poured and running over their rims. He pushed them closer with his knuckles, smug. "Lucky for you, I know how to keep a seat warm. And since you went through all that trouble" —his eyes flicked to the tankards I carried— "looks like you get to drink both."

I set the ales down, the wood damp beneath my palms. "Generous," I said, taking a slow sip from one, "but I think you're falling behind."

He barked a laugh, snatching up one of his own and draining half in a gulp. "Behind? I'm winning. You've got catching up to do."

I swirled the ale in my mug, watching the foam collapse in lazy circles. Two in front of him, two fresh in front of me. He'd made sure of it. A man could talk about roads and duty all he wanted, but this wasn't about conversation, it was about drink. About seeing how many it would take to floor me.

I lifted the mug again, letting the edge brush my lip without drinking. My gaze stayed level with his. "Maybe you're the one who can't keep up."

His grin widened, pleased with the challenge. "Now that sounds like fighting words."

Henry leaned back, balancing his mug on one knee, the foam already gone. "So, Anna." He said my name like he was tasting it. "Where's a girl like you come from? Not Asholt, that much I can tell. You've got the look of someone who's seen more road than hearth."

I traced a finger along the rim of my mug. "Maybe I have."

"Caravan girl?" His grin crooked. "Merchant's daughter? Run off from some rich house with your jewels tucked under your cloak?"

The guesses came too close. I plastered on a smile. "You've a good imagination."

"Imagination, sure." He tapped his temple. "But I've an eye for people. And you ..." He leaned in, bold, searching my face with that weather-worn squint. "You've got a story."

I took a long drink to give myself time. The ale was bitter on my tongue, but it filled the pause when words wouldn't.

What could I say?

That I'd been a prisoner, that my name sat on a bounty slip, that every road I walked on was shadowed by the ones who wanted me back?

That the ruby against my collarbone felt like a quiet tether to Art, even now?

My throat tightened. "Everyone's got a story," I said at last. "Doesn't mean it needs telling."

He chuckled, shaking his head. "You're a hard one to pin down."

I forced a smile, though my chest felt hollow. With Art, the silence had never felt like this. Heavy, brittle, every word weighing against what might slip free. With him, it wasn't easy, but it was safer. He didn't pry, he just listened.

And that was easier than this man's endless prodding.

Henry downed another swallow, unbothered. "That's all right. I like a challenge."

He leaned back, shoulders broad against the lantern glow. "Been here two years. Roads are quiet now, but I've had my share of skirmishes. Bandits mostly." He smirked, as if proud of the memory.

"Steel's one thing, but most don't expect a Caster keeping watch in a backwater like this. Wind's quick, and faster than steel, if you know how to use it." He lifted his empty mug and with a quick flick of his wrist sent a lazy current across the rim. The foam shivered, sloshing against the sides.

My brows rose despite myself.

He grinned wider. "Not much glory in guarding sheep and farmers, like I said. But when the air moves at your call, people think twice before drawing steel. That's enough to keep the roads safe."

I set my own mug down carefully. "Or to keep the tavern entertained."

He laughed. "That too."

His hand lingered on my forearm, warm and heavy. I started to move away, but before I could, a faint stir brushed across my cheek.

Loose strands of my hair lifted off my face as though a gust had slipped through the square. Only the air was too focused, too deliberate, tugging against my temple and curling across my lips.

Henry grinned at my surprise. "See? Even the Wind thinks you shouldn't hide that face."

I caught the strands with my free hand and shoved them back, jaw tight. "I don't need your Wind for that."

His grin only widened, smug and unbothered.

I smoothed the last of my hair back, my ale half finished at my elbow. The amount of bodies around us had grown thicker, laughter high and uneven as the fiddler's tune stumbled into something faster.

I stood, lifting my tankard in a small gesture, drank, and then set it down. "It's been a fun night, Henry. But I think I'll call it here."

His grin faltered, then returned as though pasted back in place. "Already? Don't tell me Asholt's too much for you."

I offered a polite smile. "Not too much. Just enough."

Before he could answer, I turned and slipped between the benches, weaving past a cluster of dancers and smoke from the spits. The square thinned toward the edge of the fountain, where only a few couples lingered with their drinks. The music dulled here, muffled by distance.

I'd reached the edge when boots scuffed behind me.

"Not even one more?" Henry's voice carried too easily. He caught up with the easy swagger of a man who thought no one ever told him no, hands loose at his sides, grin still plastered wide. "You don't strike me as the type to turn in early."

"I said it was a fun night," I answered, keeping my steps even. "I didn't say it had to last forever."

He lifted a hand, fingers twitching with casual precision. A quick breeze stirred, not the cold one off the valley, but tighter, bound to his will. It pressed against my legs, tugging at my shirt, pushing back against each step.

I stopped short, heat prickling my skin.

Henry tilted his head, his grin turning sly. "See? Even the Wind wants you to stay."

I shoved past the current with a breath, jaw tight. "Stop it."

"Easy," he said, chuckling. His fingers flexed again, tracing a lazy arc through the air. "Just a little bit of fun."

The air coiled at once, swirling faster as his hands moved. Strands of my hair snapped across my face. Fabric whipped against my arms, the circle of Wind tightening until I was forced to brace my stance.

Henry laughed, raising both hands now, palms wide as if pulling invisible strings. "Not bad, eh? Quicker than steel. Nobody walks away when the air's mine."

And then—

It stopped.

The swirl collapsed in an instant, the air falling still as though it had never moved. My hair dropped limp against my cheek, the square quiet except for the crackle of firepits.

Across from me, Henry staggered as though struck. A controlled gust slammed his chest and drove him back into a post, his breath leaving him in a grunt. He blinked, stunned, while the villagers nearby burst into laughter.

I turned, pulse hammering. Art stood a pace away, his hand just lowering from a precise motion. His jaw was set tighter than usual, eyes colder, the faintest edge of anger breaking through the calm he wore like armor.

"You mistake power for permission," he said, voice cold.

Henry had no reply.

Art didn't wait for one.

He turned and walked back into the dark edge of the square, the air still restless in his wake, leaving Henry looking at the ground, and me staring after him, the echo of his words playing in my mind.

I shoved through the thinning crowd, my boots striking harder against the stone than I meant, pulse pounding in my throat.

"Art!"

He didn't slow, his shoulders set, the lamplight catching in the edge of his hair as he strode for the darker fringe of the square.

I caught up with him, breath quick, my words cutting sharper than I'd intended. "I could've handled it."

He stopped then. His jaw was tight, eyes colder than I'd ever seen them. "By letting him shove you around?"

"I wasn't letting him," I snapped. "I was waiting for a chance."

His voice cut back. "Waiting isn't handling."

The heat rose in my face. "And what, you think you had to humiliate him for me? Make sure everyone saw you step in?"

His gaze flicked back to the square, then to me again, voice flat as steel. "Better they laugh at him than watch him press you further."

"You think I can't handle myself? I've lived through worse than some drunk soldier's hand on my arm. I don't need you stepping in every time someone looks my way."

For a moment, something flickered in his eyes—anger maybe, buried deep under the weight of restraint. "You're right," he said finally. "You don't need me."

He turned without waiting for an answer, his figure swallowed by shadows as he strode down the empty street, leaving me alone in the fading glow of the lanterns.

22

rtemis

A The stables smelled of hay and damp earth, the chill of morning still clinging to the air. A lantern guttered low, throwing a thin gold light on the plank walls. My breath fogged when I spoke to my horse, and his ears flicked, patient as ever.

I'd been there before first light, my horse already saddled, tack checked twice, then a third time. Leather creaked under my palm, oiled and familiar. I ran a cinch, tugged the breast strap, slid a finger under the girth, checked the bit ring and the stitching along the reins. I wiped a fleck of grit from the stirrup and did it all again. The motions kept my hands busy, even if my thoughts refused to still.

Her words from the night before hadn't left me. *I don't need you stepping in every time someone looks my way.*

They pressed like a blade against my ribs, sharp and unrelenting.

Maybe she was right. Maybe she didn't need me, not the way she thought. What future was there in leaning on someone like me? I'd lived too long on the road, carrying more scars than stories, leaving wreckage behind me whether I meant to or not. I'd seen what being close to me cost others. Even now, with her, every step I took seemed to draw danger closer.

And there was the other truth, the one I couldn't speak. If she knew what I was—*what I truly was*—would she still look at me the same way? Or would she see only the years between us, the burden I'd carried long before she was born? I could shoulder a hundred wounds without flinching, but not that. Not the moment she turned from me because she finally understood.

My hand drifted to the small weight beneath my sleeve.

The wolf's head charm rested warm against my palm when I drew it free. I turned it slowly between my fingers. The lantern light caught along the edges of the carving, the wolf's muzzle lifted as if scenting the wind.

Boots sounded on the packed dirt behind me.

I closed my hand around the charm and slipped it back beneath my shirt before I turned.

Celeste stepped into the aisle, her hood pushed back, the ruby at her throat catching in a stray shaft of light. She didn't look at me at first, just at the stall where her mare waited, stomping at the straw.

She moved with practiced efficiency, brushing down the mare, checking the cinch, but her motions were too quick, almost brusque. The brush snagged once in the mare's mane and she yanked harder than needed before smoothing it with a guilty pat. Her jaw stayed tight, lips pressed thin, shoulders rigid under her cloak. Even her steps were clipped, boots striking harder than the hushed quiet of the stables called for.

She kept her eyes on the leather and buckles, never on me. But the stiffness in her back, the way she pulled the reins a fraction too taut before loosening them again, said more than she intended.

A silence hung heavy between us, thicker than the scent of hay.

"You meant what you said?" Her voice cut through the quiet.

I tightened the last strap on my horse before I answered. The words I should have said came to mind easily enough.

Yet none of them made it past my teeth. "I meant enough."

She paused, one hand on the reins. "Then why are you still here?"

A hundred answers crowded my mind, all of them wrong. I'd tried to leave before dawn, but every step away twisted into something I couldn't stomach. That I knew where she was heading—toward walls and chains she couldn't tear down alone.

Because I knew what walls did to a person.

The thought of her falling back into the hands of men who would break her, cage her, strip the light from her again was more than I could bear. I'd worn chains once—different irons, but the same slow erosion of self. I remembered how long it took to learn how to breathe again after escaping them. How surviving alone left marks I would never forget.

But it wasn't just the fortress. It was me. The life I'd carved alone on the road, the scars I carried that never stopped taking from those near me. I could bear her anger, but I couldn't bear the look she might give if she knew the truth and decided she wanted no part of it.

For a second, I almost told her anyway. That I couldn't leave because the thought of her chained again would destroy me.

But I didn't say it.

"The roads don't care what we meant," I said instead, flat. "It only keeps going."

Her eyes narrowed, searching mine, but I gave her nothing more. She swung onto her saddle without another word. I mounted my horse, the silence between us heavy and uncomfortable, and together we rode out of Asholt with the morning mist curling low across the fields.

The road stretched long and narrow through the fields, wagon ruts filling with water from the night before, mud clinging to the hooves of our horses. The mist burned away slow, giving way to a gray sky heavy with clouds.

She didn't look at me, and I didn't look at her. Every word from last night stood between us like a wall neither of us would climb.

By midday the air turned. A cold wind swept low across the fields, carrying the smell of rain before the first drop even struck. The sky darkened in slow degrees, heavy clouds sagging low, and the horses grew restless under the pressure.

The rain started in scattered drops, soft at first, soaking into the ruts and grass. Then the storm broke all at once, a hammering downpour that slicked the road into mud and sent rivulets coursing off the fields. Water ran from the horses' manes, plastered their ears flat, and streamed down our cloaks in cold sheets.

Celeste hunched in her saddle.

I kept my eyes ahead, hands tight on the reins. I almost let her fight the rain alone.

Almost.

She'd made her stance clear enough last night, and pride cut both ways. But the sight of her cloak sodden, hair plastered to her face—something in me twisted. For a brief moment, I saw her not on the road but in a cell again, water dripping from stone, her breath shuddering in the dark.

The thought gutted me.

With a breath, I nudged my horse closer, lifted my hand once, then let it fall again. The air bent to me, the rain curving as though it struck glass. A thin barrier shimmered around us both, dulling the storm to a muted hiss.

Her head whipped round. "How are you doing that? You're not even ..." She lifted her hands slightly. "You're not holding your hands to keep Casting."

"Not holding it, no," I said. "At least, not with my arms."

Her brow furrowed. "So you can just … make it happen? Without channeling it down your arms? What about the lessons?"

"It isn't that simple." The barrier flexed under another hard gust, the water breaking and sliding off its curve. "Most Casters can refine their control to a point. A skilled Wind Caster might blow across his lips and stir a breeze without lifting a hand. But the strength won't match what he could summon through his arms."

She studied me, her voice low under the patter of rain. "But you could make it stronger than that."

I kept my eyes on the road. "Stronger, yes. My core runs deeper than most. But even mine has its limits. A windstorm poured from my hands will always outmatch a gust from my lungs."

The silence stretched again. The rain hammered against the barrier before it ever touched us.

"So … how are you keeping it in place?" she asked, studying the faint shimmer overhead. "You've held it this whole time. Where are you channeling it, if not through your arms?"

Curiosity edged into her voice, the guarded tension easing into the familiar cadence.

I breathed slow, feeling the current flow through me, steady as the rain. Teaching was simpler than untangling what lay between us. "You're thinking of Casting as if it starts in the hands," I said. "That's where most stop, because that's all they're taught. But the flow begins deeper. Each element moves differently through the body, and the body shapes where it goes."

She frowned. "So the flow changes depending on the element?"

I guided my horse around a rut, the barrier flexing to follow. "Fire pushes. Heat and pressure has to be vented, so Casters drive it down their arms and out through their hands. Wind's the same. Projection. That's why most settle into that path, because it's the cleanest outlet."

She chewed her lip. "But Water's not the same."

"Water isn't just energy. It's weight. Shape. A Water Caster can turn their energy into liquid just like a Fire Caster burns theirs into flame. The difference is what happens after. Fire burns through the energy that makes it, spending everything at once and leaving nothing behind to carry. Once it's made, Water has to be borne, held, and driven—and most Casters lack the strength to do all three."

I guided my horse around the rain-slicked ruts. "That's why most of them rely on rivers or lakes. They aren't spending their strength to create the Water, they're simply guiding what's already there. Starting Water from nothing costs far more than steering what's already in motion."

"But you made it without a source. You had to create it yourself and still held it together long enough to freeze it solid."

I felt her eyes on me, but I kept mine on the road.

"Not nothing. There's always moisture in the air, in the ground. I gathered what was there—but that alone wouldn't hold."

I let out a breath. "The rest I forced into shape with my own Casting. Think of it like a net. You tie together what's already there, strand by strand, but there are gaps. I wove those spaces shut with my own energy, turning it into Water."

I shook my head. "It's hard to explain. Closest I can come is this: I followed flame's path, the way a Fire Caster pushes outward, but I just replaced it with Water instead. Even then, it only works if your core can bear the strain."

She stayed silent for a long moment, the rain sliding down the barrier around us. A faint smile tugged at the corner of her mouth. "So the rules are more like suggestions for you."

I didn't answer, just let a faint breath of amusement slip past.

"I understand the channeling. But you still haven't told me how you keep it steady."

"Wind gives it shape," I answered. "It bends the drops outward, pushes them aside before they touch. But Wind alone leaks. So I weave Water through it. Thin enough to catch what slips through, to close the gaps."

"So it's two elements, working together."

"Both," I nodded. "One without the other would falter. Together they hold."

She was quiet for a moment, watching the barrier as the rain hissed against it, sliding harmlessly to the ground. "Most Casters couldn't manage this."

I let out a slow breath, some of the weight easing from my shoulders. "You're right."

Her eyes flicked toward me, cautious but curious. "Could I? If I learned Water and Wind Casting, I mean."

I glanced at her, then back to the road. "Maybe. But it takes refinement and control so fine, you can feel where the element frays and stitches back together before it unravels. Most never reach that point."

She leaned back a little in her saddle, though I saw the spark in her expression. "But you think I could."

I didn't answer right away. The rain continued to fall, constant and patient. "I think you could," I said finally.

The road stretched on, mud slick beneath the horses. For once, the silence of the morning didn't feel strained.

Celeste shifted again, and I knew that meant another question was coming. "If it takes years for more elements to awaken, and from the training and the strain, how long did it take you to master each of them? How many years between Water and Wind?"

I glanced at her, the corner of my mouth tightening. "Wind came first."

Her brows lifted. "Oh. I thought—" She broke off, shaking her head. "Wind first, then. Still ... how long between them?"

I gripped my reins a little tighter.

The number caught like a rock in my throat. Long enough for her childhood to pass.

But what would she see in me if she knew the truth?

"It's not when you start that matters," I said instead. "It's how much you refine it."

Her mouth pressed into a thin line. "That's not an answer."

I kept my gaze forward.

She let out a loud breath. "You always do this. Every time I ask something real about you, you dodge it or twist it into some neat little lesson. And maybe that's fair." Her grip tightened on her reins, the leather creaking under her fingers. "I don't really know you. Not well enough. And I understand that."

Her frustration bled into something softer. "I just thought..." She shook her head, rain glinting off her hair. "I thought by now you'd trust me with more than riddles."

The moment stretched, heavy with the hiss of rain.

When she spoke again, her voice was quieter still. "Maybe I rushed things. It all happened so suddenly, and maybe I read the wrong signals. I can live with being wrong about that."

Her eyes flicked toward me, holding mine despite the wavering in her tone. "But you're the one who told me there couldn't be half-truths between us. That this only works if we're honest. So at least be honest with me now."

I kept my eyes on the road. I'd fought Casters stronger than me, survived chains and fire and blades. None of it felt as dangerous as this.

"Don't twist my words," I said at last. "When I told you there couldn't be half-truths between us, it wasn't a bargain. It wasn't me asking you to lay me bare. You think this short stretch between us is enough to undo a lifetime of silence? Well, it isn't. Trust doesn't mean trading scars, Celeste. It means I keep mine buried so you don't have to carry them."

"That was for you," I went on, quieter. "For your training. For your Casting. I can't teach you if you're hiding pieces of yourself, not when Ardor runs through you the way it does. I needed your honesty to keep you alive. But my secrets—" I let out a breath. "My secrets don't change what you have to learn."

I drew in a short breath, the words dragging out of me. "So don't mistake me. I'll give you every truth you need to survive, but not every truth I carry. Some things stay mine."

The barrier held, the rain bending off its curve in silver sheets, and the horses pressed on through the muck. For now, that was enough. Keep moving. Keep the storm at bay. That was all I could give her.

But the tension between us was heavier than the storm itself, pressing down until every breath felt weighted. She didn't speak again, and I didn't risk a glance her way. If I looked, if I gave her even a step more, I might unravel what little I'd managed to hold back.

I kept my eyes forward, fixed on the road vanishing into the downpour. Secrets had kept me alive this long. They would keep her alive, too, whether she hated me for them or not. Yet the thought sat heavy in my chest, a pressure I couldn't shake—if that secret ever burst its banks, it would sweep everything away.

23

C*eleste*

The rain kept falling, but I hardly noticed it anymore.

Art's words stayed with me as we rode. The way he'd drawn his lines so cleanly—secrets, scars, silence. As if burying them was some quiet kindness he was offering me.

"You've taught me a lot," I said at last, my voice level beneath the rain. "And you've saved me more than once. I'm grateful for that. But I didn't start surviving when you found me."

My hands tightened on the reins.

"I didn't lay those things bare because it was easy," I continued. "I did it because I need this to end. Because I need to stop running from it. You don't owe me your past. I can respect that you want it buried. But you need to respect how hard it was to unearth mine."

He didn't answer right away.

The sound of hooves filled the space between us. And for a long moment, that was all there was.

"You're right," he said finally. "You kept yourself alive. I didn't give you that. And I don't dismiss what it meant to say those things."

He let out a slow breath. "I'm not asking you to carry my silence. I'm only asking you to let me carry it myself."

For the first time since last night, the space between us didn't feel like distance. It felt like something we'd chosen to carry together.

We rode on without speaking. The horses pushed through the mud, hooves squelching in the ruts, the road stretching beneath the low gray sky.

A gust rattled the shimmer overhead, harder than before. Art's voice broke through. "This storm's not easing. We'll need shelter soon."

I nodded. My mare slogged through the mud, her ears flicking with every rumble of thunder.

The road narrowed between dripping trees. The downpour intensified, hammering the barrier until it groaned like cracking glass. My cloak clung cold to my shoulders, even with Art's Casting holding the worst of it back.

By the time the hills started rising around us, my thighs ached from the saddle and the air tasted of wet stone. I kept my eyes on the blur of gray and green until Art slowed, lifting a hand.

"There," he said.

At first, I saw nothing but another swell of earth. Then the line of it broke, shadow carving a dark mouth into the hillside. Not a cave but a hollow where time had eroded the stone. Rain streamed across its lip, dripping down in narrow rivulets, but the interior yawned with the promise of dry respite.

We urged the horses forward. The ground sloped beneath us, slick stone under their hooves, but the hollow was wide enough to fit us all. Roots dangled from the ceiling, the air cool and damp, carrying the smell of moss and wet stone. The sound of the storm dulled, fading into a muffled hiss.

It wasn't much—a wound in the hill's side—but it was shelter.

And for now, it was enough.

The horses shifted in the hollow, steam curling faint from their coats in the damp chill. Art tethered them close to the wall where the rock cut deepest, then turned his focus to the ground. With practiced motions, he gathered the driest brush tucked under the overhang and piled it into kindling.

I leaned against the wall, arms folded, watching. "You really think you're going to start a fire in this?"

He didn't answer right away. A flick of his fingers, a whisper of heat, and the brush caught in a low crackle. Orange light flicking against the stone. His expression didn't change, but the faintest glint in his eyes gave him away.

"Is that fire, or just your ego?" I muttered, though the warmth was welcomed.

The storm outside drummed harder, a relentless percussion against the earth. Water streamed at the cave mouth, rivulets running together into shallow pools that sunk into the ground. Art crouched by the fire a moment longer, feeding it until the glow steadied, then sat back against the wall with a slow exhale.

"This storm won't break quickly. We stay here, ride it out." His gaze turned toward me. "Better use the time for something useful."

I narrowed my eyes. "Useful?"

"Practice," he said simply. "Reach for Enervation. Learn to feel your core before the next fight drives you there."

A short laugh slipped out of me, sharp and incredulous. "So that's what this is. Your way of getting me to shut up."

The corner of his mouth twitched as though he was fighting down a smile. "And miss all your charming commentary?"

I rolled my eyes and let out a scoff. "Wonderful. Collapse on command. That's exactly how I wanted to spend the afternoon."

"You know this is for your own good. Every push makes your stronger. You'll eventually get used to it … Kind of."

My glare held, though I pressed my lips together, refusing to give him the satisfaction of a smile. I sighed, dragging my hands down my face before settling back against the stone. "Fine. But if I wake up with a headache, you're getting one too."

"You've been giving me headaches since this journey began," he said lightly, but there was something restrained beneath it.

I shot him a look, but he'd already turned back to the fire as if the words slipped out without weight.

"All right," I muttered, settling cross-legged. "Let's get this over with before I change my mind."

Art leaned back against the stone, one knee drawn up, eyes focused on me. "Same as always. Don't burn it all in one burst. Control first, power second. Let it drain slow until you break."

I rolled my eyes again but lifted my hands anyway, light sparking faintly in my palms. "You know, most people would just say 'good luck' before asking someone to pass out in front of them."

"Most people don't survive it either."

That shut me up. I focused, pulling the light into a finer point, brighter, then releasing it in flickers. The pulses were small at first, then grew larger. Small sparks, then wider flares.

Time blurred. My arms trembled with the constant shaping. The fire crackled steadily, the storm outside rising and falling in waves against the stone.

"Again," Art said. His voice stayed calm, patient, even as sweat dampened my hair and trickled down my temple. "Control the size, not the strength."

Time lost its edges. My shoulders ached, every muscle taut from holding steady. The light sputtered sometimes, too strong or too weak, but his voice kept pressing me forward. Each correction pulled another thread of strength from my chest.

By the time my core neared empty, my breaths came shallow, every flare of light a strain. The world narrowed to the faint shimmer in my hands and the rasp of his voice.

"Almost there," he said quietly. "Don't fight it. Let it drain. I'll catch you."

The glow guttered out. My arms dropped uselessly, chest hollow, my body swaying as darkness closed in.

Strong hands caught me before I hit the stone, lowering me gently against the wall. His voice followed, low and certain in my ear.

"Easy. I've got you."

The warmth of the fire blurred, and the dark closed in.

When I stirred again, the fire was a bed of glowing coals and the storm outside a gentle patter.

My head felt thick, every limb heavy, as if I'd slept for days. The stone at my back was cold, though a blanket covered my shoulders. I shifted, blinking against the dim light.

Across from me, Art sat with his back against the wall, the firelight catching on the edges of his profile. His sword was set aside this time, replaced with a small leather-bound book balanced on his knee. Charcoal darkened his fingertips. He didn't look up right away, his hand moving quickly as he worked.

"You're awake," he said at last, his voice quiet enough not to press against my headache.

I swallowed as I sat up. "How long?"

"Long enough." He shut the book and set the charcoal aside. "The storm's passed. We'll move when you can stay in the saddle."

I rubbed my temples and groaned. "You were very clear about the risks. You just forgot to mention how miserable it makes you feel afterward."

His mouth twitched. "You've done it plenty times by now. What's a few hundred more?"

"Wonderful," I muttered, dropping my hands in my lap. "So the rest of my life is just headaches and dirt naps. Truly inspiring."

The fire snapped softly, the storm outside now little more than a drip from the overhang. I let my head tip back against the stone as I closed my eyes, the ache still buzzing in my temples but fading, slow and stubborn. My body felt wrung out, but warmed by the flames.

Art hadn't moved much, only stoked the fire once. When I finally cracked an eye, he was leaning against the wall again, his sword within arm's reach, the notebook once again balanced across his knee. His hand moved smoothly over the pages, like he'd forgotten I was even there.

I watched him for a beat, curiosity pushing through the haze of exhaustion. That book was never far from his hands. Every time he thought I wasn't paying attention, he'd be scratching away in it.

Finally, I broke the silence, my voice scratchy. "You're always scribbling in that thing. You write more than you talk," I muttered dryly.

This time he let out a breath that was almost a laugh.

Curiosity finally got the better of me. I pushed myself up and padded over, brushing the dirt from my palms. "Fine then, if you won't talk, I'll see for myself."

He made no move to stop me as I leaned closer. He tilted the notebook and flipped through the pages—dozens of them, filled with beautiful, intricate lines. Stags in mid-leap, birds with their wings fanned wide, the curve of a riverbank traced with delicate care. Every line was precise, detailed, almost alive.

I blinked. "Saints ... These are beautiful. You've been carrying this around all this time and said nothing?"

He shrugged. "They're just drawings."

"Just drawings?" I traced a finger above the air over one of the pages, afraid to smudge the charcoal. "These are better than most tapestries I've seen. You could sell these and never have to swing that sword of yours again."

A faint huff escaped him, but his thumb stayed pressed firm against the edge of the page, hiding the one beneath.

My eyes narrowed. "And what's this one you're guarding like a secret?" I asked lightly.

He didn't answer.

I reached, quicker than he expected, and flipped the page before he could stop me.

My breath caught.

It was ... me.

Sleeping, head tilted against the stone, hair spilled loose around my shoulders. Every line was soft, carefully shaded with patience.

I froze, staring at it, my pulse a loud drum in my ears.

He'd drawn me. Not just a sketch, not the rough outlines he gave a tree or a ride of hills, but me as I was a little while ago.

Warmth crept up the back of my neck.

It stirred something in me. He had a way of staying close without ever claiming the space, of making the storm feel smaller just by being there.

And now this. A sketch tender enough to feel like a confession—one he'd never call by that name.

It was maddening. Flattering and infuriating all at once.

"You drew me beautifully," I said, uneasy. "I wish I felt that way."

Art stayed silent.

He took the book from my hands carefully, as if the page might bruise if he closed it too fast. His thumb lingered at the edge of the paper, charcoal-smudged and still.

The fire popped softly behind me.

"I started drawing so I wouldn't forget things that mattered," he said, finally.

I waited, my chest tightening.

"I was young. Before the road and before I became what I am. I drew anything that held still long enough. Trees. Homes. The way light sat on stone at certain hours. It wasn't serious. Just ... something I was good at."

His gaze moved to the fire. "Later, it became useful. I drew faces for coin. Missing children. Criminals. People someone wanted tracked down. You don't forget the faces once you've drawn them. Even when you wish you could."

The thought came unbidden: In another life, it might have been my face he was asked to draw.

"Then I'm glad you drew me. I just hope I'm not a face you wish you could forget."

He thumbed the edge of my image once before he closed the book. His eyes met mine at last. "You won't be."

24

A*rtemis*

The rain followed us for days.

A persistent, needling rain that soaked through wool and leather and patience alike. It came in waves—sometimes in mist that clung to the air, other times as freezing downpours that forced us to find shelter.

We lost a full day in a roadside inn when the clouds broke open without warning. Another night beneath the barn's sagging overhang with three other travelers and their nervous horses.

There were moments where I could have taken the rain off us. But I didn't. There were too many eyes on the road now.

Merchants and caravans were heading south, wagons heavy with winter stores. Farmhands drifted in the same direction, relocating for the season—tanneries, repair crews, whatever temporary work they could find. The more traffic we passed, the less freedom I had to Cast without inviting questions I didn't want asked.

So we rode damp more often than dry.

By the third morning, the storm finally bled itself out. The sky cleared at midday, sunlight spilling across the road in pale gold. The air still carried a cool edge, but it felt clean. Washed.

I let my horse slow to an easy pace.

The tension between us had smoothed somewhere along the road. The brittle edges from that night had worn down under shared leagues and genuine laughs.

Celeste rode a few paces ahead, the sun catching in her hair where it slipped free from her braid. She glanced back at me over her shoulder, squinting against the light. "You know, a little less rain would've been appreciated."

"I'm aware," I replied.

"And yet."

"There were too many eyes."

She gave an exaggerated sigh. "Such a shame. All that power. Used for … restraint."

"I prefer to think of it as wisdom."

She shook her head. "Tragic. A legend on the road, undone by caution." She looked skyward in exaggerated thought. "I'll be sure to sing songs about you."

I let the faintest smile show.

My eye then caught something moving ahead of us.

Three men stood near the bend where the road dipped shallow toward a wall of ash trees. One of them waved both arms overhead.

Celeste followed my gaze. "Trouble?"

"Possibly."

As we drew closer, the scene resolved.

A cart stood crooked off the side of the road. One wheel lay several yards away in the grass. Two draft horses were hitched to a tree a few paces away, ears flicking at flies.

A boy—no more than eleven—hovered near the rear of the cart, hands blackened with soot. He straightened when he saw us.

The man waving lowered his arm as we approached. Broad shouldered, with thick wrists and hammer-callused hands. His beard was shot through with iron-gray hairs.

The cart's rear was stacked careful with crates and wrapped bundles. Even from horseback I could pick the tools: two hammers secured with leather ties, tongs with varying jaws, a wrapped anvil horn peeking out from beneath oilcloth.

A blacksmith.

I brought my horse to stop a cautious distance away.

"What's the trouble?" I asked.

The older man inclined his head. "Our axle collar split. Wheel came loose a ways back. We caught it before it sheared entirely." He wiped his hands on his apron. "I've the tools to mend it. Just not the forge."

His gaze shifted toward the cart's sagging corner.

"She's too heavy to lift alone. If I could ask for your assistance in helping my lads raise the bed high enough, my boy can seat the wheel back on the axle."

I followed his look.

The rear corner of the cart leaned low, the naked axle jutting out at an awkward angle, smeared with mud and old grease. The iron collar around it cracked through the center.

Celeste's gaze moved from the axle to the boy.

He had already rolled the wheel closer, grunting under its weight. It was taller than his hip and rimmed in iron, the spokes caked with road grime. He kept glancing toward his father as if waiting for instruction.

The blacksmith cleared his throat as he looked from me to the back of the cart.

"I should've unloaded her before we tried," he admitted. "That's on me. But at this angle ..." He gestured to the sunken wheel well. "Those crates are heavy. If we start pulling them off now, we'll shift the weight and possibly put pressure where it shouldn't be. Might even split the axle clean through."

He walked to the sagging corner and pressed his boot against the beam. The cart gave a soft groan in response. "She's bearing wrong. All the strain's sitting here. I'd hate to do much more than this." He looked at me again. "If you'd be willing, we could lift her as she stands. Just enough to take the weight off the axle. My boy's quick with his hands. He can guide the wheel back onto the spindle before we lower it."

The boy straightened, as if he'd been waiting for the chance to prove it.

I studied the beam a moment longer.

I gave a single nod. "All right."

Relief passed over across the blacksmith's face.

Celeste was already moving, guiding her horse to the tree where the others were posted.

We tied the horses to the ash tree beside theirs, the animals shifting and snorting as we secured the reins. Then we stepped toward the sagging corner of the cart.

I positioned myself near the rear beam, and the two other men moved into place opposite me. The blacksmith took the heaviest corner without comment. Celeste stepped beside one of the other men, setting her hands beneath the wood.

The boy rolled the wheel closer, bracing it upright against his thigh.

"On my mark," the blacksmith said.

We bent.

"Now."

The cart groaned as we lifted, wood fibers straining under the sudden shift. Mud sucked at my boots as I drove upwards, shoulders pulling against the load.

The boy darted forward, rolling the wheel onto the exposed spindle. He crouched low, guiding the hub with quick hands.

"Almost there," the blacksmith groaned through gritted teeth.

The wheel slid home with a dull, solid *thunk*.

"Got it!" the boy called.

We eased the cart down carefully. The wood shook with a tired creak, the weight redistributing through the axle once more.

I stepped back, rolling my shoulders.

The blacksmith let out a breath. "You've my thanks."

Celeste brushed dirt from her palms and glanced at the wheel, her brow furrowing. "Will it hold like that?"

The blacksmith's mouth tightened. "For a short stretch, perhaps," he admitted. "But not far. The collar's split through. Even seated, the hub won't stay true under load."

He crouched near the axle and tapped the cracked iron ring with his knuckle.

"Bit of irony in it. I've iron stock in the crates. The tools to shape it. Could forge a new collar before supper." He gave a faint, rueful smile. "Just haven't the forge. Or the fire to bring the iron to heat."

The boy shifted awkwardly at that. "I'm sorry, Da," he muttered. "If I could hold it hotter—"

The blacksmith shook his head. "None of that," he said gently. "I've spent my life shaping iron with coal and sweat. You've been given something special. I only wish I knew how to guide that part for you."

Celeste tilted her head. "You're a Fire Caster?"

The boy nodded, a little self-conscious now. "A small one."

"Small is still something," Celeste said warmly.

The blacksmith gave her an appreciative look. "He's learning. Just not strong enough yet to heat iron through. Not without burning himself empty before it reaches a working glow."

He straightened slowly, wiping his hands again out of habit more than need. "I've poor manners. Apologies for not introducing myself proper. Name's Ulf." He nodded toward the boy. "This is my son, Alvis."

The two men who helped lift the cart stepped forward. "Erwin," said the broader one of the pair.

"Humbert," added the other with an incline of his head.

Ulf gestured between them. "Hired blades. Road's been rougher of late. We're bound for Mutebrook."

I lifted my gaze a fraction.

"The Firewright Guild," Ulf clarified. "They keep proper Caster forges. Stone-lined hearths, stronger bellows, reinforced vents. Places built for those who can heat iron with their hands."

He placed his hand on Alvis's shoulder. "I taught the boy my trade since he could hold a hammer. But he awakened this year." There was pride in his words. "And I'm no Fire Caster."

Alvis looked somewhere between embarrassed and pleased.

"A smith who can Cast properly ... He'll go farther than I. Shape steel cleaner. Work faster. Craft pieces in a few days that would take me a week to finish." He glanced toward the stacked crates. "That's why the cart's so heavy. Tools of mine. Some iron stock. Blacksmith guilds expect their apprentices to arrive with more than empty hands."

Celeste's gaze drifted to me. One brow lifted just slightly.

I rolled my eyes.

Her mouth curved in a knowing smile.

I looked back to Ulf. "I can Cast Fire. If that would make the difference."

Alvis's head snapped up.

Ulf's expression changed—hope flashing there so quick it almost looked painful.

"You'd be willing?" he asked carefully.

"I won't promise a guild forge. But I can bring iron to heat," I replied.

Ulf exhaled slowly. "Then you'd have my gratitude twice over."

Celeste folded her arms, watching me with open amusement now.

I ignored her.

Ulf hesitated a moment longer.

"I should warn you," he said carefully, "it won't be quick. I'll need to dig the pit, shape a stone hearth. Craft a proper bellow if I'm to keep the heat steady." He glanced at the road, then back to us. "A few hours at least."

"We're not pressed," I said.

Celeste gave a small shrug. "We've ridden worse delays."

Ulf studied us once more, as if wondering whether we might change our minds. Then he nodded. "My thanks."

He chose a patch of bare ground well away from the cart and the trees—smart enough not to risk catching root or branch should the heat flare wild. Erwin and Humbert fetched shovels from the cart while Alvis carried tools with careful reverence. Within minutes they were cutting into the earth.

I watched from the shade of an ash tree as they worked.

They dug a shallow bowl into the ground, lining it with flat stones pulled from the ditch. Ulf directed his son with precision, correcting hand placements, angles, the spacing of the stones.

Long after, Ulf laid a leather out across a crate lid, cutting and stitching with swift, competent movements. Slowly, I could see the bellow taking shape.

Celeste had drifted a short distance away, her blade in hand. She moved through her stances, feet setting, shoulders turning, edge aligning. The sun caught the steel each time she pivoted and swung.

She had grown steadier, less frantic in her footwork.

Erwin and Humbert eventually left the pit and wandered toward me, wiping soil from their palms.

"She been training with a blade long?" Humbert asked, nodding toward Celeste.

"Long enough," I said.

Erwin watched her complete a turn, blade snapping into guard with crisp motion. "Moves clean," he said.

"She trains daily," I replied.

Erwin's mouth curved. There was a restless energy in him now. He stepped away from us before I could comment. "Miss!" he called to Celeste. "You care to test that edge?"

She lowered the blade and looked toward him.

"I've wooden practice swords in the cart," he added. "Been drilling the boy on the road. Wouldn't mind seeing how you fare."

Humbert sighed beside me. "Forgive him. Erwin's blood runs hot."

I watched Celeste.

She smiled. "All right."

Erwin returned moments later with two wooden blades, tossing one to her. She caught it clean, adjusting her grip with easy familiarity.

They circled.

The first exchanges were quick—wood striking wood in a sharp crack that echoed off the roadside stones. Erwin came in fast, forcing her back. He clipped her shoulder, then scored her thigh before she slipped a strike past his guard.

She adapted to his pace quickly. Better than she'd been able to months ago. Her timing had improved. She no longer overcommitted when baited.

Erwin drove in with another flurry meant to overwhelm.

She slipped under it, tapped his ribs cleanly, and reset.

Humbert let out a low whistle. "She's quick."

"That's what she keeps telling me," I said.

If this had been steel instead of wood, it would already be over. And if she had been free to Cast, it would not have lasted long enough to call it a fight.

But it wasn't, it was wood. And she was holding her own, reading him better as they continued to exchange blows.

Erwin pushed harder, relying on strength and forward momentum. Celeste adjusted without panic, letting his weight work against him. She pivoted, leading him on, no longer chasing openings that weren't truly there.

He lunged.

She slipped aside and caught his wrist with the flat of her blade before tapping his shoulder in the same motion.

A point, if they were counting.

Humbert gave a low chuckle.

Just like with her Casting, she had learned faster than I expected.

They traded again, harder now.

She clipped his shoulder. He caught her thigh on the return.

Erwin scored once across her forearm. She answered with a strike to his hip that would certainly leave a bruise.

They went on like that for several minutes—each finding openings in the other's guard, each refusing to yield the edge for long.

When they finally stepped apart for breath, both bore the marks for it. Faint welts rose along exposed skin. Sweat darkened Erwin's collar. A strand of Celeste's hair clung to her cheek, her chest rising and falling with each breath.

She would wait until we were back on the road before Healing those.

Erwin grinned, wiping his mouth with the back of his hand. "You've got teeth."

Celeste smiled back. "So do you."

Beside me, Humbert shook his head. "He'll be sore tomorrow."

"So will she," I said.

Ulf came from the direction of the forge pit, brushing dirt from his palms. "It's ready."

I walked with him without looking at Celeste again.

Alvis stood near the shallow stone-lined bowl they had shaped into the earth. The crude bellows lay fitted with a narrow wooden pipe angled into the pit's base. Charcoal had been stacked with care, larger piece at the center, smaller ones layered tight around them.

Effort had gone into this.

Ulf held the cracked collar in his hands. "New one will take time. But better that than trusting a split."

He crouched and placed the broken ring beside the pit.

"I've iron stock cut to width already. Was meant for shoe bands." He glanced up at me. "We'll need it hot enough to bend clean. Hotter than common coal can manage alone."

Alvis stood straighter when I stepped closer. His eyes tracked my every movement.

I knelt at the edge of the pit.

The charcoal smelled dry and earthy. The ground was still damp beneath it from recent rain. I pressed my palm directly on the stacked coals, feeling the empty space where heat would soon gather.

"How steady can you hold a bellows?" I asked the boy.

"As steady as you need, sir," he answered.

Ulf gave him a small nod of encouragement, then inclined his head toward me. "Whenever you're ready."

I crouched at the edge of the pit and extended my hand toward the charcoal once more. The first flicker caught deep beneath the surface.

Ember-red flame spread through the bed, then brightened. Heat rolled upward in short waves as I fed it, keeping it concentrated in one area.

Alvis worked the bellows carefully, sending air into the base of the pit. The flames deepened, dull orange color brightening.

I fed it slowly.

Ulf held the strip of iron with tongs while the fire climbed around it, the metal dark at first, then dull red.

Alvis edged closer.

"Watch the color," Ulf told him.

The boy nodded.

Ulf turned toward me. "Hold it there."

So I did.

The iron deepened to cherry red, then flared brighter.

"Now."

Ulf drew it from the forge and laid it across the horn of the anvil, raising his hammer.

I held the heat steady between rounds, feeding the fire each time he returned the iron to it. The ring began to take shape between blows. Ulf worked with the ease of long practice, each strike hitting exactly where it needed to land.

As time passed, Celeste drifted over at some point. I felt her presence there without looking.

By the time the collar was rounded true and fitted to the axle, sweat glistened on Ulf's forehead, and ash clung to my sleeves. The sun had slipped low, the sky softening to violet and gold as the last adjustments were made.

Ulf stepped back, studying the fit. "That'll carry him to Mutebrook."

Alvis looked from the axle to me, barely containing his excitement.

Ulf exhaled and looked my way. "We'll not test it in the dark. Share our fire tonight. You've earned at least that much."

We accepted.

They drew the cart closer to the trees, and watered and brushed down the horses. Ulf insisted on contributing what they could spare—salted beef, hard cheese, a heel of dark bread wrapped in cloth. Celeste added dried apples from our own stores without comment.

Erwin rebuilt the pit fire into something meant for comfort rather than iron. The flames rose easier now, less demanding. Humbert produced a small flask from somewhere inside his coat and passed it around without ceremony.

Stories followed.

Road stories, mostly. Broken axles and frozen rivers. Bandits who thought better of their odds. A guild master who could hear a flaw in steel before the hammer ever touched it. Ulf spoke of his own journey to the blacksmith's guild—one not meant for Casters, where steel was worked by hand alone—when he himself was a boy. How as a young man, he had walked to the nearest town with nothing but wrapped tools and letter of introduction his father had bartered for.

Alvis listened like a boy standing at the threshold of his future.

Celeste sat close enough that her shoulder brushed my knee when she moved. She laughed at something Erwin said and the sound carried clean through the trees.

At some point the circle loosened. Humbert drifted off to check the horses. Erwin began carving at a scrap of wood with idle focus. Ulf and Alvis spoke over the newly set collar again, discussing adjustments they might make once they reached a proper forge.

Celeste leaned back on her palms beside me, gaze lifted toward the open sky. She then lowered herself until her head rested against my thigh. Her hair spilled across my leg, warm from the fire.

I let my hand rest against her hair. My fingers brushed along the crown of her head, slow and absent, as if the motion required no thought at all.

She didn't move away.

Across the fire, Ulf glanced up once. A small smile reached his lips before he turned back to Alvis, resuming his quiet lecture about grain in the steel.

The flames cracked softly. Somewhere beyond the trees, a night bird called.

Celeste's breathing evened out, not quite asleep, but close to it.

The road would call again in the morning. But for that stretch of night, there was only the warmth of the fire, the scent of ash and iron lingering in the air, and the gentle weight of her resting against me.

I watched the embers dim. And let it last a little longer.

25

We bid them farewell and return to the road the next morning. The road sloped upward, the mud clinging to our horses' hooves and pulling at every step.

To our right, a narrow track wound down into a shallow hollow where a cluster of homes leaned together, their thatch roofs sagging under the weight of the rain. Smoke curled stubbornly from a few chimneys, twisting into the gray sky. From here, the hamlet looked almost hidden, pressed low against the land as though it wanted no part of the wider world.

I noticed only the drip of water from my hood, the dull ache in my legs, and the tired rhythm of hooves pulling us forward.

Art's gaze cut toward the hamlet. He didn't say anything, but I knew the thought was the same as mine.

Quiet roads weren't always safe ones.

I straightened in my saddle, stretching the stiffness in my back. And then I heard it: the faint rhythm of something heavier than rain. A cadence, dull at first, like distant thunder.

Hooves and boots.

The sound became clearer as we neared the crest of the hill. My mare's ears flicked, head lifting as she caught it too.

Art slowed, one hand lifting in a quiet signal to halt.

And then they appeared.

Over the rise came the first glint of steel, dulled by the storm but unmistakable. A line of figures took shape against the gray sky, ranks tight, their banner heavy with water but still dragging behind them in stubborn color.

Soldiers.

Not just a handful. A patrol.

They marched with a slap of boots against the wet earth, spears lifted, mail and leather darkened by rain. They were far enough that I could make out their shapes but not their faces.

In another dozen paces, they'd see ours.

The hamlet huddled below the hill, its crooked lanes and sagging roofs too close, too exposed. There was nowhere to hide.

My pulse thudded hard against my throat.

There were twenty at least. Some mounted, others trudging in their wake, armor dull from the damp but no less heavy for it. Spears and blades caught what little light broke through the clouds.

And above them, snapping hard in the wet breeze, flew the banner of AurenVale—two jagged volcanoes side by side, both in eruption: one spilling fire, the other crowned in storm and lightning. Between them burned a lone star.

The mark of the Triarchy.

The banner that had taken my brother from me.

Art's shoulders tightened, though his hands never left his reins. He spared the hamlet one last glance, then leaned toward me. "Keep riding. Don't look away, don't fidget. Just move forward."

A knot formed in my stomach. "Will they stop us?"

"They might." His eyes never left the banner. "If they do, let me talk. If they press you, tell them we're husband and wife from Dunwade. That we're heading for Rodin to visit your sick father." The words came fast, as though spoken with a blade to his back.

"And you?" I asked.

"A blacksmith." His mouth twitched into a grim smile. "I've had a quick apprenticeship."

The patrol spread wider across the road as it neared, mud churning beneath boots, hooves striking hollow against the wet ground. They weren't charging, not yet, but the set of their ranks spoke of practiced order.

Of men who knew how to pen prey.

Art's voice slipped one last time across the narrow space between us. "Eyes down, Celeste. Breathe. Let me handle it."

The soldiers drew closer, close enough now that I could see their faces through dripping helms, rain streaming down the iron. Close enough that the banner snapped sharp overhead, flame and storm twisting against the gray sky.

And still we rode forward.

The soldiers closed the last of the distance, their officer at the front astride a great black warhorse, its shoulders rolling beneath dark, rain-slick hide. His helm bore a black plume, soaked through but still lifting faintly with each gust. His sharp voice cut through the wet air.

"Halt."

The word dropped like an axe.

Art reined in, slow. I followed, my mare tossing her head as if she felt the scrutiny of their eyes just as I did. The patrol fanned out, steel and mud hemming us on every side.

The officer fixed his gaze on Art. "Where are you bound?"

Art dipped his head, his voice slipping into the rough cadence of a tradesman, thick with the sound of hard years. "Rodin, Captain. Passing through, that's all. My wife's father's taken ill. We're on our way to see him before his time runs out. I've a forge waiting there as well. No business but our own."

The man's eyes narrowed, his horse stamping beneath him. Then his voice turned disdainful. "Captain is a title for soldiers. I am a Magister. Forget that distinction again, and you'll find out what separates us."

Heat pricked my skin. From where I sat, I wouldn't have been able to tell the difference—steel was steel, cloaks were cloaks. Their ranks might as well have been written in another tongue.

Art bowed his head once, as if conceding the point. "Magister, then. Forgive the mistake."

The Magister gave a thin smile, light drops running down his helm. "You'd do well to remember that. Titles matter. A Captain follows the chain. A Magister *is* the chain."

Art's jaw worked once. "With respect, we've no quarrel here. We're worn, and the road's long. Better we keep on and leave no burden for your men."

The Magister's tone hardened. "You'll turn aside. Now."

Rain hissed against the stillness. My hands tightened on the reins until my knuckles burned.

Art gave the briefest glance my way, then guided his horse toward the track. I swallowed as the patrol wheeled in behind us, closing the road until there was nowhere left to go but down.

We turned from the main road, horses pulling us toward the narrow track that sloped into the hamlet. Behind us, the soldiers fell in, their line pressing close enough that I could hear the creak of leather, the clatter of spear hafts. The banner snapped wet above them, flame and storm twisting.

Art didn't look at me, his gaze fixed on the path ahead, but his voice reached me all the same. "Samuel and Anna," he said, repeating the names we'd agreed to use.

The hamlet opened beneath us, crooked lanes and sagging thatch huddled low against the earth as though trying to hide. Smoke trickled weak from a handful of chimneys, and the damp smell of manure clung to the air.

The soldiers didn't wait. The moment the first boots hit the edge of the lane, voices rang out.

"Out! Everyone out of their homes!"

"Gather in the square!"

"Move, now!"

Doors creaked open, shutters banged back. Faces pale with fear blinked into the gray light. A boy clutched his mother's skirts; a farmer still held a hoe in his hands, knuckles white around the haft. The patrol spread through the lane with practiced ease, driving them forward with curt orders and harder looks.

And all the while, we kept moving with them, two strangers folded into the herd.

The order came crisp from behind us.

"Dismount."

Art swung down first, his movements calm, unhurried. I followed, my boots sinking into the muck as the reins slipped through my gloves. A soldier took the lead rope without a word, guiding our horses aside while the rest of the patrol funneled us forward.

The square was little more than a muddy open space where the hamlet's lanes bled together. Smoke from the few chimneys curled into the damp air, thin and pale, as if afraid to rise. One by one, the villagers shuffled out. Farmers in rough-spun tunics, wives with shawls pulled tight, children huddled close against their parents.

The soldiers moved among the houses with cold efficiency, kicking doors open, pulling shutters wide.

A voice called, "All clear," and a young teenage girl emerged from the last cottage. She stumbled as he shoved her, but a woman, presumably her mother, caught her, holding her close.

The Magister wheeled his horse into the square's center, plume dripping water down his helm. He surveyed the crowd in silence for a moment, letting the weight of his presence drag across us like a blade's edge.

Then his voice rose, firm and practiced. "AurenVale has need of its people. The realm bleeds at its borders, and only the strong can stem the tide. The Triarchy calls not just for good men and women, but for Casters most of all."

The words carried, striking hard in the damp stillness.

"Casters are worth more than any number of common soldiers. Step forward, and you will be paid well. Silver enough to keep your kin fed and your homes standing. Refuse, and we will take what strength we can find. Healthy men. Healthy women. Any who can serve. Whatever the realm requires."

His horse tossed its head beneath him, nostrils flaring, but his voice stayed firm, commanding. "AurenVale is generous. Do your duty, and you will be rewarded. Hide, and others will pay the price in your stead."

The villagers stood frozen, faces pale, eyes darting but never landing. A man coughed once, harsh and empty, but no one spoke. No one moved. Only the drizzle filled the space, pattering soft against helm and shawl alike.

The Magister let the quiet stretch, eyes sweeping the crowd. When no one stirred, his voice rang out again, his tone softening with false warmth. "Healers—if any are among you—your worth is beyond coin. Serve the Triarchy, and you will be rewarded as saviors of our people. Refuse, and your gifts will be wasted on hovels and fields while soldiers bleed for your safety."

His words came cold. But the villagers only stood tighter, their silence hanging heavy in the damp air.

At last, he leaned forward, voice lowering. "If fear binds your tongues, then hear this: AurenVale rewards more than just those who step forward. Tell us of another who bears the gift. Point the way, and silver will be yours. Hide them, and the punishment will be theirs ... and yours."

The silence that followed felt like a suffocating weight. Eyes darted, not at the soldiers, but at each other. Evaluating. Wondering.

The stillness broke with the shuffle of boots in mud.

An old man stepped forward, his back stooped, hair gone thin and gray. His wife's hand shot out to catch him, her voice cracking, "No, stay!" But he pulled free, trembling more from age than fear. The crowd parted around him as if the very air were brittle.

The Magister straightened in his saddle, eyes narrowing.

Not satisfaction, but something close. "Good," he said, the word clipped. "What is your gift, old one?"

The man lifted his chin, though his voice wavered. "Water. Always been Water."

A flicker of disinterest touched the Magisters face. He gestured curtly. "Show me."

The old man raised his hands, catching the rain on his palms. The drizzle bent to his will, gathering into a single trembling sphere. It swelled, growing to the size of a melon before it hovered, quivering, between his fingers. A thin rivulet slipped loose and spattered into the mud, but he held it long enough to prove the truth of it.

The Magister gave a single nod, as if the man's life had just been tallied and settled. "Brave," he said. He flicked his fingers, and one of the soldiers stepped forward. A small purse of coin was pressed into the wife's shaking hands.

Her eyes brimmed, lips trembling around a protest she couldn't voice. The Magister ignored her. His gauntleted hand closed firm on the old man's shoulder, steering him toward the line of soldiers.

The villagers looked on, the only sound the drip of rain and the faint jingle of coins in a bribe no one wanted.

The soldier shoved the old man forward, and the crowd seemed to recoil as one. The girl clung to her mother's skirts, sobbing openly now, her small shoulders shaking.

The Magister's lips twisted, the faintest ghost of a smile, but there was no kindness in it. "A Water Caster," he said, as though tasting the words. "A good start." He let that sink in before his tone turned harder, edged with iron. "But not enough. The Triarchy asks again: If there are others gifted among you, step forward. Do so, and you will be rewarded beyond any farmer's wage."

No one moved.

No one spoke.

Only the rain answered, whispering down the thatch and dripping into the mud. Eyes slid toward us every once in a while, giving questioning looks, as if asking why we were there.

The Magister exhaled through his nose. He straightened in this saddle, gaze sweeping the huddled villagers until it caught on a boy half hidden behind his mother, all elbows and knees, too young yet to shave, but strong enough to wield a hoe.

The Magister pointed at him, his gauntlet gleaming wet.

"Then perhaps," he said, voice cold with mockery, "we take the able-bodied in their stead." His hand came down again, landing squarely on Art, standing proud despite the rain. "Or him. He looks fit enough to swing a sword."

My breath caught. Art's jaw flexed once, but he didn't flinch. Without so much as glancing at me, he spoke in that rough, workman's burr he had slipped on like a second skin.

"I'm a smith, Magister. That's how I've served my country all my life by making the iron your soldiers carry. They let me keep my wife at my side because of it. We're bound for Rodin. Her father's taken ill. We've no business but family."

The Magister studied us, rain streaking down his breastplate. For a moment I thought he might wave us through.

Then he lifted a gloved hand and waved us off, a short, humorless laugh escaping him. "You'll serve your country another way, then."

The Magister's gaze lingered on Art a beat too long, then he turned in his saddle, lifting his voice over the rain. "Thames. Bring the Ashpire Stone."

One of the mounted soldiers swung down, boots splashing into the muck. He moved with a heavy, purposeful tread, water sluicing from his cloak. From the pouch at his side he drew something dark, something that caught the thin gray light and drank it in.

A stone. Black as pitch, jagged as broken glass, veins of red running through it like molten fire caught mid-flow. Big enough to fill a man's hand, yet the soldier carried it easily, raising it high for all to see. The red threads pulsed faintly in the dim, curling and shifting as though alive.

A shiver ran over my skin. I didn't know what it was, only that the air seemed to lean away from it.

I turned to Art.

He hadn't moved, but the change in him was as sharp as a blade drawn in the dark. His hand hovered a breath too close to the hilt at his side.

The villagers stirred uneasily. The word rippled through them, heavy with a meaning only some recognized.

I didn't. Not fully.

But I understood the way Art's breath slowed, the way the muscles in his forearm flexed against the leather of his bracer. That whatever that thing was, it wasn't just a stone.

26

Artemis

The recognition rose like a bruise on the back of my tongue the moment Thames lifted it for the square to see.

A Warden's Stone.

Black glass veined with red. Ashpire. Cut from Mount Avarrek's throat, where the rock still remembered fire.

The official term for it was the Ashpire Stone, but it was more commonly known as a Warden Stone. A tool used by some Wardens when taking on students, to test whether the spark of a core was there to begin with.

Different names, same hunger.

It never gave power—only forced it out.

Wardens used it to find out what a child was made of. One hand on either side and a slow pull. If the core answered—on the edge of waking—the Stone drank power and gave the lesson back as an ache and shaking hands.

If it didn't, it drank something worse—breath, warmth, the will to stand.

It was never kind, even in good hands.

In soldiers' hands it was even worse.

Thames cradled it one-handed like a trophy. The red threads inside the glass stirred with the Stone's constant pull, the slow bleed it took from those who held it, even without meaning to feed it.

I felt that draw the way a smith felt heat through the leather. The air around the Stone bent, not much, just enough that rain slid off in a hiss and the hair on my forearms rose.

They were desperate, then. Desperate enough to bring a Warden's trial into a muddy hamlet and call it law.

The Magister sat on his horse like a preacher, pleased with the fear he'd brought.

The villagers couldn't name what they were looking at, but their bodies knew. They edged back as far as the square allowed, pushing against one another under the dripping eaves, eyes fixed on the red glow in the glass.

Mount Avarrek.

I could see it as Thames drew nearer. A crown of black rock, rivers of glass cooling into knife-sharp stone, veins of red-like molten script.

Ashpire drank whatever element you put into it. Fire. Light. Water. That was why Warden's bound it in iron and kept it under checks: to slow the absorption and keep eager boys from burning themselves hollow.

No iron here.

No checks.

Just leather and the soldier's grin.

Celeste stood stiff beside me, jaw set, though I caught the way her breath caught. She'd likely never seen a Stone before. And that meant, if they called her name, it would have to be mine that answered.

The Magister gave a sharp nod, and two soldiers waded into the crowd. They seized the boy he'd marked earlier, little more than a youth, barely past his first beard, and tore him from his mother's arms. She cried out, but the spear haft dug into her back as a warning.

The boy stumbled, mud splashing up his shins, as they dragged him before Thames.

Thames stripped the glove from his right hand, the leather falling wet against the muck. He cradled the Stone barehanded now, its jagged edges bit deep into his palm, as though eager for skin. The veins of red flickered faintly, as if waiting.

"Place your hand on it," the Magister said. His tone was flat, almost bored, as though ordering a sack be weighed on scales.

The boy shook his head once, trembling, but a soldier behind him shoved his shoulder. He lifted his small hand, hesitated, then laid it against the crown of the stone.

Thames smiled thinly, and I felt the moment he fed it power. The Stone woke like a furnace bellowing, the veins flaring red, twisting in their glass prison. The air bent around it, heatless yet searing all the same.

The boy jerked. His eyes rolled back. His knees buckled as though the marrow had been stripped from his bones. He collapsed into the mud with a sound I hated—soft, final, like meat hitting the block.

His mother screamed, shoving past the line until a spear blocked her way. The boy twitched once in the muck, then went limp.

I knew exactly what the Stone had taken from him.

A Caster holding it alone would feel only the slow bleed—the steady pull of a core draining into the glass. Enough to leave hands trembling if held too long.

But the Stone was never meant to sit quiet. Not when another Caster fed it.

That was when the pull doubled back. Whoever held the Stone opposite them had their core wrung against their will. Strong ones could fight it for a time. Weak ones stumbled, drained.

And for the ones whose cores didn't stir at all … They had nothing to resist with.

When a Caster fed the Stone while their hands were on it, it took something else.

Strength. Breath.

Sometimes more.

Thames held the Stone high again, the red still burning bright in its center. He looked proud, like he'd proven himself somehow.

The Magister's gaze swept across the villagers, hard and cold. "This is what it means to lie. To waste our time. To hide your gifts. A non-Caster weakens us all."

The crowd shrank in on itself, every face pale, every body shivering from cold and fear alike.

And beside me, Celeste's breath caught.

The boy's mother was still screaming when the Magister lifted one gauntleted hand, palm outward. His voice cut through her cries, flat as cold iron. "Enough. Take the boy away and give him back to his mother. Grab the next one. I don't care who."

The words dropped like stones into the square. The soldiers obeyed without hesitation, pushing back into the huddled crowd.

Panic rippled through the villagers, mothers clutching children tighter, men trying to make themselves small behind women and children. A farmer was yanked forward by the collar, his heels digging trenches in the muck as they dragged him toward Thames.

I didn't watch the man. My eyes stayed on the Stone, but I angled my voice just low enough for Celeste's ear. "If this turns wrong, you keep riding for Rodin and don't look back."

I felt her stiffen beside me. "What are you—" she began, but her words were cut short when the farmer's hand was forced against the Stone.

The red veins flared again. A moment later, he dropped like a sack of grain, limbs twitching before stillness claimed him. The villagers recoiled, and another scream tore through the air, a wave of fear breaking through the square.

Celeste's voice came again, sharper, edged with panic. "Art—what's the plan?"

I kept my eyes forward, watching Thames lift the Stone once more for the crowd to see, his smirk spreading like rot.

My voice was steady, though I felt the knot tightening in my chest. "The truth? I don't know. But you keep to yours."

I finally risked a glance at her, just enough to catch the flash of worry in her eyes before I looked away again.

"Be careful," I murmured.

The square trembled with the last man's collapse. Mud clung to his cheek, his body limp, and still no one stepped forward.

Then a voice split the silence, high, cracking with desperation.

"Viola!"

Heads snapped toward the sound. The crowd parted just enough to reveal the man who'd shouted, his face already draining of color—but the damage was already done.

A mother shrieked, "No!"

The soldiers moved quick, shoving bodies aside until they seized the girl from earlier. The one they'd dragged from her cottage; young, near the edge of womanhood, her wide eyes bright with panic.

"No, please! Not her!" Her mother clung to Viola's skirts until a spear haft slammed her back, knocking the wind from her. Viola screamed once, high and raw, as they tore her free.

They dragged her forward, her feet slipping in the muck, until she stood before Thames. He grinned like a wolf, lifting the Stone in front of her. Its red veins glowed eager, hungry.

"Hand," the Magister ordered.

Viola's lips trembled, but she obeyed, pressing her palm against the jagged crown.

Thames fed it, and the Stone came alive, veins flaring in a spiral of molten light.

Viola staggered, knees dipping, but she held. Her jaw clenched, but she did not break. As long as Thames fed it, she was bound to answer the pull, forced to pour her own ability into the glass.

Thames finally cut the feed.

When at last she tore it away, she swayed but did not fall.

The Magister leaned forward in the saddle, studying her with new interest, bored no longer.

"Well? What are you?"

Viola's chest heaved, her lips quivering as though the answer itself might damn her.

"Fire," she whispered.

The Magister's hand lifted. "Show us."

Her mother sobbed, but Viola raised a trembling palm. She drew in a ragged breath, and then a tongue of flame sparked to life. Small at first, flickering like a candle in a storm, then swelling into a steady blossom of heat, hissing as the rain touched the edges, steam curling into the gray air.

The square fell silent, every eye fixed on the glow in her hand. Even the soldiers stilled, their faces hard but their gazes intent.

The Magister's mouth curved at last into a smile, thin and satisfied. "A Fire Caster," he said, as though he'd found a jewel buried in the muck.

He flicked his fingers, and one of the soldiers stepped forward, pressing a purse into the mother's shaking hands. She clutched it without looking, her other arm wrapped around nothing but air where her daughter had stood.

Viola was already being pulled back toward the soldiers, her flame snuffed out with a hiss, her face pale and set.

The Magister turned his horse, surveying the crowd with fresh hunger. "Now this," he said, "is worth the price."

The Magister let the silence linger, his satisfaction coiling in the air like smoke. Then his voice rang out again. "You've seen the proof. You've seen the reward. Now, once more, I ask. Who among you will step forward for the realm? Who will serve the cause that keeps your borders from burning?"

His gaze swept the crowd, pausing here and there on a bowed head, on a face too pale, on hands that fidgeted in the wet. His tone darkened.

"Do not think one girl enough. AurenVale bleeds. The Triarchy will have what strength is owed. And if no more step forward" —his eyes flicked to Thames, the Stone burning red in the soldier's palm— "then the Ashpire will decide."

The murmur that rolled through the villagers was thin, desperate. Fear had their throats shut tight, but one man found his voice, hoarse with anger. "There's no one else!"

He pushed forward, mud splashing against his boots. His fists trembled, but he lifted his chin all the same. "You've taken what we have. There are no more Casters here."

The Magister's plume dipped as he tilted his head, studying the man like a spider might a fly. "No more?" he asked, calm as steel. "Then perhaps you lie."

"I don't!" the man snapped. "There's none left!" His eyes darted suddenly, desperate to turn the blade away from his own throat.

His hand shot out, pointing through the press of bodies. "What about them?"

A dozen faces turned. I felt the weight of it hit like a hammer. Celeste and I stood out in the crowd, strangers folded into a herd.

"They're not from here," the man spat, his voice cutting through the hush. "Maybe they're the ones you want!"

The Magister's head turned, slow as the grinding of a millstone, until his eyes fixed on us. "You," he said at last. His voice was low, but it carried. "You told me you were a smith. Yet I see no forge here. No hammers, no smoke, nor steel. This is no place for your trade."

The villagers edged back from us, fear and relief mingling in their eyes, glad the attention had turned elsewhere, glad it wasn't theirs to bear.

I kept my shoulders loose, my hands easy at my sides. No fight in them. Not yet.

"We're not of this place," I said again, letting the rough cadence of a workman rasp through my words. "I never claimed it. My wife and I are from Dunwade. Passing through only, on our way to Rodin."

The Magister's gaze narrowed.

"Her father lies dying in the city. That's where we're bound, and the only reason we're on this road. I've a forge waiting for me besides. We've no ties to this village."

Beside me, Celeste held still as stone, her hood shadowing her face. But I caught the edge of her breath.

The Magister's eyes lingered, weighing us as though the Stone itself sat in his gaze.

He let the implication hang, then he softened his mouth into something like reason. "These two aren't of your village," he said, turning so the crowd could hear him as much as we could. "You claim no more Casters here. Very well. Then it's only fair the strangers take the same test. The realm asks the same of all."

He flicked two fingers. A few soldiers started forward, angled toward Celeste.

I caught her eye briefly, offering a small, reassuring smile, then stepped forward before they could reach her. "My wife first, is it?"

Let him see what he wanted to see.

I kept my hands visible. "Magister."

He reined his black destrier a fraction, eyes narrowing.

"What reward," I asked, "goes to a man's wife if he proves himself more valuable than any here, Caster or otherwise? If I take your test and stand where the rest fall, what does AurenVale pay her?"

"Nothing," he said, his tone cutting. "A man who hides until pressed earns no coin. You had your chance when I asked, yet you failed to step forward."

I held his gaze. "And yet, you paid a mother for a daughter who never spoke a word. You paid for the hint of worth. Surely then, you see the value in me naming mine plain. You want a quota. I can give you more than that."

The Magister's brows drew tight.

"One demonstration from me and you'll have met your count for a month. More than that, you can release the old man, even the girl. Take me in their place, and still leave this rabble satisfied you've done your duty. That's a fair bargain, my lord."

The villagers stirred uneasily at that, a murmur rippling through them. I felt Celeste's eyes burning at my back, but she did not speak.

The Magister studied me for a long while, rain streaking down his faceplate. Then, at last, he let out a thin huff that might have been a laugh. "You think highly of yourself, blacksmith. Bold words for one unproven. You must consider yourself very ... important."

His gauntleted hands twitched on his reins, then he leaned forward. "Very well. If you can prove your worth, I'll pay your wife what I'd pay a powerful Caster. If you're telling the truth."

If I impressed him enough here, the Magister would take his prize and ride on. Celeste would be nothing more than a blacksmith's wife again.

The Ashpire Stone burned brighter in Thames's hand, hungry for the test.

I stepped forward, mud sucking at my boots, the crowd parting as though the Stone itself burned a path for me, guttering red in Thame's bare hand. He turned his grin on me, smug and eager.

I stopped a pace away and lifted my gaze to the Magister. "Best be ready to open your purse," I said, voice flat as hammered iron.

A flicker crossed his face—amusement, maybe contempt, but he nodded. "Then prove it."

I set my palm against the jagged crown. The Stone was both colder than ice and hotter than flame. Beneath my skin it stirred, veins pulsing, red twisting like molten threads waking from sleep. I felt Thames feed it immediately, pouring his gift into the glass. The pull came quick, a river trying to drag me under.

He expected me to drown in it.

Thames always fed the Stone first, letting him set the pace and take control. And he trusted his strength too much to think anyone could push back.

The Stone bound both of us the moment our hands touched it; once the feed began, either we both stopped—or neither of us could.

He knew the rule. The smugness in his eyes said as much. He just didn't think it applied to him.

I pushed back. Not with fire. Not with storm. Just with what I was.

The Stone flared, veins writhing like serpents, and Thames's smirk faltered. His jaw clenched, breath hissing. He fed more, breath sawing hard in his chest as he tried to drown me in the draw. The Stone's hunger grew, clawing deeper.

But it didn't drink me.

It drank him.

His eyes went wide, the first crack of fear breaking through. His hand twitched, trying to pull away, but he couldn't. The red inside the glass pulsed wild now, like a furnace pushed past its limits, veins twisting black at the edges.

Then Thames broke.

A strangled gasp tore from his throat, and his knees buckled. The Stone flared one last time in his grip before he crumpled into the mud, limbs jerking in a fit. Convulsions racked his body, eyes rolling back, foam flecking his lips.

The square was silent but for the hiss of drizzle on steel and mail.

The Stone remained in my grasp. I let it go cold, the glow in its heart guttering without Thames feeding it. Then I turned my gaze back to the Magister, unblinking.

"Need more proof?"

The Magister's face didn't crack. No outrage, no barked command. Only the faint lift of a brow as he studied Thames writhing in the mud, then me, still standing, breath even.

"Impressive," he said at last, the word flat.

His gaze lingered on Thames, then rose again. "He is not weak by any means. Thames has proven himself more than once in service to Auren-Vale. Yet here he lies like a boy undone." The Magister's eyes narrowed, voice carrying across the square. "And still, that alone does not prove your worth."

The villagers pushed closer together, watching with wide eyes, their breaths held tight.

I let the silence stretch a moment before I spoke. "Then put more to the test. One after another. I'll show you the measure of me against them all. If it's proof you're after ..." I held the Magister's gaze. "It's proof you'll have."

The Magister's gaze flicked past me, over his own line of men. They shifted, unease rippling through their ranks like wind through tall grass.

None stepped forward. None wanted to. They'd seen the way I stood, the way the Stone had barely touched the surface of my core. The way my hand hadn't even trembled.

The Magister's lips thinned. "Not necessary."

He leaned forward in his saddle, wet plume dripping dark trails down his helm. "Tell me," he said, voice calm but edged, "what ability do you possess?"

"Fire," I said.

"Fire, is it?" The Magister's brows flicked, quick as a spark, before he smothered the reaction. "And what use has a blacksmith have for Fire Casting, I wonder?"

I let my mouth tug into something close to a smile, though it didn't reach my eyes. "The best use there is. I learned it standing at my father's forge, when the bellows were too heavy for my arms. Fire answered me before iron did. Been feeding flame ever since."

A ripple went through his men at that. Fire wasn't rare, but it carried weight. Soldiers respected it, feared it. The Magister narrowed his eyes. "Words," he said. "Show me."

I stepped away from the huddle of villagers, boots dragging through the muck until I had clear ground. My palm opened, fingers loose.

For a breath, nothing. Then the air thickened, heat pressing back against the drizzle, curling the rain before it touched my skin.

She wouldn't be the one they dragged away today. Better me than her.

I gave the Fire its freedom.

It roared out in a wide cone, blasting skyward. Sparks spat like stars before the gray swallowed them. The square lit in violent color, the wet thatch glowing red. The Magister's horse shied beneath him, nostrils flaring wide. A murmur went through the villagers, half awe, half fear.

I shut it down as quick as I'd started it, the flames choking out until the drizzle returned to pattering against my shoulders. I lowered my hand.

I looked back to the Magister.

The Magister's smile came slow, like a man savoring his own cleverness. "Pay the wife."

A soldier stepped forward, pressing a heavy purse into Celeste's hands. Heavier than the others. I saw the way her fingers closed tight around it, the way her chin dipped so no one would see her eyes.

I turned back to the Magister. "Let her keep the other coin as well. For the girl. For the old man. You've no need of them if you have me. I'm worth more than both combined, and you know it."

His smile thinned. "You speak boldly, smith. But even you can't win this war alone." He let the silence bite before he added, "They come with us. Impressive as you are, it isn't enough to leave the others behind."

I held his gaze. The rain fell between us, steady as a forge fire. Then I gave the smallest nod, no room for argument. I handed the Ashpire Stone to the closest soldier as I turned to look back at the villagers.

Celeste stood stiff at the edge of the crowd. I crossed to her, the mud pulling at every step, and drew her into one last embrace. She clung to me tighter than I wanted her to, and I bent my head until my lips brushed her ear.

"Do as I said," I whispered. "Go to Rodin. Keep your name. Don't look back."

Her breath caught, but I didn't give her the chance to answer. I pulled away before her strength became my weakness.

The Magister barked his order, and the soldiers moved like a single body. Boots and hooves dragged the square back into motion. Thames was flanked by two soldiers who hauled him upright and shoved him onto his saddle.

They gave me my reins, but not the right to mount. I walked among them, my horse following at my side like another captive.

The villagers watched in silence as we left, the weeping of a few mothers and wives smothered beneath the rain's steady return.

And then the hamlet was behind us, and all that waited ahead was mud, steel, and the Triarchy's leash.

27

The weight of the purse felt less like gold and more like loss.

The Magister's men pulled Art farther down the road, their armor clattering in rhythm with the horses' hooves. He walked among them, reins in hand, his own mount trailing behind, close but no longer his to claim.

His back was straight, his stride even, as if he had chosen this path himself. As if he hadn't left me with nothing but a whispered command and gold I didn't want.

Anger burned under my skin, hot and ugly. The Triarchy had taken my brother. Now they were taking Art too.

Rodin.

That was where he told me to go. To keep walking, to keep my name hidden, to bury myself in the noise of the city until he came ... If he came.

But every step the soldiers took with him felt like a rope tightening around my throat. My stomach twisted, my fingers digging into the purse until my nails bit through the leather.

I could follow. If I hurried, if I caught the tail of their line, maybe I could slip among the carts or keep to the hedges, close enough to watch, close enough to ... what? Save him? What chance did one girl with Ardor Casting have against a wall of soldiers?

Soldiers who might wield their own element at that? If that had been the way forward, Art would have taken it himself.

I closed my eyes. The memory of the Stone still burned in my mind: the boy crumpling into the mud, the farmer convulsing, the way Viola's flame had barely lit before they snuffed her out and claimed her. That was the future waiting for anyone who defied the Triarchy. If they saw me as more than a smith's wife, if they even guessed at what I was, then what?

Art told me to go. To be careful. To remain as Anna. He had trusted me enough to let himself be taken.

But what if obedience was just another kind of cowardice?

I told myself once that I'd do it alone. That I'd find a way back to Faylen, if it meant breaking against the walls that held her. I believed that before Art. Before he stepped in and made my fight his own.

And now he was gone with them because of me.

The rain thickened, soaking through my cloak, plastering my hair to my cheeks. Villagers trickled back into their homes, doors shutting against the weight of silence, leaving me to stand alone in the square with mud clinging to my boots and doubt clinging to everything else.

A voice cut through the rain.

"You there—girl!"

I turned, half expecting more trouble, but it was only a woman standing under the eaves of a cottage, a kerchief wet with rain knotted beneath her chin. Her eyes held something softer than the rest of the village, something that hadn't yet been drained out by fear.

"You shouldn't be out in this!" she called. "Come inside."

My fingers tightened on the purse. "I can't," I said, shaking my head. The words felt like stones in my mouth. "I must go."

The woman stepped closer, the mud dragging down her skirts. "At least until the rain stops." Her voice wasn't unkind, but it left no room for argument. "You'll catch your death standing out here."

I opened my mouth to refuse again, to tell her that I wasn't hers to look after, that I had a road to Rodin and nothing else, but the weight in my palms, the ache in my chest, and the rain pouring down stole the words before they could form.

The woman stepped down from the neighbor's eaves and beckoned me to follow. Her skirts dragged through the muck, her scarf sagging under the rain. Lines marked her face, but not the deep creases of age. A woman no longer in her first youth, the traces of years written in work and worry.

Her home was further down, tucked at the bend of a lane, but the square hadn't yet emptied. As we passed, I caught sight of the farmer who had collapsed under the Stone, now laid out near the edge of the square where the others had carried him. His wife was kneeling in the mud beside him, her face buried against his chest, sobbing loud enough to cut through the rain. He hadn't stirred.

A few men crouched close, speaking in low voices, while others readied themselves to lift him. One pressed his fingers against the side of the farmer's throat; another shook his head. Their words carried just enough for me to catch. *Too old … May not last the night.*

I forced myself to look away.

"What about the boy?" I asked, my voice thin in the rain. "The one they pulled first."

The woman glanced at me, her mouth a grim line.

Her expression softened, if only a fraction. "He woke. His mother was crying so hard I thought her heart would burst, but she carried him home." She gave a small smile. "Joyful tears, that time."

I let out a breath. It didn't undo the image of him convulsing in the mud, but it loosened something in my chest all the same.

The woman gave me a look, but said nothing more as she led me down the crooked lane where her cottage waited, a faint curl of smoke rising from its chimney.

The cottage was small, but warmer than the gray world outside. Fire pulsed low in the hearth, where a pot already hung above the embers. The woman ushered me in, shutting the door behind us, and for the first time since the square, I felt the sound of the storm soften to something distant.

She busied herself with the fire, coaxing it to life, then set about warming water in a dented kettle. "You'll have tea," she said, not quite asking. Her voice was plain, the sort of tone that expected agreement.

"Yes," I managed, my throat dry. "Thank you."

She nodded toward the chair. I sat, the stiffness in my legs easing as I did. She poured the steaming water over leaves, and let the scent unfurl in the air, sharp and bitter, but clean. Carrying the cups to the table, she set one in front of me before settling in the chair opposite.

"My name is Mireth," she said after a moment, her hands wrapped around her cup. "I'm sorry for your loss. A husband taken like that ..." Her voice thinned, but she shook her head, leaving the rest unsaid.

The words caught in my chest.

Husband.

The title sat heavy between us. I forced my lips to shape the name I'd been given, though it stumbled out uneven. "Anna," I said.

My fingers tightened around the cup, grateful for the heat. "My name is Anna."

The lie tasted bitter, almost as bitter as the tea.

The cottage smelled of damp wood and smoke, the warmth seeping slow from the hearth.

She didn't waste time on silence. "How long have you and your husband been married?" she asked, tilting her head as though it were a harmless question.

I blinked into the steam, buying time with a sip that burned my tongue. "Not long," I said carefully, though the word felt fragile in my mouth.

Mireth's eyes softened, but they didn't turn away. "I heard what he told the Magister. About your father. I'm sorry, Anna. To have to come all this way to console your father and now losing your husband. It's too much for anyone."

I nodded, but the lie grew heavier in my chest with every word she gave back. Husband. Father. A life that wasn't mine stitched together by Art's quick tongue, tightened by her sympathy.

She reached across the table, her hand warm against my knuckles. "You've been given more grief than any woman should bear. You'll stay as long as you need. Let the rain pass and your strength come back to you."

I swallowed against the heat rising in my throat. "Thank you," I whispered, though the words felt crooked.

I felt her eyes lingering, ready to ask more, with the lie already strained thin in my throat. Before she could press further, I lifted my head and asked, "Do you live alone?"

Mireth blinked, then let out a soft laugh as though she knew exactly what I was doing, but answered anyway. "No. This is my father's home. He's gone to Redwick for a time, visiting my aunt. I stayed behind to mind the house and keep the livestock alive." She shook her head, a wisp of hair slipping loose from beneath her kerchief. "It isn't much, but it keeps us fed." Her gaze softened. "My mother passed when I was still young, so it's been just the two of us. Father and I make do."

She sipped her tea, then gave a crooked smile that carried more weariness than mirth. "Though if I don't find a man soon, I'll end up an old spinster.

But all the good ones are either married already or have been dragged off to fight in this blasted war."

I cleared my throat, trying to keep her words from circling back to me. "Do you keep many animals here?"

Mireth smiled. "Hens, a few sheep, two goats. And a cat that comes and goes as he pleases. Stubborn creature, but Father says a barn without a cat isn't worth keeping."

I nodded, grateful for the ordinary sound of it. "Are there many families left in the village? How did you avoid conscription until now?"

She leaned back a little, her cup cradled between her palms. "Most families here have been rooted for generations. A few children left, chasing work in larger cities like Rodin or farther still in Vitel, where the Triarchy sits. But most stay. We're a tightknit place, quiet, not worth much notice."

Her gaze darkened. "The lord of Rodin's seen to that, I think. He's kept a long arm over these parts. Paid his quotas another way. And truth be told, we're too small to matter much. A few farmers and shepherds don't fill an army. Better to leave us where we are, tending our fields and sending wool and grain into the city."

Her voice lowered, as if even the walls might overhear. "But if they've come here now ... it means even the small places aren't safe. Desperate men count every body, no matter how few. I've never heard of them using a stone like that before. My father served when he was young, and he'd have told me if such a thing was part of taking young men and women. No ... That was something new."

She gave a small shake of her head, as though to scatter the thought. "Whatever it means, it isn't good."

I hesitated, then asked, "The two who were taken ... Were there ever any more Casters here?"

Mireth's brow lifted, and for a moment I thought she'd seen too much in the question. Then her expression softened, her voice lowering as if she were offering comfort.

"You mean whether your husband spared another? He did." She set her cup down, fingers brushing the rim. "What he did stood for something. The Magister saw it. Respected it, in his own way. They left one behind, a child. Only eight years old. A young Earth Caster who just found his abilities."

My throat tightened, but Mireth kept on. "It isn't common, you know, to have so many in a place like this. First old farmer Jarl, then Viola, and now Young Braden." She shook her head. "When I was a girl, Jarl was the only Caster in the whole village. And now, within just a few years, there are two children showing gifts."

She looked toward the shuttered window, rain drumming against the wood. Then her gaze dropped to her cup. "I feel for Bridget, though. Poor woman lost her son when he chose to leave. She must worry every day that he's been conscripted by now. But ... he never showed signs of a gift, so maybe he's safe."

The light outside had dimmed to a bruised blue. The rain had slowed, but the air that seeped through the shutters was colder, heavy with the smell of wet earth. I hadn't realized how long we'd been talking until the fire had burned down to embers and the shadows in the corners of the room stretched long and dark.

Mireth pushed back her chair and stood, brushing her hands on her skirts. "It's late now. You should stay the night here." She nodded toward the small hallway. "Take my room. I'll sleep in my father's."

"I couldn't—" The words tumbled out, but she cut me off with a look that left little room to protest.

"You'll take it," she said, though her voice was gentle. "The road to Rodin is no place to start after sundown, not with all that's stirring these days."

I hesitated, but the truth was, my body ached and my thoughts were knotted enough without another stretch of lonely road.

I gave a small nod. "Thank you."

Mireth smiled, her eyes shining in the firelight. "You're a strong woman. I can tell. Stronger than you realize, maybe. I'm sorry for what's been taken from you." She didn't linger on it, only let the words settle over us like a blanket.

Her home wasn't grand, but it was well kept. Sturdy beams, a clean hearth, shutters still whole. Better than Calla's house had been, though perhaps only because it had been spared what others had not.

I followed her down the narrow hall, the purse still heavy on my waist, and for the first time since the square, allowed myself to hope I might close my eyes without hearing the Magister's voice in my head.

The room Mireth gave me was small but neat, the quilt smoothed flat across the bed, a wooden chest tucked beneath the window. I set the purse on the stool by the door and lowered myself onto the mattress.

I lay back, staring at the beams overhead. My thoughts slid, unbidden, to Art.

Where had they put him now? A cot, if he was lucky. More likely the mud, with nothing but his cloak for cover. The memory of his straight back stung harder now that I pictured him shackled to their march.

And Faylen.

Every day stretched longer between us. Every turn, every delay pulled me farther from her cell. I had sworn I would go back, that I would not leave her behind. Yet here I was, under another roof, chasing another road.

I closed my eyes, pulling the quilt up to my chin. Tomorrow I would choose again. Rodin lay ahead, and I had to believe it would bring me closer to both of them, not farther.

Sleep found me slowly, in fits and starts, until the gray light of dawn broke against the shutters.

By morning, the smell of porridge and fresh bread drifted down the hall. Mireth had laid the table, and the fire stoked bright again. She pressed a bowl into my hands before I could protest, and we ate in companionable hush.

When the meal was done, I gathered my cloak and reins, ready at last to take the road north.

I shouldered my pack and Mireth followed me to the door, her hands folded tight in front of her.

"Thank you. For everything," I said.

Her kind eyes softened once more, the lines around them deepening. "Safe travels, Anna. May the road be kinder to you than it's been so far." She touched my arm, her voice low. "You're stronger than you think. Don't forget that."

The words caught in my chest, and I didn't trust myself to speak. I only nodded, then stepped out into the cool morning air.

My horse waited in the lane, breath puffing in white curls. I swung onto the saddle and gave Mireth one last look, raising a hand in farewell before turning back toward the narrow road that wound out of the village.

The climb was quiet but for the creak of leather and the muffled thud of hooves on soft earth. At the ridge, the road split: South, where Art had been taken under the Magister's banner; and north, the road to Rodin, the one he told me to follow.

I reined in and sat still, the morning air cold against my face.

My chest tightened as I stared at the northern track.

Rodin.

Our goal from the beginning. The place he told me to keep to, and the one he trusted me with. Somewhere near its walls, Faylen was waiting, counting on me. Every delay had already stretched thin. How many more before her hope broke entirely—or worse, before she was no longer there at all?

But the road south burned in my chest.

Each league I put between us would only deepen the cut. He had pulled me back from death's edge, stood for my village, taught me when I thought I was beyond saving—not as something owed, but as something shared. As if we were already fighting the same war.

And now he was gone under their banner.

My fingers tightened around my reins. I could almost hear his voice in the hush of the morning: *Go to Rodin. Don't look back.* The choice pressed hard as iron; north or south, duty or loyalty, trust or defiance.

My breath caught, the choice crashing hard against my ribs.

I looked north once more, to Rodin. Then back, south, to the road he had taken down.

And when I turned my horse forward, it was not toward the city.

It was toward him.

Toward Art.

About the Author

Steven never planned to write a book. After a conversation with his wife, he sat down one day and started writing—and didn't stop.

He and his wife live with their four dogs, splitting time between everyday life and traveling abroad. From Iceland to Italy, they're always looking for their next destination. When he's not traveling, Steven is at home working on *The Aberration Cycle*, a series that grew far beyond what he ever expected.

A fan of fantasy in all its forms, he enjoys both novels and manga, drawing inspiration from each. His wife, Sarah—an avid reader—was his first beta reader and remains an essential part of his writing process.

Afterword

Do you want to continue exploring the world of The Hallow?
Scan this code to subscribe to the Aberration Cycle newsletter:

www.aberrationcycle.com

www.ingramcontent.com/pod-product-compliance
Lightning Source LLC
Chambersburg PA
CBHW051305130726

47987CB00004B/1665